The Gilded Cage of Woman

The Gilded Cage of Woman

JAYNE CATHERINE CONWAY

GREENLEAF
BOOK GROUP PRESS

The Intimate Memoir of Margaret Bryan (1757–1836)

Published by Greenleaf Book Group Press
Austin, Texas
www.gbgpress.com

Distributed by Greenleaf Book Group

For ordering information or special discounts for bulk purchases, please contact Greenleaf Book Group at PO Box 91869, Austin, TX 78709, 512.891.6100.

Design and composition by Greenleaf Book Group and Kim Lance
Cover design by Greenleaf Book Group and Kim Lance
Cover image used under license from The Print Collector/Alamy Stock Photo

Publisher's Cataloging-in-Publication data is available.

Print ISBN: 979-8-88645-206-8

eBook ISBN: 979-8-88645-207-5

To offset the number of trees consumed in the printing of our books, Greenleaf donates a portion of the proceeds from each printing to the Arbor Day Foundation. Greenleaf Book Group has replaced over 50,000 trees since 2007.

Printed in the United States of America on acid-free paper

24 25 26 27 28 29 30 31   10 9 8 7 6 5 4 3 2 1

First Edition

Dedicated to my own dear uncle Eric Walker, who was often bemused as to why his Nannie lived in a laborer's cottage but spoke fluent French. This curiosity eventually led us to the remarkable and long forgotten story of Margaret Bryan.

Bryan House, London
September 2, 1826

Dear Harriet Emma,

You are but a little girl, and I have only met you once, but you stole my heart the minute I laid eyes on you. I can still smell the sweetness of your hair from the lock I hold in my hand. I am not sure what the world has told you about me. Not that it matters, as I wish you to remember me in my own words, which you will only read long after I have departed from this earthly world to reunite with my heavenly Creator.

I have decided, arrogantly or otherwise, that the story of my life may be worthy of some memorialisation to you, to perhaps change the lens in which you live your own. It is my hope that my story might inspire you to continue to challenge the political establishment, to allow women greater access to higher education, and for the world to ultimately embrace the idea of women having a fairer share of occupational pursuits beyond fashion, music, and needlepoint.

I trust you will use discretion in whom you share this work with, as it may offend and expose many. It is my hope that by leaving this manuscript in trust for many years that most characters mentioned will have also passed into the afterlife. It is certainly not my intent to cause damage or injury to anyone. My sole intent, rather, is to explain how difficult my personal and professional life has been, simply due to my sex and the cruel confinements this binary and arguably random assignment has put upon me. I wish with all my heart as you read this that you have enjoyed much greater freedoms in your own life to pursue the passions that spring from your heart and that you have suffered less than I in your pursuit of them.

Tout d'amour,
Mamie

1

I T WAS AN OPPRESSIVELY HOT JULY DAY in 1767 when we wound our way through the twisted lanes of London, from St. Luke's Church in Finsbury to the bustle of Fleet Street. I was ten years old. We had just left Sunday services, so the streets were noisy and lined with people entertaining themselves as a distraction from the sweltering heat. The overwhelming smells of the city had also become more pungent, as the horse dung almost boiled against the streets beneath us. With St. Paul's Cathedral just behind us, I briefly spotted two circus clowns, both perched on wooden stilts, sparring with each other. I momentarily stopped to watch the two swaying in the wind, wondering who might meet their demise first. "Margaret, come. Don't get distracted, my love. I have a surprise for you," my very old great-grandmaman, whom everybody in the world called Mamie, beckoned to me.

I shuddered, turned obediently, and squeezed her hand as we pressed on. Whilst I loved the excitement of the city, I always had the good sense to be somewhat afraid of its peculiarities as well.

"There, Margaret, just up ahead, the building with the big oak door; that is where your surprise awaits," she quietly said as she was rooting in the pockets of her old-fashioned skirt for what I assumed was a key. Finally successful, she inserted the ancient object into the keyhole and pushed gently on the beautiful oak door.

The first thing I felt once inside the enormous room was the blinding light from the windows above, which must have been at least twenty feet high in the air.

I squinted and raised my forearm over my eyes, trying to look up at the vast ceiling. I could see nothing at first, but the sound, the sound was deafening: *tick-tock, tick-tock.* I remember so vividly the pounding in my chest.

When my eyes had somewhat adjusted to the light, I held my breath as multiple time-measuring pieces came into visual clarity, chiming in harmony like the piano I had been taught to play. Except the music in this room felt like the entire world heard in unison. *Tick-tock, tick-tock.*

"Margaret, your uncle is a world-renowned clockmaker and mathematician. He has made clocks for nearly every royal court on the Continent. Look at this long case over here," I faintly heard her say, as I put my hand on my chest to indicate that I was having trouble breathing.

Now turning to look at me, Mamie suddenly changed her tone. "Oh, Margaret, I am so sorry; you can't breathe. I always forget how delicate your little lungs are. I should never have brought you down here in this oppressive heat. Sit down for a moment, my love, and rest. Let me see if I can find you some water." I could always hear a hint of Mamie's Irish accent in her voice when she got agitated.

As she helped me onto a nearby stool, the room began to spin like a planet on its axis, and I closed my eyes and just listened to the chiming: *tick-tock, tick-tock.* I am not sure how long I indulged in the moment, but when Mamie finally came back with a glass of water, she stopped about three feet short of me and slowly put her hand to her mouth.

"My God, Margaret, my God in heaven, I think you have the gift. I have always felt it, known it, since you were a little girl," she said, moving her fingers across her lips slowly, as the words were still coming out of her mouth. She didn't say anything else for at least a minute, but just stared at me, until she very quietly whispered, "Margaret, I think you understand the music of mathematics. Oh, my love, you need to understand from whence you came."

Tap, tap, tap, my brain continued. *Tap, tap, tap,* as I heard the clocks synchronising, not knowing whether to be flattered or afraid.

"Let us go home; you are not well," she then said. "I will explain, but not today. I will say this today, though: You are of Huguenot descent and come from a long line of mathematicians, mathematical instrument makers, and clockmakers. I have always thought one's sex didn't matter in the understanding of such concepts, but you are now proof that it is so."

2

M AMIE PULLED THE GREAT OAK DOOR shut and locked it behind her, checking it at least twice. She then shoved the ancient key deep into her skirt pocket, and we started to make our way to my uncle Samuel's home, where Mamie also lived. We walked in complete silence, holding hands. I felt that she was gathering her thoughts and I should be respectful, but I couldn't stand the suspense. Even though I still felt poorly, I finally broke the silence.

"Mamie, what is a Huguenot?"

She stopped on the footpath and turned to smile at me. "Margaret, you bear your papa's patience level as well. Thank goodness they won't let you be a mariner of the sea, as I am certain we would never hear from you again. Let me try and explain a little bit," she said, turning around again to continue walking. "But I really want you to take the time to understand the entire history of our family. Our relatives came from the European Continent, specifically Northern France, nearly two hundred years ago and practised a different kind of Christianity than that sanctioned by the King of France at the time, who was a Roman Catholic. The Huguenot religion is based more on a direct relationship to God than with an organised church. It was the desire of the French king, though, to be loyal to the Catholic Church in Italy and have all his subjects practise Catholicism in deference to the pope." She then stopped to look down at me. "The pope is sort of like Italy's king. So, all those of any other religion in France who refused to convert were subject to dreadful circumstances, including imprisonment and death. Sometimes they even moved a soldier into your house to watch over you."

I shuddered at the thought.

"Many succumbed to the king's demands, understandably, just to try to stay alive. Our relatives, however, flatly refused. They were very fortunate, though, as their men had been educated in advanced mathematics at Le Leuven University."

"Why just the men, Mamie? Why aren't girls allowed a proper education like that?"

Mamie sighed. "That is just the way it is, Margaret, but it doesn't mean you can't try. Ironically, it was a woman who would get them and all of us out of the sordid mess eventually. Elizabeth I, then the Queen of England, welcomed our relatives to her shores, as men with highly sought-after mathematical skills, to advance British innovation capabilities. They left everything they owned behind, though, and many died on the ships trying to cross the English Channel."

"Don't tell me that, Mamie. Papa goes to and fro from there all the time, and it was not that long ago."

"Shhh, I am not finished. You are a precocious little one," she admonished me before continuing. "That very valuable mathematical blood now runs in your veins, Margaret. I am sure I have seen that today. Let this be our little secret for now, though. I will tell you all about the mathematicians who came before you on another day, but today let's celebrate the Sabbath with our family and all the blessings this great country we call England has given us." She kissed the top of my head and gently squeezed my hand, and then we pressed on. You never really walked with Mamie; it was more like an efficient trot. Legs, she'd told me, were the primary mode of transportation in Ireland, so I just tried to keep up with her and breathe, all at the same time.

I already knew Mamie was the historian of the family. She was born Elizabeth Thompson in Dublin, Ireland, in 1683. Her mother died in childbirth, and she was raised by her father, Francis Thompson. She came to London at the tender age of sixteen by an arranged marriage to a London clockmaker called Richard Bryan.

WHEN WE ARRIVED BACK AT my uncle's house a few minutes later, Bryan House on Golden Lane was filled with the smells of roast beef and Yorkshire puddings. My papa met us at the door with a big embrace.

"Margaret, whatever has your mamie had you up to this afternoon?" he said, kissing her on both cheeks at the same time. "Your maman has been so worried. You really shouldn't be out in this heat."

"We went for a walk in the park, William. Can't I spend a little time with my granddaughter without menacing enquiry?" she said, bristling at him.

"Mamie, please, stop," Papa said. "We only have one child, and she is a girl with health issues. Her maman was only concerned for her well-being."

"Her lungs will be fine, but don't look past her brain, William. She is beautiful, but she is also very clever. She comes with the mathematical blood; I have seen that myself," Mamie responded, bristling at him again, and then barreled full steam ahead into the kitchen to help with the Sabbath meal's preparation.

3

THE NEXT TIME I VISITED Bryan House on Golden Lane, Mamie called me to her room as promised, and specifically to her bed, closing the door behind her. The bed was already littered with at least one hundred pieces of paper, all lying on top of the worn patchwork quilt with the morning newspaper.

"From top to bottom," she said. "Six generations of mathematicians, instrument makers, astronomers, and clockmakers, some of whom worked for Christopher Wren himself. They would have been founding members of the Royal Society if they hadn't died in the Great Plague."

She had records of them all in some sort of order, which, after brief observation, I am quite certain only she understood.

"So, it started with the Thompsons from the Continent, then my husband, then your grandfather, then your uncle . . ." Her voice then dropped off as she started to touch all the papers, as if it had all happened yesterday.

"Mamie, we must write all this down. I would like my own children someday to understand from 'whence they came.' Can you help me organise this in some sort of timeline?" I asked, already looking for dates on the fragile, almost burned-looking pieces of paper. "Mamie, can I ask you why my papa never wanted to be a clockmaker?" I continued trying to arrange the papers on the bed, now putting them in order by the brownness of the colour of them.

It was the birthright of my papa, William Bryan, to become a Freeman of the Worshipful Company of Clockmakers. Unlike my uncle Samuel, though, he had no interest in clockmaking nor in hobnobbing with royalty and the privileged gentry, either, although I would not learn all that until much later.

Mamie simply answered, "Even as a little boy, your papa used to spend hours at the docks of the Thames, watching the boats come in and out, always asking where they were coming from, where they were going, or how long it took to get there or back."

It was indeed my papa's dream to see the world, particularly the vast new world of the American colonies. He became a mariner when he was only thirteen. Whilst he didn't have my uncle Samuel's clockmaking talents, he was a keen astronomer and mathematician, having received much of the same training from his papa that his brother had. On board the ship, Papa was often head mariner. His primary responsibility was to carefully monitor the ship's position against its desired course, plotting the night sky against the crude trading maps of the day and then triangulating them with known physical markers on land or at sea. Papa once told Mamie he so loved the adventure of the sea that he would never ask a woman to marry him and thus burden her with such a lonely life. "My only wife will ever be the sea, so you need to pester someone else about more grandbabies," he used to tease her.

Of all the exotic ports of call Papa visited during his mariner lifetime, it was in a tiny town in Suffolk that he finally succumbed to his heart when he spotted the most beautiful woman he had ever seen: Jane Laurent, my maman. She had long, shiny black hair and dark skin. They were both twenty-three years old. She was as smitten with him as he with her, and they married in secret less than a week later. Like Papa, my maman was also of Huguenot descent. After they married, they lived in a thatched cottage by the sea in Ipswich. It is there, in that cottage, that I was born in 1757 and where I lived until I was three years old. We then moved back to London so Maman and I could be closer to Papa's family whilst he was at sea.

Whilst we all worried about Papa when he was away, we welcomed the well-rehearsed traditions of his returns: As soon as we got word what day Papa's ship was due in port, Maman began preparing the French feast. We would start baking the bread and the pastries first, and then she would cure the meat in a French herb that she could only buy at a special shop in the Spitalfields. Then, when the day finally arrived, we would go to the docks to wait, sometimes for hours at a time. I used to count the portholes in the ships to amuse myself and try to make an equation to guess how many portholes there were simply by the apparent length of the ship. Next, I would count them for real to see how far off I was, taking notes to readjust the assumptions to the original equation.

When Maman would finally spot the flag of Papa's ship coming into port, we would make our way down to the docks. "William, William," she would shout as loudly as her soft voice would allow, waving both hands in the air as she anxiously scanned the crowd of sailors looking for Papa's familiar face coming down the gangway. When we eventually found him, Papa would scoop me up into his arms and carry me on his shoulders, telling me that I could fly all the way home.

We would sit around the enormous kitchen table and eat for days. I always sat on Papa's lap in *his* chair in front of the roaring fire. Papa would tell stories of his latest adventure and smoke his pipe. We often asked Mamie, Grandpapa, and my uncle's family to join in as well. I remember 'overhearing' my uncle Samuel once telling Maman at one of these feasts how much better her cooking was than my auntie Anne's. I often reminded Maman of that as she was preparing those meals, and she always answered by saying, "Shhh, Margaret, that isn't nice." I will admit, I was terribly proud of her. There was never a scrap left at the end of those magnificent French meals.

Papa also always brought me a little present from whatever strange or familiar place he had just returned from. I still have many of those presents to this day, although I have now forgotten where many of them came from. There is one particularly precious one, though, that is never far from my side, whether that be around my neck or in my pocket. It is a silver locket he bought for me in the Spanish Americas. He gave it to me on my twelfth birthday with a lock of Maman's hair inside it.

In 1770, tragedy struck though and upended my entire world. When I was only thirteen years old, my papa died of consumption, perhaps better known as tuberculosis. It was the most feared disease of the time, and arguably still is. I recently read it now kills one in every eight people in Britain. We still to this day have very little information about what causes it. But its spread has certainly been getting worse, as large amounts of people have started to move to the cities from the country. This could not be truer than in London, where people are starting to live on top of one another. The 'consumption death' is a horrible one to witness, with wretched coughing filled with dark-coloured blood and a general wasting away of the body cavity. I could hardly bear to be around Papa at the end and see him in such a wretched state of pain. Within days, my grandpapa John Bryan was dead of the same disease. I couldn't eat nor sleep for days. Mamie came over to our house to sleep in my bed with me for at least a week and help take care of Maman. The entire family was in bits.

"Maman, what will we do, where will we live? What will become of us without Papa?" I cried, crawling for the first time in bed with her since Papa's death, but Maman just wept and shook her head.

"Ma chérie, I do not know. I do not even know if I'll have the will to live without your papa to take care of us." It was at that exact moment that the sun began to set in her bedroom, and a blinding light entered the room through a small gap in the heavy draperies. It was only then that I really saw Maman's face since Papa's passing. It looked tired for the first time, like stone—hard and pitted. She then just said, "Please, let us just rest for a while." I climbed out of her bed and kissed her forehead, trying to hide my tears. I then closed her bedroom door behind me so she could go back to sleep.

4

MAMAN RARELY LEFT HER BED AFTER my papa died. I took care of her like *I* was the maman with a sick child. I pulled a cot into her room so I could sleep with her, hear her wake, and give her more medicine. I knew the medicine was potent, as it put her back to sleep immediately and smelled horrible in the sticky, brown bottle. I propped her up with enough pillows so at least she could read the newspaper or a book if I was doing something else. I also surrounded her bedroom with things that reminded her of Papa, including dragging his chair all the way up the stairs by myself. I always touched Papa's pocket watch that she kept on the bedstand when I sat on the bed with her. Somehow, I thought it magically gave me more strength.

Papa, we miss you; we love you so.

I fed and bathed Maman every day and attempted to keep the rest of the house going at the same time. It certainly felt like a lot of responsibility for being only thirteen years old, but what was I going to do? My only saving grace in that dreadful time was my auntie Anne and Mamie, who came often to check on us. Auntie Anne was better than Mamie at it; I think maybe the Irish culture is just different. Mamie just never had a lot of time for people feeling sorry for themselves.

"Jane, you can't go on like this. You need to get out of bed in the morning and get out for a good walk. Why don't you come and stay with us for a while, and I can help you get back on your feet?" my auntie Anne said to Maman. But it was clear she was no longer in control of her own body, or perhaps her own mind, anymore.

"Please, Anne, you don't understand. It's not of my will to be like this. I really can't get out of bed." Then Maman started to cry and my aunt wrapped her arms around her and held her like her own child. The tears started to well in my own eyes just watching, as I just didn't know how long we could cope like this.

Then, one late afternoon on a cold autumn day, I tried to wake Maman to take her medicine, but she wouldn't move, not even a stir. At first, I feared she was dead. I took the vanity mirror off the chest of drawers and pressed it against her mouth. I saw she still had breath and kissed her forehead. My chest tightening, I knew I had to go for help, but it was snowing and starting to get dark. I reached for my woolen coat and pulled on my boots, then fought the front door not to blow me flat on my back just to get out onto the street. Ordinarily I would have found my way quite easily to my uncle's house, but it quickly became unfamiliar territory with the snow, the wind, and the darkening sky. *Travel east, Margaret; follow the sun, Papa said. Look at the sky, follow your instincts.* By the grace of God, my cousin William found me about halfway there, and we were all safe and sound in my uncle's home before nightfall.

Maman and I would now call Bryan House on Golden Lane our home as well. Inside the safety and comfort of Bryan House on Golden Lane, Auntie Anne and I took care of Maman together. We alternated bathing her and feeding her. Well, we tried to feed her. Whatever medicine they gave her to help her sleep also took away her desire to eat. This made me especially sad, as it made me remember and miss those beautiful French feasts with Papa and the rest of the family even more. "Pastries—anyone for more French pastries," I could hear her saying.

Maman also liked me to read to her often, particularly when she was feeling lonely, and always in French. "Ma chérie, would you sit and read to me for a little while?" she whispered one afternoon, reaching for my hand after pretending to eat the middle of a jam sandwich.

"Judge a man by his questions, rather than his answers"—Voltaire was her favourite. Maman was far more complicated than many people—particularly Mamie—ever gave her credit for. It was one of the reasons my papa fell in love with her: the rebellious French spirit of hers that fed off the words of the infamous liberal philosopher. They would read Voltaire together for hours upon his returns from the sea.

Despite the constant worry about Maman, Bryan House on Golden Lane was otherwise filled with laughter and love, which made me feel very much alive. As an only child who now lived with her aunt and uncle and their entire family, it felt a bit as if I'd died and gone to heaven. Not to disparage Papa's memory, but I now had six siblings to play with, and I was big sister to baby Thomas, who was only one year old.

"Baa, baa, black sheep, have you any wool? Yes, merry have I, three bags full," I used to sing to him, and tickle his tummy, which always made him giggle. Thomas was also learning to walk at the time. He would make me hold each of his tiny hands in the air as he tried to get his footing, wandering all over Bryan House on Golden Lane for hours 'discovering,' until I couldn't straighten my back upright.

As well as my new extended family, my uncle also had young clock-making apprentices who worked for him littered about the house and his clockmaking shop at any given time, at first a bit older than me and then, over time, a bit younger than me. At Mamie's encouragement, we would often 'quietly listen in,' when my uncle was giving them their maths lessons in his clockmaking shop. We would secretly walk down to the shop together holding hands and would then quietly sneak in the back door.

The minute I was inside, I felt a bit like what I think Maman felt like when she took her medicine: at *peace*, I suppose is the word. *Tick-tock, tick-tock*—that was my medicine. The music of mathematics: *tick-tock, tick-tock*. I breathed it in and then swallowed it every time I walked into that room. That is, before I got to the smells of the wood chips and the disgusting varnish that made my eyes water.

When I say Mamie and I would 'quietly listen in,' that never implied with my uncle's permission. 'Quietly listening in' usually meant hiding like mouses behind the very large oak bookcase at the back of the room. It was one such day, after we thought my uncle had gone home, when I was alone in the clockmaking shop with Mamie. I was fingering the pendulum of his latest masterpiece when we heard the front door open. Looking up, startled, I saw it was my uncle. "Margaret, you must stop this, and Mamie, you need to stop encouraging her," my uncle said, annoyed. "What can you do with all this knowledge? This is a man's profession! Margaret, you should be going to dances and socialising with people your own age. Your mother would be so angry with me if she thought I'd offered any encouragement."

I put down the beautiful pendulum and looked up at him. "Uncle, you've never encouraged me, not once, not ever, so there's no need to worry Maman," I said softly, tears welling up in my eyes. Reaching for Mamie's hand, I headed for the back door. Mamie started to say something, and I just put my index finger to my lips. Whatever dreams she allowed me to believe, I didn't want to upset Maman in any way. However unwell she was, her only remaining mortal wish was for me to get married and to have a family.

Mamie did vow to protect us if my uncle ever got really cross. Mamie was bold by any measure, but particularly for a woman, like she was just too old to let anybody tell her what she could and couldn't do. As much as to say, *I changed your nappy a hundred years ago, so you don't get to supervise me.* She would secretly 'borrow' my uncle's books from his library to help me practise my maths and astronomy lessons in her room. She understood more of the maths than she ever let on to the men in her life: father, husband, son, or grandson. She could always point me in the right direction whenever I got stuck—often when I had assumed she was asleep. A long finger would just come out from under the patchwork quilt and turn to another page and point. I used to hide the maths books under her bed, not mine, in case we ever got caught. It was all a secret game that belonged only to Mamie and me, and it was nothing short of magical.

Mamie and I spent so much time together alone, particularly in her bedroom and in secret at the clockmaking shop, that my cousins probably thought I monopolised her time, but I am not sure that is fair. Nobody ever said anything to me, anyway. I knew everybody else was feeling sorry for me, so I suppose I just took advantage of the opportunity. Mamie also told me more than once that I was her favourite, but I kept that to myself. "Shhh, that isn't nice," I heard Maman say.

Mamie was indeed a character. Not only was she always up to mischief when it came to trying to advance my mathematical education, she was constantly playing pranks on everyone in the house. We all were fair game. She once told me that when she was a little girl growing up in Ireland, she took the family chickens from the coop and put them one by one in the neighbour's barn so her papa couldn't find them. When it was finally discovered what she had been up to, given away by the fact that she was covered in mud from head to toe, the neighbour didn't want to give the chickens back. When her papa finally shamed the man into admitting to what was rightfully his, he then had to carry the fowls back to his own coop himself. Mamie said he was so cross with her that she wasn't allowed to leave the house for nearly a month. She also told me she couldn't eat chicken anymore, as the whole event had left an unpleasant taste in her mouth. She could be hysterical, but she had little shame. I didn't have the nerve to ask her why the same philosophy didn't apply to eggs as well. Perhaps it was only a dead chicken that was now considered offensive.

In addition to completing my astronomy and maths lessons behind her bedroom door, we also eventually rewrote the entire family diary together from all her disorganised notes. I did finally figure out her order for the notes, divided first by how much she loved the person and second by how successful their career had been. Once I had the 'guide,' it was now obvious why her husband, Richard Bryan, was always at the top of the pile. I should mention how much in love they were. Richard Bryan left all his money to Mamie when he died, which is still very unusual in British society.

That diary holds so many lovely stories about my family and all its rich history. I cherish it to this day, still wrapped carefully in a piece of Mamie's patchwork quilt, but it is the Elizabeth Thompson and Richard

Bryan love story I always read when I am feeling a little melancholy. Even though it is a beautiful love story in its entirety, my favourite part actually reminds me of Mamie's sense of humour. As proud as she was of her mathematical and clockmaking Thompson ancestors, her arranged marriage to her beloved husband, Richard Bryan, who was a perfect stranger to her, was transacted in the currency of sheep. Her father, Francis Thompson, while having a birthright to the Freedom of the Worshipful Company of Clockmakers, chose a different occupation. He was a successful merchant trader in Irish wool, working in the Huguenot community of Dublin in the late seventeenth century. But when the 1699 British Woolen Act passed in parliament, forbidding the prospective export of Irish wool outside of Ireland, the entire industry collapsed overnight. It is then that Francis Thompson arranged for his beautiful and educated sixteen-year-old daughter's hand in marriage in exchange for his freedom into the Worshipful Company of Drapers, allowing him to freely trade wool on English soil. "Sheep, dreadful, smelly sheep, is what brought my love to me. Can you imagine?" I remember Mamie laughing out loud, telling me the entire sordid sheep story in perfect French, as I desperately tried to write everything down.

5

A S THE YEARS PASSED AT Bryan House on Golden Lane, I became resolved regarding my future of a traditional life of marriage and children. I simply wasn't interested if it meant I couldn't do something useful with the mathematical education I'd been quietly amassing over the years, hiding in the cobwebs of my uncle's business. Admittedly, Mamie was my sole advocate, but somehow with her encouragement, all seemed possible, despite not having a clear path nor destination to aspire to—except, perhaps, to become one of my uncle's clockmaking apprentices, which seemed unthinkable at the time, given his apparent feelings about even my very presence in his shop.

Then, one bitterly cold day in January of 1776, my world, or at the least the sacred dreams within it, fell apart. I crept into Mamie's room, as I often did to pray with her, and closed the door behind me. The air was still, which seemed odd.

"Mamie," I whispered, "Mamie, are you awake?" There was no response. My chest began to tighten, and my heart began to pound. "Mamie," I said louder, trembling as I reached for the mirror on her bed table. I pressed the mirror against her mouth—no breath. Once, twice, thrice, no breath. I put down the mirror and started to cry. I didn't tell anyone else for a little while. I had already closed the door, and Auntie Anne always acted like somewhat of a guard at Mamie's door when we were in there together. Instead, I just cried and cried for what felt like hours, with her hands—those long fingers that used to point to the right page in the maths book—entwined with mine.

I remember at one point reaching for the diary, also on her bed table, and finding her name written inside. I picked up the quill and started to write inside, *Died peacefully, January 21, 1776, ninety-three years old* in dark black ink as a tear dropped to the page and smeared the moment. I finally tucked the diary into my skirts, brushed the tears off my face, and then slowly opened the door to find Auntie Anne to break the news. I was inconsolable for weeks.

With Mamie now gone, despite all my prior dreams, I suddenly felt my day of reckoning was now inevitable. I assumed at some point a suitable husband and an 'attached life' would be chosen for me, even if I didn't actively participate in the process of being acquired by 'one or it.' Then, seemingly to seal my fate, another tragedy struck. After her own heartache and failing health, in the spring of 1777, Maman developed dropsy. It was clear she was in unimaginable pain. A vile yellowish fluid took over her entire being, distorting her beautiful French body into an unrecognisable version of its former self.

"Mamie," I prayed on my knees, holding Maman's hand, "please take Maman; she doesn't want to be here. She is in a lot of pain. Please take her to Papa soon."

Mamie didn't take long to hear me, as Maman's battle to be in the kingdom of heaven was swiftly won. The last thing she said to me was "Margaret, you will marry a good man and have lots of babies, won't you? I could only ever have you. That would make your papa and I very proud."

I didn't say a word. *I am not sure I can tell her that, honestly.* I just squeezed her hand, elephant tears falling from my eyes onto the bedclothes, and nodded my head. She then closed her eyes for the last time. There was a deafening silence when she was finally at peace, finally with my papa. I saw that heavenly reunion for myself. I was just twenty years old, though, and I had no idea who or what was in store for me now.

$$6$$

"MY LADY, YOUR UNCLE WISHES to see you in the drawing room. There's a young gentleman waiting."

Looking up at the servant, annoyed to have been interrupted in the middle of trying to replicate a mathematical theorem, I replied, "Yes, of course, just give me a minute." *Not another one. How do I put a stop to this?* Whenever I was summoned to appear before these potential suitors, I pinned my hair back tightly in a bun and tried to look as uninterested as indeed I was. I certainly had no intention of providing even an ounce of encouragement to the other side.

"My apologies," I said, curtseying before my uncle as I entered the drawing room.

"My dear Margaret, no apologies necessary. Please welcome Francois Dubois Esquire," my uncle replied, politely gesturing for me to sit down. "He will be joining us for dinner tonight, and I thought you might enjoy his company privately for a few hours beforehand. Perhaps you could play the piano for him."

I started to feel anxiety. I'd never been left alone in the presence of any of these 'potential husbands' before. I instinctively looked at my aunt for a signal of relief and wasn't pleased with the result. She was clearly avoiding eye contact with me entirely.

"Yes, of course, it would be my pleasure to entertain Mr. DuBois with the piano before dinner," I almost announced, lacking any enthusiasm whatsoever. They then left us in the drawing room, and I played the piano for two hours without interruption, until the same summoning servant let us know that we were now expected in the dining room. Mr. DuBois honestly never said a word the entire time. There could be no matter of doubt, though, that the music had been deafening by design.

In all fairness, Mr. DuBois turned out to be a lovely man when he was finally able to present himself at dinner. He was just never intended to be *my* lovely man and that needed to be made clear. Admittedly, I had not been at my best, banging on the piano, but I was furious that all of this had obviously gone on behind my back. *What century does my uncle think we live in?* The formal meal was then only filled with the indigestion of the uncomfortable conversation that was inevitably to follow.

After the dinner finally concluded, my uncle and Mr. Dubois went into the library to have a drink, and I heard Mr. Dubois leaving about an hour later. My aunt and I were doing needlepoint in the drawing room, hardly looking at each other, let alone speaking to each other, when a servant finally broke the deafening silence.

"My lady, your uncle wishes to speak with you in the drawing room privately."

Be strong, Margaret, I thought, taking in all the breath I could ingest. I'd hardly had a chance to sit down when my uncle launched into speech.

"Margaret, your aunt and I have been thinking about your future. I know you enjoy your mathematics and your books, but you need to start thinking about your future and a marriage to a husband of some means. We think that man is Mr. DuBois. You seemed to have a compatible nature tonight, and he has a very promising career ahead of him. I think it is a fine match."

"A fine match?" I spat at him. "How do you match something before you know what colour it is? I will have no part in this medieval practise of complete ignorance." I immediately walked out of the room to try and find my aunt, which I eventually did, in tears, in her bedroom.

"Were you really a party to this?" I cried out to her. "I just lost Mamie and now Maman, and now I am to be sold to the highest bidder?"

"No, Margaret, that is not what is happening here. I never—no—he is a kind man, but I understand why you are upset. I cannot comprehend what it would be like to marry a man you didn't love with all your heart. Your uncle and I married without either of our parents' permission, underage and in secret. Let me deal with this issue of Mr. DuBois on my own with your uncle. He will not force you into anything, I promise you. I would not stand for that, but what will you do with your life? I mean, are you not interested in getting married at all?"

I softened, now realising she was as upset as I was. "Auntie, Mamie told me that I had the intellect to be a mathematician, an astronomer, and even a clockmaker, or all three, just like the six generations of men that preceded me. She told me I have their gift and that my sex doesn't matter in my ability to study and comprehend advanced mathematics. So that is what I want. This world will not let me do that and have a traditional family because I am a woman."

"Margaret, sometimes I worry Mamie put too many unrealistic ideas into your head."

"That may be true, but they are now there, and they have no place else to go. So, if I must choose, I choose to have an occupation studying advanced mathematics and this mysterious concept we casually refer to as the movement of time and space. That is what I am passionate about; that it is what runs in my blood and my bones, as much as my religion does. Please understand it is not my intent to be disrespectful, but it is my intent to be heard. If you can hear me, I desperately need your help. You are the only person on earth who could get my uncle to consider making me a proper clockmaking apprentice."

She looked solemn but eventually spoke. "Well, your uncle has never been able to say no to Mamie about anything. Let me talk to him, and we will pray to her in the meantime." She turned around and closed the door behind her.

After my aunt had left the room, I sat on her bed and stared at myself in the mirrored bureau. I had said it out loud now. I knew my aunt was telling my uncle of my decision, in that very moment. I also knew he was going to be livid with me. I thought about Papa and then Maman. Certainly at least she would be equally as furious, given what I had implicitly agreed to on her deathbed. I slowly knelt to the floor, put my elbows on the bed, and began to pray to Mamie.

"Mamie, are you awake? Mamie, I may have gone too far. I need your help. This isn't a game anymore. This is my life. Show me the way—show me the way to get them to understand why I must do this."

My uncle was indeed livid with me, beyond even what I thought might be a reasonable punishment for what I will admit was rude, whatever the circumstances might have been to justify it. He wouldn't speak to me or be in the same room as me for weeks. He would pass me in the hallway, bristling as if I were an unwanted ghost occupying space in *his* house.

"Margaret, he will soften," my aunt assured me. "He will come around. It is just going to take some time."

"Is she qualified or not, Samuel?" I overheard my aunt asking my uncle in the kitchen a few weeks later. "If Thomas or any of your other sons showed a tenth of the interest in your business that Margaret does, you'd be doing cartwheels. Why does her sex have to matter so much? She's clearly got a natural inclination for the subject matter, and she's practically your daughter. Give her a chance, for heaven's sake!"

"It is not that straightforward, Anne. We have a responsibility to secure a future for her. We will not be here to take care of her forever," I heard my uncle respond. I was now officially in no man's land, no pun intended. I just sort of shuffled through the house without purpose for weeks, waiting for whatever was going to happen to finally happen.

Without warning, though, things started to tilt my way. Looking for my uncle in what appeared to be a drunken stupor, a colleague of his accidentally found me buried in one of my uncle's physics books. Puzzled, he started to say something to me, when he was suddenly interrupted by the parlour maid, who was clearly agitated.

"Sir," she said, "Mr. Bryan is in the drawing room. Pardon me, my lady. Please, sir, let me take you to him." The two then turned their backs to me and left the room.

The incident may have been missed entirely from my story but for the man's voice becoming so loud that I could now hear him bellowing from the drawing room. I opened the library door quietly to get a better position.

"Samuel, why do you allow that odd niece of yours access to your library and all your expensive books? She's 'vixen-like' and only likely to mix up your filing system, and anyway, there's no point. Any man with half a brain knows women are incapable of understanding such complex subjects as advanced mathematics and physics."

I wanted to barge in and tell him right then and there that the only man whom I knew with half a brain was him, but of course, I did not.

"What's wrong with you, John?" I then heard my uncle shout. "I will not tolerate my niece being referred to with such vile and disrespectful language. You know what Margaret's been through. It would serve you well to stop drinking, at least during the light of day. You need to leave, now." I heard the front door open, shut loudly, then nothing.

On one level, the man's comments didn't really bother me. I already knew what he said to be ridiculous, simply through observing how frustrated my uncle became with his apprentices' inability to grasp even the most basic of mathematical concepts—concepts that I would digest and be capable of replicating after a single afternoon's lesson. Quietly crying, I put the book back on the shelf, *in the exact place it was supposed to be*, and went upstairs to my bedroom.

About an hour later, I heard a knock on the door.

"Margaret, your uncle wishes to speak to you in his library," I heard my aunt say from the other side of the door.

Well, I didn't know if this was good news or bad news, but at least it was news. I knew I needed to pull myself together regardless and face whatever consequences were coming my way.

"Coming," I answered, using the bottom of my skirts to dry my tears.

When I arrived in the drawing room, my uncle was in his chair in front of the fire smoking his pipe. He again launched into speech, which initially was so startling I almost lost my composure. I quickly sat down and straightened up to look directly at him. He didn't seem to notice.

"Margaret, I need to apologise for my behaviour these past few weeks. Your decision to discard Mr. DuBois so casually was disrespectful to both of us. I now understand that you were trying to make a point to stop this fruitless effort of trying to find you a suitable husband, as your aunt has informed me of your decision to alternatively pursue an occupation."

I suddenly felt my heart begin to pound. *Where is this going? Could it be he's changed his mind?*

"I will tell you that I don't agree with it nor understand it, but I do now respect it. With my complete support, I am offering you a full clockmaking apprenticeship, which you are free to begin immediately."

Oh, Mamie, you heard me. I started to cry uncontrollably. I knew I was making my uncle uncomfortable again, as he got a bit twitchy, and I thought I may have even seen a tear starting to form in his eye. Fortunately for both of us, my aunt was now in the room, embracing me with a full-body assault.

"Thank you, Uncle. Thank you, Uncle. I will be the best clockmaking apprentice ever born" was all I could get out.

This made him laugh out loud and say, "I am sure you will be, Margaret."

I then made him put it in writing and sign it, for fear of a future reversal. "You have to sign here, Uncle, on this piece of paper," I said, handing him the quill pen, which made him laugh even louder and give me an awkward embrace.

$$7$$

T RUE TO HIS WORD, MY UNCLE laid out the formal
responsibilities and requirements for the apprenticeship, exactly
the way he would have with any young man, both of us knowing that this formality was only for us. Unlike my male counterparts,
I'd never be eligible to achieve my freedom—my right to trade—as part
of the Worshipful Company of London Clockmakers, or of any other
comparable guild anyplace else either, for that matter. This was fine with
me, though. I'd never been as interested as my uncle in the actual pro-
duction of clocks. Like my papa, I was more interested in understanding
the mathematical and astronomical concepts behind them, particularly
navigation and timekeeping. My ambition, then, was not to make clocks
or navigational equipment, but rather to teach the concepts in a way
that ordinary people could understand them. It was my ultimate dream
to publish that knowledge in books, which would then give even more
people *and more women* access to an education in the sciences.

It would be remiss of me not to mention the awkward moment when
my uncle took me through the moral requirements of the apprenticeship,
including the complete prohibition of drinking alcohol and fornication.

"Margaret, your apprenticeship will be terminated immediately for any
indulgence—however seemingly small or harmless an act might seem—
in either the acts of imbibing alcohol or engaging in sexual fornication."

Auntie Anne just happened to be in the library when we were having
this very serious conversation. Well, at this, she just burst into laughter—doubled over and holding her side, I should add.

"Samuel, if there's a man alive who can coax Margaret out of her books
to indulge in any human vice, let alone alcohol and sex, then he should be
allowed to claim his rightful prize," she finally managed to get out.

My uncle looked confused and annoyed. I think my aunt knew immediately she had hurt his feelings.

"I am sorry, Samuel." She straightened up and looked more serious. "Samuel, I know that isn't funny by itself, but she has just worked so hard for this. That is all I meant, nothing else. She will be your most loyal pupil. My apologies for interrupting you two. I shall respect your privacy in the future," she finished, closing the door behind her.

My uncle still looked confused and then just decided to carry on with the sacred oath of which I quickly obliged, at the obvious risk of it not reaching its necessary conclusion, to secure my formal apprenticeship.

It was for seven years as my uncle's apprentice that I studied mathematics, clockmaking, and astronomy, and side by side helped him to make longcase clocks. Fortunately, mostly due to Mamie's efforts, I had very little to learn from the academic side of the apprenticeship—except to push my knowledge far beyond what anyone else would have been able to reach—what with the nearly ten years head start I had living in the shadows of my uncle's clockmaking shop before I gained my apprenticeship.

This practised knowledge was also useful in helping my uncle with his other apprentices' academic studies. I had long since been responsible for Thomas's mathematical education, but soon after I began my formal apprenticeship, I began to realise the strength of my teaching talents, particularly my ability to explain complicated mathematical concepts in a simpler way without requiring intimidating equations. There was one young apprentice of my uncle's called Pierre who hated mathematics. He was probably only thirteen years old at the time. I have no idea who thought a clockmaking career was a good idea for him, as I have never seen anyone more miserable in the assignment. My uncle was equally as frustrated, but neither party seemed to be able to undo whatever agreement had been reached to secure and fulfil this commitment to each other. I liked Pierre, and honestly, I felt sorry for him. I decided then to make it my mission to help him understand this world of mathematics and clockmaking—at least enough to get a pass on whatever examination he was going to be required to take to gain his freedom into the clockmaking guild.

After my uncle's maths lessons were over, Pierre and I would go into the back of the shop, very nearly where Mamie and I used to 'quietly listen in,' and I would go over the day's lessons with him. My uncle hardly seemed to notice at first, other than to thank me for taking the time to be kind to another. I think my uncle had already concluded that Pierre wasn't capable of ever understanding the maths, but he was mistaken. Pierre just needed to understand the maths through pictures, not equations. He then somehow learnt how to translate that back to doing, in his own way. It was miraculous, and I have never felt more alive to have been a witness and a party to such a transformation. I had certainly been passionate about teaching prior to this experience, but Pierre taught me how to teach and write in a different language: the language of pictures. He ingested pictures the way I heard *tick-tock*.

"Margaret, whatever have you done to Pierre?" my uncle jokingly asked me a few months later. "He is nearly my top academic apprentice now—besides you, of course. Perhaps you are better at this teaching thing than I am. You know it has been an irritation and a distraction for me my whole life. Would you be willing to take on the academic component of all my apprenticeships going forwards?"

I felt my face get warm and felt a feeling of pride wash over me, which I am quite sure I had not felt before. *Mamie, I hope you're watching. Maybe you could let Maman and Papa know as well?*

I smiled, trying hard not to get emotional. "Uncle, thank you so much for your confidence. That means everything to me. Yes, I would love that. I will begin to structure the lessons immediately, with a formal syllabus for your review."

For a moment in time, in the protected cocoon of my uncle's clockmaking shop, my sex didn't seem to matter much at all. There was never again a mention about whether I would ever marry, but instead an implicit understanding that this, my occupation, was now my destined path.

SEVERAL MONTHS LATER, THOMAS DID tell his father that he had no interest in clockmaking, and that, like my papa, he wanted to be a mariner of the sea. Embracing him awkwardly as grown men do, my uncle just said, "Well, it is not my first wish to have you be a slave to the sea, but I understand your calling. Margaret's papa had it himself. Your maman and I will pray for your safety. You will write often, won't you? Please let us know where you are and how you're faring."

He then casually turned to me. "Margaret, we have a lot of work to do, and there is a new apprentice arriving this afternoon," so ending the entire conversation.

Thomas quietly thanked me later that day for the joy I gave to his father, working by his side, day after day. I knew I was going to miss Thomas terribly. He had unquestionably, over the years, become a brother to me. Not that I didn't love nor care for my other cousins, but he had been just a baby when Maman and I came to live with them. I had helped him learn to walk. I felt like I was second maman to him and he was big brother to me, if all that is possible beyond one's imagination.

When Thomas announced his desire to be a mariner, I couldn't help but think of the long absences during my own childhood when my papa was at sea. Not only did we miss him, but we always feared for his safe return. We finally bid farewell to Thomas in 1785, when he moved to Liverpool to begin his career as a journeyman of the sea. I avoided the big send-off at the stables, having given him my farewell privately the night before. I looked on from a distance, though, watching him mount his horse, and I thought about the baby I used to sing to and the boy I used to teach mathematics to. Now my brother was a man and going out into the world to navigate the perils of the sea.

Be careful, Thomas, my love. Please be careful.

8

E IGHT LONG YEARS PASSED AS Thomas circled the globe via its vast oceans, as my uncle and I built longcase clocks side by side together. Whilst we saw Thomas from time to time when his business brought him to London, we were all surprised when he arrived back at Bryan House on Golden Lane in the autumn of 1793.

"Helloooo," I heard with excitement. This was always the way Thomas would announce his arrival home, as he would then waltz into the house with presents for everyone. This time, though, apparently his present was a wife. "Meet my new bride," I heard him proudly announce, and then my heart stopped. I raced down the stairs to discover that the rest of the family had suffered the same reaction.

When we were all assembled, he held a toast of champagne and said, "I would like to introduce you all to Sarah Bryan, my beautiful wife." She was, indeed, beautiful but seemed out of her element. I started to feel sorry for her. I immediately looked at Auntie Anne for help, but she looked as bewildered as I felt. Uncle Samuel awkwardly started to step forwards to welcome Sarah when Thomas's speech continued, much to everyone else's chagrin.

"I have another announcement to make as well. I've enlisted under the Duke of York's command. We're going to fight the French aggression on the Continent. We'll be leaving immediately for Ostend to join the Flanders Campaign," he finished with great authority.

Well, if my uncle Samuel had taken Thomas's decision to become a mariner rather than a clockmaker in stride, both he and my auntie Anne were devastated by the news of him becoming a soldier. There were voices raised, which was unusual.

"Thomas, as your father I will not allow this. You are disrespecting me and your mother with such a cruel and thoughtless decision, without even asking our opinion. We have not raised you this way. We are Huguenots! We are peacemaking people of God, not warmongers. We believe in the enlightenment of the mind, not the wielding of the sword. That is the very reason our families came to England to begin with. In the name of your French forefathers, please! I am forbidding you to leave London. In fact, I am forbidding you to leave this house."

I watched as Sarah, his new bride, looked on in horror, wondering, I'm sure, what kind of family she'd just married into. Thomas and Sarah (née McLaughlin) had met in Liverpool just a few weeks earlier. I must admit, at the time, I'd thought the marriage decision itself rather impulsive, before Thomas's military enlistment clearly superseded it. Eventually, though, as they do, emotions settled down, since it was abundantly obvious that Thomas wasn't going to change his mind. His new bride would come to live with us whilst Thomas was on the battlefields of Europe, and we would just have to pray for his safe and uninjured return.

It was, however, lovely for me to have another young lady in the house, even though at twenty-four years old, she was twelve years my junior. The rest of my aunt and uncle's children had long since left Bryan House to start their own lives. Sarah and I fast became friends, and before long I could barely remember a time when she wasn't there.

Thomas came home for Christmas that year for a few days, and it was one of the loveliest times of my life. It was a white Christmas for the first time in many years, and there were now many grandbabies running about the house. All our men were home from the front, whether that be water or war, and my uncle looked healthier than he had in years. It was indeed a time to celebrate.

9

T HE YEAR 1794 TURNED OUT, however, to be painful and tumultuous for us all. It was also a year, though, that presented me with a new and very interesting opportunity. In the early spring, we learnt that Sarah's older sister, Elizabeth, had been widowed. Her husband, George Dalton, also a colleague of Thomas's, had been killed in France in the war. When Thomas asked my uncle if she, too, could move into Bryan House on Golden Lane, both he and my aunt agreed at once. Well, if I was terribly fond of Sarah, I was immediately drawn to Elizabeth in a different way. I soon learnt that, like me, she had a passion for teaching.

Even to this day, I'm not sure what Elizabeth and Sarah's childhood had been like, and neither of them certainly liked to talk about it. What I did know, though, was that they were orphaned at a relatively young age. They were fortunate to have been taken in and well cared for by some sort of distant family member, as they were both well-educated by the time they came of age. Elizabeth was also governess to a prominent family of gentry in Liverpool before she met her husband. Probably for all those reasons, Elizabeth would often volunteer at the local orphanages after joining us at Bryan House, teaching the younger children how to read and write a little bit. She was always happiest then, telling us about the various children and their progress since the week before.

"Margaret, you should volunteer as well," she said to me one evening at suppertime. "Why don't you come down to the school with me next week? You're such a natural teacher. I hear you with the apprentices, and sometimes even I understand some of your strange mathematics, you explain things so clearly."

My uncle was now surrounded by a house full of women, and we'd developed a lovely routine that felt a bit like precision clockwork. Suddenly, however, in late June, my uncle Samuel's health started to decline rapidly, and by the middle of July, the unthinkable happened: He, too, died of consumption. We knew he had been ill for some time, but the end was fast and cruel by any measure.

Whilst my relationship with my uncle had been distant and somewhat awkward when Maman and I had first come to Bryan House on Golden Lane, all that changed when he granted me my apprenticeship. He simply forgot that I was a woman, simultaneously discovering I spoke the same language of mathematics that he did. We just worked side by side, often saying nothing at all to each other, just the *tick-tock, tick-tock* of the mathematics.

Now he and all that were gone. Our routine, the hum and smell of the clockmaking shop, his bristling—all gone. I felt like something was choking me, an object stuck in my throat that wouldn't let me breathe. I literally had no idea what life would be like without him, nor did I know what would become of the occupational protection he'd afforded me for so many years.

The funeral was atrocious. The rain was pelting so hard we could hardly find our way to St. Luke's, and trying to get the casket from the church to the grave without incident was a complete nightmare. It was the most unceremonious day for the most ceremonial man I had ever known and loved. I knew there was a reason Thomas couldn't be there, but I was upset about his absence regardless. I mean, really, what could have been more important?

Thomas came home for a visit about a week later. He found me in the clockmaking shop trying to clean things up, for what I now assumed would soon be re-let to some other London clockmaker. Thomas was gracious enough to bang on the door as opposed to his usual "Hellooo," as I was in no mood.

"Margaret, it's me, Thomas," I heard.

"Thomas, so lovely to see you," I said, opening the enormous oak door. "So sorry this awful news brings us together." I kissed him on both cheeks with a fistful of rags in my hand. "Sorry, I probably smell. This varnish is asphyxiating as well. I was trying to be useful. I am not sure what you want to do with the remaining clocks. I can finish them if you would like at the house, but I want to make sure everything else is in order."

Thomas then grabbed my hand gently and said, "Margaret, stop. I know you are in pain and that you are scared. Let me put you at ease. Papa has left you a sizeable inheritance, including ownership of his seaside home in Margate on the Kent coast."

"What?" I said quietly, at a loss for words.

We will not be here to take care of her forever.

Well, this is the way my uncle had done that in death: He had found a way to take care of me forever. The true weight of my loss now fell so hard upon me, I just collapsed into Thomas's strong and able body and started to weep.

"Please, Margaret, come back to the house. There is time for all this later." Thomas had my uncle's carriage waiting outside the door, which he carried me into in a puddle. I finally allowed myself to grieve, and I slept for three days.

When I was able to pull myself somewhat together, I realised that I was now a woman of some means, at least the means to take care of myself. I was a little awkward and embarrassed around the rest of the family at first. Somehow, I felt like I'd taken something that wasn't rightfully mine. Thomas sensed my apprehension and immediately put me at ease.

"Margaret, nobody in this family begrudges you any of this. You've earned it in spades." He then paused thoughtfully and asked, "What will you do with your life now, though?"

Before letting me respond, he surprised me by offering his own opinion. "I've been thinking about it myself, and at the risk of meddling, I think you should open a school, maybe even a boarding school, and take Elizabeth with you to help. I think that's why Papa left you the seaside house in Margate: It's perfect for a boarding school. I know your passion is truly teaching, and now you could run your own school, if you want that."

I was taken aback, and I didn't say anything at first. Thomas seldom ever freely offered his opinion on other people's lives, mostly because he despised other people interfering in his. I'd never had such an ambitious thought in my life as to open my own school, but now that he was suggesting it, I thought, *Why not?*

"I'll need your help," I said. "I think, if it's possible, I'd like to open a boarding school that educates young ladies in mathematics and astronomy."

As supportive as Thomas had been on the school, he didn't hesitate to discourage me on the curriculum front. "Margaret, I'm not sure where you will find fathers willing to foot the bill for a scientific education for their *daughters*, which by all accounts will have little to no value at its logical conclusion."

"Let me see to that part myself." I then hurriedly left him for fear of more dissuasion on the matter of the curriculum and went to find Elizabeth to ask her if she'd be my partner in the new school. As Thomas had aptly pointed out, we'd need a traditional curriculum as well, and Elizabeth would be perfect to manage that.

I finally found Elizabeth in the back garden. "Elizabeth," I shouted, slowing down as I reached the end of the garden where she was weeding the rosebushes. "I just spoke to Thomas, and he thinks I should start a school with my uncle's inheritance. I wanted to know if you would like to partner with me in it."

Elizabeth seemed surprised and certainly waited a moment to say anything. "I don't know, Margaret. That seems very ambitious. Does Sarah know anything about this? I would have nothing to contribute financially."

"I'm sorry, of course you wouldn't, and neither had I less than a week ago. No, the money is there already. Think about it, talk to Sarah, and of course you will get paid. It is nice to have your own money, even though I can hardly get used to the idea myself." I left her then. I didn't want to push and was still getting used to the idea myself.

It wasn't but a few hours later that Elizabeth knocked on my bedroom door. "Margaret, may I come in?"

"Of course," I answered, clearing off part of the bed, filled with the beginnings of my planning notes, so she could sit down. I could tell by the look on her face that her sister had given her whatever encouragement she needed.

"I'm all in," she said, with the biggest of smiles on her face.

"Well, let's dig in," I said. "Start putting down your thoughts on a traditional curriculum. Thomas is dissuading me, but I want to teach mathematics and astronomy to young ladies and then publish my lessons in a textbook."

"Oh, Margaret, that is really ambitious, but if anybody can do it, it is you."

WE TRIED VERY HARD TO MAKE the Margate school location work, but we quickly learnt it was both an inconvenient location for our pupils and the staff we were trying to hire to help run it. We actually moved out there for several months and spent a lot of money on advertising, but we just couldn't seem to get a plan together that we felt had any chance of success. After six months of utter frustration and not much progress, I finally conceded that we needed to be closer to London. Thomas suggested that the house in Margate could be leased, and we could use the income to secure our own leasehold in a London location. Ideally, I wanted proximity to the Royal Observatory in Greenwich Park, where I could continue to advance my mathematical and astronomical research.

By the autumn of 1795, Thomas had secured a lease in a beautiful building in Blackheath for us, just across the heath from Greenwich

Park and the Royal Observatory. After months of preparation, Elizabeth and I opened Bryan House, Blackheath, for the 'education of young ladies,' in the spring term of 1796. I was about to celebrate my thirty-ninth birthday.

10

BRYAN HOUSE, BLACKHEATH, was a beautiful new building just outside the village and on the heath. It even smelled new, or alternatively, it didn't smell old, like the fireplace soot that gets into every nook and cranny of everything. There were ten rooms upstairs on the top two floors, a large library, drawing room, dining room, and kitchen on the first floor, and sizeable servant quarters in the back as well. It wasn't as nice as Bryan House on Golden Lane, but it was a very proud start for two women trying to open a school of their own at the end of the eighteenth century.

We had only been open for a few months, and I was confident we'd be profitable by the end of the year. We had a full complement of staff: A married couple, Mr. and Mrs. Murphy, took care of the upkeep of the house, including preparing the meals, and Mr. Murphy was kind enough to serve as my coachman occasionally. I typically liked to drive my own phaeton, though, as it was always an opportunity to clear the gears of my mind from getting jammed. Elizabeth had hired more academic staff, so we now had a music instructor and two other part-time teachers. As planned, Elizabeth was responsible for the more classical components of the curriculum, and I was writing and teaching the astronomy and mathematics lessons. I'd also built a personal laboratory on the top floor of Bryan House, where I probably spent more time than I should have.

All told, I couldn't have been more delighted with myself. I wrote frequently to Thomas to let him know how well things were progressing and thanked him at every opportunity for all his support in helping me open my school. Those letters were hard during the war years. I worried about him constantly, and the reports in the papers were grim with news of the European battlefields. Thomas's return letters were always brief, typically sending news of the family, which I knew already. But he always included a few thoughtful words of praise and encouragement for me as well. I knew he was sparing us from the atrocities of the European battlefields. We just hoped and prayed he'd come home alive.

Despite the tolls of the French wars, the mood in Britain was marginally more hopeful by the spring of 1796, as the Prince of Wales had finally, legitimately, married the year prior. His new wife, Princess Caroline of Brunswick, better known as the Princess of Wales, had also just given birth to a legitimate heir to the British throne, Princess Charlotte. The press's happy news of the princess's birth, though, was quickly overshadowed by the growing animosity between her parents—which, by each of their own designs, was now becoming an increasingly public joust.

I won't make any attempt to dilute the vile nature of the Prince of Wales, George IV and Caroline's husband. He is an utterly disgusting and immoral man—a known womaniser, gambler, drunkard, and any other demonising adjective you can think of. He'd been illegally married to his Catholic mistress, Maria Fitzherbert, for years, with whom he had sired two children. But George IV, as heir to the British throne, needed a legitimate heir and, more importantly, significant help from the British Parliament to pay his outrageous gambling debts. Not only was he still illegally married to the widowed and very Catholic Fitzherbert when he married Princess Caroline of Brunswick, he also had a mistress on the side by the name of Lady Jersey. These were just the women the papers knew about. Lady Jersey had been the couple's matchmaker, to Lady Jersey's sole advantage in that Caroline had been forced to take her on as a lady-in-waiting so her husband could spy on her. The arranged marriage had been a complete farce, intended only to meet the prince's financial needs and produce a legitimate heir for the British throne. Now, with those tasks completed, Prince George had no use for poor Caroline. She found herself alone in a foreign country without friends or acquaintances and exiled from the London Ton and the Royal Court. The only advantage Caroline had was that she greatly garnished the sympathy of the press and the British public, and did she ever learn to use that to her advantage.

BY EARLY SPRING, THE PAPERS were reporting that the royal couple had officially separated and the Princess of Wales's new residence would be at Montague House, which was located just inside Greenwich Park, directly across the heath from Bryan House. Well, it wasn't as if Blackheath didn't have other notable residents, but this was the Princess of Wales. I didn't have much time to think about it or to provide protocol to my pupils, because less than a week later, the entourage from London arrived at Montague House. Caroline of Brunswick, the Princess of Wales, was now an official resident of Blackheath, and our very royal neighbour. Her daughter, Princess Charlotte, however, would apparently have a separate residence, where she'd be supervised and educated by a governess chosen by her father. It was clear who was making those ridiculous rules.

How embarrassing for the world to know that your husband, and the father of your only child, thought you couldn't take care of your own baby.

With hindsight, I'm not sure what my expectations were of having a royal neighbour. I probably thought she'd keep to herself, and all we'd be aware of would be her staff serving her every need from afar. But this wasn't to be the case, and it certainly wasn't who Caroline Amelia Elizabeth Brunswick-Wolfenbüttel was nor would ever be. About a week after she moved in, we received our first unannounced visit from Caroline, who'd been taking a walk by the heath towards town. Our windows had been open, and when she heard music coming from the drawing room, she entered the gate and knocked on the door.

"Helloooo," she called out in a heavy German accent that reminded me of Thomas's salutation. Then, pushing on the heavy door and letting herself in, she shouted, "It's the Princess of Wales; may I come in and listen to your music?"

Elizabeth looked like she was going to faint. Thank goodness we'd heard of Caroline's relocation, or I'd have probably sent for the authorities for fear of an impostor. Elizabeth quickly recovered from her intense surprise and politely offered, "Of course, Your Majesty. I mean, Your Royal Highness. Yes, of course you may listen to the music. May we also offer you lunch and tea?"

"I prefer wine at this hour, if you'd be so kind," Caroline answered.

Wine! I didn't know if we even had a single bottle in the house—certainly not one fit for the Princess of Wales. I felt my face getting warm and my palms starting to sweat. After what seemed like an eternity, I finally heard Elizabeth coming up from the cellar.

"We are in luck," I heard her say.

Thanks be to God, I thought, feeling a great sense of relief.

I then looked over at the four young girls, who had been taking turns practising their piano lessons in the drawing room before the princess's unexpected arrival. They were now sitting in perfect alignment on the bench in the hallway. They looked like pigeons on a fence, except they were petrified pigeons, as though one could fall over at any time and smash into a million pieces.

"Girls," I said, trying to smile without looking like a petrified pigeon myself. "Pull yourselves together. What a lovely surprise for the Princess of Wales to come and visit with us. Which one of you would like to play for Her Royal Highness first?"

Complete silence. Thank goodness Mary was amongst the group. As much as I found her manners a little lacking, she was afraid of nothing.

"Mary, why don't you go first," I suggested. I watched Mary begrudgingly peel herself off the bench to take her place at the piano in the drawing room—not, however, without wiping her runny nose with the sleeve of her dress on her way to get there. I cringed. She then began to play—in fairness, without any hesitation. The rest of us followed her into the drawing room in singular formation.

It was a strange afternoon, for sure. Caroline drank the entire bottle of wine in about an hour as she listened to our pupils practise their piano lessons in the Bryan House drawing room. I must admit, I was terribly proud of our pupils. That was quite some pressure to be under, but they performed beautifully. I personally thanked Mary afterward, as did Elizabeth, for having the confidence to go first. I also tried to address the runny nose incident. Elizabeth had clearly thought the additional effort futile.

The wine seemed to relax Caroline, although she said very little other than "The wine is delicious, ladies, and your pupils have much talent. I'm very grateful for your kind invitation."

My first impression was to feel sorry for her, and certainly I was confused as to how she thought we had invited her to barge in and upend the entire afternoon schedule at Bryan House. She was as awkward as the papers had described her, and her English was atrocious. *Why wasn't this German princess better prepared for such a role?* From what I'd read in the papers, it had always been a strong possibility, because of her lineage, that she'd be chosen as a royal bride and potentially the Queen of England. Yet, no one had even taught her to dress properly. Whilst I appreciated that such women apparently had little value to these royal men, I'd have thought their role in producing their heirs might have at least justified some sort of investment in basic hygiene.

I soon learnt that Caroline's French was better than her English, so we mostly spoke French to each other. Because of my Huguenot descent, French had been the first tongue spoken in my family since at least 1699, when Mamie had been brought to London to marry Richard Bryan.

How the history books will remember Caroline, I can only speculate. I am quite sure the royal family will vilify her, but I do hope the records will also include some insight into her positive qualities, of which she had many. Whilst she was certainly without any sense of decorum, there was a childlike nature about her that encouraged those around her to engage in her level of 'playfulness,' which had she not been the Princess of Wales, I am quite sure would have been deemed completely inappropriate by all.

Did I mention she sat on the floor—I mean the ground—when she stopped by to listen to the music lessons at Bryan House? The girls just followed suit, besides, of course, the one playing the piano. After all, what on earth was I going to tell them—"You can't sit on the floor with the Princess of Wales"? I just looked at Elizabeth, who looked away as quickly as she could, trying not to burst into laughter.

Caroline's love of children was also immediately apparent, as was her constant anxiety about how often she was allowed to see her own daughter, Princess Charlotte. Her strongest attribute, though, was her tenacious courage. She simply carried on, no matter what blows she was dealt—ironically, a very British trait, albeit her German ancestors might take issue with that. Her courage was raw and untamed, and the press and, ultimately, the British public adored her for it, many of whom felt the exact same way as she did about the royal family, and especially her husband, the Prince of Wales.

Caroline came often to visit us at Bryan House that year. Initially, she was just interested in listening to the young ladies practise their piano and singing lessons and probably looking for a bit of company. Eventually, though, she began to show an interest in my teachings on astronomy. At the time, I assumed her proximity to the Royal Observatory in Greenwich Park must have sparked this interest, and, indeed, she told me she'd met the Astronomer Royal and his family.

One day, such a conversation with her seemed less benign, though. "Margaret, I find these astronomy lessons you teach these girls interesting, but also strange. I don't have much of an education myself, and certainly I should have had more. There are powerful men out there, though, who believe that intelligent women who study the occult are the devil's spawn. Have you heard of the Salem witch trials in America? Are you ever afraid someone will think you are a witch?"

I was taken aback, and I didn't know how to answer her. It was certainly 'unfiltered' Caroline, which was always served 'cold.' I was also starting to feel a bit scared. Naturally, Elizabeth and I had been concerned and had several conversations prior to opening the school as to how the curriculum would be received—more, though, from the point of view of whether there would be a demand for the curriculum as opposed to something more sinister. What frightened me, though, was whether Caroline had overheard a conversation elsewhere regarding the curriculum at Bryan House. Whilst she wasn't welcome at the official court in London, she still went to social events that were also attended by some of the most important and influential men in Britain. I decided, however, not to ask her that question. I didn't know whether it would offend her and, more importantly, I wasn't sure I wanted to know the answer.

Instead, I just said, "I can understand how the maths curriculum might be misunderstood by people unfamiliar with it, but no, I don't worry about anybody drowning me for being a witch. If I let myself worry about such unimaginable events, I'd never get out of bed in the morning."

Caroline smiled. "Ma chérie, I often don't get out of bed in the morning for no particular reason at all."

11

T HE WORRY DID KEEP ME UP at night for several months, although I never mentioned it to Elizabeth. Fortunately, my irrational fears that there was some sort of male conspiracy trying to ruin Bryan House were put to rest by the end of the summer when Caroline came by for a visit.

"Margaret, there's a friend of mine whom I think you'd like to meet. Her name is Georgiana Cavendish, the Duchess of Devonshire. She shares a similar passion to you for the study of the sciences, which is unusual in women. Do you know of her?"

Of course, I knew who the Duchess of Devonshire was. Anyone who had ever read a newspaper knew who she was. She was born Georgiana Spencer into a wealthy family of gentry to begin with but later married the most eligible bachelor in Britain, William Cavendish, the 5th Duke of Devonshire, on her seventeenth birthday.

"Yes, of course I know who the Duchess of Devonshire is. She is arguably the most influential socialite within the entire London Ton and Royal Court, before you get to her liberal politics," I replied to Caroline. "I had no idea she had an interest in the sciences. All the papers ever want to talk about is her political influence on the Whig Party and what she's wearing. I suppose, though, she may have been influenced by her uncle, Sir Henry Cavendish. He's an influential Fellow of the Royal Society, at least according to my late uncle. I can't imagine why she'd want to meet me, though."

"You underestimate how interesting you are, Margaret," Caroline said. "I'm sure she'd be delighted to make your acquaintance. She has recently suffered some serious health issues and is looking to spend more time in the country to recover without the intrusion of the London press. I've offered her accommodation at Montague House for as long, and as often, as she wants to stay. Bryan House would also be a welcome distraction for her. It certainly has been for me."

I myself had just recently read that the duchess had suffered an extraordinary eye infection that had resulted in some blindness in one eye and some subsequent disfiguration to her face. I couldn't, however, imagine, blind or not, the effort of trying to entertain a conversation with such a woman. I was regaling the conversation to Elizabeth a few hours later when she just interrupted me and said, "Of course you must meet her, Margaret. You'll be cross with yourself if you don't, just because you are nervous about it. You do know she is a published authour many times over, don't you? Maybe you should ask her to come here, to Bryan House. Show her your laboratory; that will help put you at ease."

I knew Elizabeth was right, so the next time Caroline visited, I volunteered to show the Duchess of Devonshire my private laboratory. Caroline seemed very pleased. As promised, I met the Duchess of Devonshire, Georgiana Cavendish, or Gee, as her family and friends called her, at Bryan House, Blackheath, in the autumn of 1796. I personally never got used to calling her Gee. It seemed such an unbefittingly simple title for such a sophisticated woman.

As nervous as I was to meet her, she immediately put me at ease, managing the conversation as if it had been previously rehearsed. She was clever, funny, and beautiful, and she had a keen interest in the sciences, particularly botany, mineralogy, and chemistry. The scarring on her face from her eye infection was evident but not ugly, except from the perspective of wondering the magnitude of pain she must have endured to wear such a badge of honour. She eventually brought her very famous uncle into the conversation.

"Margaret, you must have heard of my uncle, Sir Henry Cavendish. He is a distinguished Fellow of the Royal Society. He's not much of a sociable man, but I'd like to introduce you to his library and to his assistant, Charles Blagden."

"Yes, my late uncle has mentioned your uncle's work at the Royal Society, with great admiration, might I add. Thank you so much for such a kind invitation," I said. "I'd be most privileged to have an introduction to your uncle's library. My uncle also told me that you had a distant relative called Margaret Cavendish, who was also a published authour in the science of natural philosophy. And he told me that she was the first woman to attend a meeting of the Royal Society in 1667."

Georgiana seemed surprised by this. It was obvious she'd not heard the story before. "Oh my," she said. "Even today they don't let women go to those meetings. How was that received?"

"Not well," I replied. "They laughed her out of the room. It's been said that Samuel Pepys called her a mad, conceited brush, or something like that."

This made Georgiana laugh so hard she almost snorted, putting her hand over her mouth, which clearly pleased Caroline. "Oh no!" she finally said. "I hope she gave it right back at him!"

So, as unlikely a trio as we must have appeared on the surface, the three of us were fast becoming friends.

As soon as we were finished with lunch, I took Georgiana and Caroline upstairs to my laboratory. I knew already that Georgiana was impressed with the school, but the laboratory was where her passions became evident. I could hardly get her to leave the room as the sun started to set outside over the heath. I also observed that it was rapidly approaching the time when Caroline started drinking. Caroline drank a lot, not that I blamed her. It may have been partly cultural—Thomas once told me that Germans drank ale for breakfast, but I'm sure that isn't true. With respect to Caroline, I think it was probably mostly out of anxiety and sheer boredom, particularly during the long periods of time when she wasn't allowed to see her daughter. When they were getting ready to leave, I discovered that Georgiana wasn't going back to London that evening and would be staying overnight at Montague House with Caroline. Then, much to my delight, Caroline insisted that I join them for dinner and the rest of the evening.

That evening, the three of us drank a lot of wine, which was unusual for me. I didn't want to appear to be a prude, and to be honest, I was so intoxicated with Georgiana that maybe the wine concealed the true source of my now apparent gaiety. I had never seen a woman so talented and beautiful, seemingly so at ease with herself and the rest of her world.

I was, therefore, very surprised when she said, "Margaret, I've so much respect for your independence. You're the only woman I know who doesn't have to answer to another earthly being. Beyond being beautiful, God has given you such enormous intellectual ability and, mistakenly or otherwise, the powers that be have given you a man's education. This gives you even greater freedoms than maybe you realise. You can make your own money, acquire your own property, and accumulate your own wealth because you're not married. I'm so envious of your life."

I was embarrassed and at a loss for words. I also didn't want to go anywhere near the marriage conversation. Elizabeth and I had decided just before we opened Bryan House, Blackheath, that I would also be 'a widow to the war with France.'

"It just softens you, Margaret, to have had a husband. Less ambitious, less pointy," Elizabeth had said. I had just agreed, whatever *pointy* meant. This was the first time I had ever been questioned about the potential fib though, and it felt uncomfortable, particularly given the company I was in.

I was eternally grateful for all the wine at this point and politely gestured for more. When the words finally came out of my mouth, I just said, "I am very grateful for the life I have, but it has not been without sacrifices, including my own children." I knew I was apologising when I shouldn't have been, but I still felt the compelling urge to do so.

I was temporarily grateful, then, when Caroline interrupted the entire conversation to say, "You don't have to give birth to a child to be its mother. In fact, I think it's better not to be the birth mother if the father is an oaf with whom you had to lie down."

Caroline now had the unrelenting hiccups. Georgiana started giggling and making 'oaf noises' as she reached for the open bottle of wine, topping us all off, before Caroline then completely caught me off guard—some translation between the hiccups being required, which I will not suffer you the details of.

"Margaret, I don't think you have ever had the displeasure of lying down with an *oaf*, have you? Could it be you still have an unbroken hole?"

Even when we sorted out what she was trying to say, I still wasn't sure if she said *hole* or *hall*, but I wasn't about to ask for further clarification. I really started to sober up now. I knew Caroline, like everybody else at Bryan House, Blackheath, believed that, like Elizabeth, I was a widow. Now Caroline was telling me she didn't think that was true. *Any ideas, Mamie?*

Thankfully, Georgiana came to my rescue, at least long enough for me to think. "Really, Caroline, I completely agree with the oaf part, but if you are going to ask Margaret such a rude question, at least ask it in French, where it sounds more genteel!"

Slurring her words between the hiccups, drinking ale from a wine glass, and snorting tobacco snuff all at the same time, Caroline then replied, "It would have been worse in German."

Well, with the German accent and all the wine, this sent us all into stitches. Then I heard Mamie: *They are your friends, Margaret.* I pulled myself together and tried to get a little serious.

"Ladies, I have a confession to make, but you must swear to keep my secret," I practically announced.

Caroline's head was bobbling more than a bit at this point, so I wasn't even sure she would remember the conversation at all, but I could see I had Georgiana's attention.

"Well then, we all have to tell a secret now," Georgiana said, "so none of us can ever betray one another. That is how the game works. I will have to think of one, so, Margaret, you go first. Caroline, you need to wake up, because I am quite certain your secrets are far better than ours."

I started. "I have told my pupils, and probably a great deal of other people, that I am a widow. That is not true; it never has been. I don't know how you knew that, Caroline, but I want to be truthful with my friends. I hate secrets, but Elizabeth and I thought it would 'soften' me a bit. 'Make me sound less ambitious, less pointy,' I think is how she put it. By the way, she is a legitimate widow. Her husband's name was George."

Georgiana reached for my hand. "I'm sorry, Margaret. I know how hard it is to keep secrets. That is the plight of every woman in England who wants to do anything meaningful with her life. Let me tell you what I did to break out of my gilded cage: I bore a child with a man who was not my husband, but who I loved and still do, very much. That is my deepest secret, and I paid painfully for the mistake. But you—your secret has let you lead your life on your own terms and with your own money. Bravo, Margaret!"

This seemed to jolt Caroline to life—literally, as if someone had poured a bucket of cold water over her head. "Oh no, Gee, you can't tell that one; that one does not count. That is the worst-kept secret in all of London. You need to think of something else."

I was shocked at her lack of compassion and held my breath, until Georgiana finally threw her head back and started laughing, saying, "Go on with you now, Caroline. That is just mean—plain old mean. Now it is your turn, and it had better be good."

All eyes were now upon Caroline, who seemed to sober up entirely at this point and then got very serious. "I hate my husband; I despise him and would like to see him stone-cold dead," she said, deadpan. This was getting stranger by the minute, or maybe I just wasn't used to being this drunk or free with my emotions.

Fortunately, Georgiana again came to the rescue. "Well, you now just won that blue ribbon from me, because that fact is really the worst-kept secret in London. Please, though, Caroline, you shouldn't go around saying things like that. Your husband is a powerful man who would like to destroy you. There are also plenty of other people who hate your husband as well. You just never know what might happen. Please keep those thoughts to yourself. Let's stop this game; it has gotten too dangerous. Margaret, your secret is safe with us, we promise. Right, Caroline? Here's to another bottle of wine," she said, gesturing to the attending servant and waving her glass in the air. "No more seriousness tonight. Tonight we drink and laugh to our newfound friendship. Friends forever!"

12

NOT LONG AFTER OUR EVENING together at Montague House, Georgiana invited me to lunch at Devonshire House, the stately London home—or perhaps more appropriately, the stately London palace—of the Cavendish family. She gave me a brief tour of the highlights, but I could only imagine it taking days to go through the place to appreciate its beauty in its entirety. It was the gold I remember the most—the gold was everywhere. It reminded me of when my uncle would complain about the cost of the gold leaf he used to complement his black-lacquered clocks with. It was everything I could do to restrain myself from trying to calculate what it all must have cost.

That afternoon, when I felt surprisingly at ease with Georgiana, I found the nerve to ask her if she would help me publish my astronomy lessons. It was a beautiful day, and we had just finished lunch on the outside terrace overlooking the sweeping Cavendish gardens, now all in summer bloom. I knew from Elizabeth that Georgiana was already a published authour of more than one book, but more importantly, I knew she had an address book that could likely finance anything in the entire world. This newfound friend—I could hardly believe my luck— this woman of immense power and privilege who truly cared about advancing the rights of the oppressed whenever she could. Could this now be my chance to ask for her help?

"Georgiana," I said, "can I ask you something? How difficult was it for you to publish your books? As a woman, I mean. I want to publish my astronomy lessons as a scientific textbook. I use them in my teaching lessons at Bryan House, so they're already written. But I've no idea how to publish them, or how to secure the financing needed, or even if any of that is possible." I finally stopped.

Georgiana smiled at me. "Margaret, I'd be happy to help you publish your textbook," she said, putting down her teacup. "It won't be an easy task, though, unless you want to remain anonymous, or even worse, use a male pseudonym. I didn't publish under my own name." She stood up at this point, almost melancholy in nature, then stared out at the chimney tops of London for at least a minute, looking pensive, as if something was irritating her that she couldn't put her finger on.

She finally spoke, and her voice seemed to get a little bit louder. "Margaret, I think you should publish under your own name, particularly given the subject matter. We'll engage Caroline as well. She knows the Astronomer Royal, who would be an important supporter. I think, though, you'll need further *softening*, Margaret—isn't that how Elizabeth put it—if you're to have a chance." She began to pace, seemingly now having moved from melancholic to annoyed. "Being pretty and precocious is the loneliest place on earth, Margaret. I know that better than anyone. Men don't understand you, and women hate you for pretending to have a man's mind and stature in a world they mostly don't participate in. The landed gentry are also nervous about a possible uprising in the masses. They're certainly not looking for intelligent women putting their lofty ideas into print for the whole world to see, especially without the supervision of a husband. The good news, my dear, is," she said, finally sitting down and touching my arm reassuringly, "there's no one better at 'packaging' someone for a coming out than me. So, we'll do whatever is needed to make sure you're published, and published under your own name. You're just going to have to trust me a little bit."

I almost didn't know what to say. "Yes, I'd like to publish under my own name, and yes, I'd be very grateful for your help. And, of course, I trust your judgement entirely," I added, not having a clue what 'packaging' someone meant.

That afternoon after lunch, as promised, Georgiana and I made our way to her uncle's library in Bedford Square. It was an unassuming townhouse around the corner from the British Museum, with a very posh red front door. Once inside, though, it was an amazing place, beautiful but simple all at the same time. There were more than twelve thousand books covering three singular subjects: astronomy, mathematics, and natural philosophy. I felt like I'd died and gone to heaven. It was the smell of the place, rather than its architectural beauty, that arrested my senses. The entire library smelled of the leather those beautiful twelve thousand volumes were bound in, as if it had happened yesterday. Like smelly varnish, it made me want to open the windows to let the knowledge out before it made my eyes start to weep with the concentration of it.

Sir Henry Cavendish was kind enough to let other scientists with fewer resources, including me, access his library. I fast became friends with the librarian, never taking out more than one or two books at a time. I particularly wanted to expand my knowledge in natural philosophy, following, I suppose, in Margaret Cavendish's footsteps. I'd have a lot to learn, though, as most of the material was beyond what I'd learnt from my uncle. I was already in a publishing mindset now and thinking about what future books might be down the road.

13

I T HAD BEEN DECIDED, THEN, that Georgiana was now in charge of 'packaging' me, whatever that meant. Nothing turned out to be more hysterical than telling Caroline about the whole project, especially this 'packaging' idea. She clearly, however, understood the meaning better than I.

"Gee, if there's anyone in this world who needs 'packaging,' it's me, not Margaret!" was the first thing out of her mouth.

Georgiana didn't disagree and simply said that in 'packaging' terms, she, Caroline, was simply always 'a work in progress.' Of course, she told her in perfect French, with a smile on her face.

She then continued, "The goal, Caroline, is to only emphasise the feminine and gentle sides of Margaret," now talking about me in the third person. "Margaret is but a dedicated headmistress, a friend, a sister, and a daughter. She has no other agenda in publishing her book other than to preserve her lessons for her own dear pupils to be able to refer to in perpetuity."

I began to feel that I wasn't even present, but I also knew Georgiana's power and recognised her knowledge of a man's world, of which I had no experience. If she was willing to help me accomplish one of my lifetime dreams, I wasn't going to be the one to get in the way.

By the following week, she'd lined up a painter for the miniature portrait that would eventually become the frontispiece of my first book. Caroline, in turn, had secured an audience with the Astronomer Royal a couple of weeks hence. However far-fetched my publishing dreams had seemed just two weeks ago, they'd now taken a giant step forwards thanks to these two women I'd come to love for different reasons and who I was very privileged to call my 'forever friends.'

As promised, Georgiana and I met the painter at the Cavendish laboratories in Clapham Common. Georgiana had thought it better not to bring the man to Blackheath. "The less he knows about you, the better," she'd said. This was also Henry Cavendish's home, but he wasn't in residence there at the time. It was apparent that Georgiana knew the painter quite well.

"Well, good morning, Mr. Shelley," she remarked as we approached the house. He was waiting for us on the front step. "Thank you so much for accommodating us at such short notice. I know your schedule is very busy." She then turned towards me. "This is my dear friend Margaret Bryan, who is publishing a book in the sciences. We would like you to paint the frontispiece to her book. The goal is to show her credibility in the subject matter, but also to highlight how beautiful and feminine she is. An unintimidating Venus, if you will. We'll go up to the laboratory on the top floor; you can use that as your studio. There should also be some astronomical props up there as well that we can use. Shall we then?" She then glanced at each of us in turn, not expecting a response. It was certainly clear that Georgiana had a plan.

When Shelley had finished painting me several hours later, along with a telescope and a globe, he turned to us, smiling, and simply said, "Voilà!" After sitting like a statue for nearly five hours, which I can tell you was more tedious than building a longcase clock, I looked at Georgiana, expecting her to be pleased.

Georgiana began to shake her head. "No, Mr. Shelley, that's not quite right. Could I impose on you, do you think, to add two young ladies to the painting as well?"

I alarmingly assumed she felt this would add more credibility to my implied motherhood and wifehood. Georgiana saw the look on my face, most likely of horror, and excused us to another room, making sure Shelley couldn't overhear our conversation.

"Margaret, darling, you need to trust me."

"Georgiana, but I don't have any children," I replied, now feeling completely uneasy. "I will readily admit I had told people I was a widow—at

Elizabeth's suggestion, might I add. Whilst I appreciate this as being disingenuous, at least my husband was supposed to be dead. Implying that I had children that are alive and well, children I am supposed to be taking care of, is a completely different level of a fib."

"Margaret, the world does not know that you have no children of your own. We don't have to say it out loud. We just need *imply* that you do."

I didn't say anything else because I had no idea what else to say. We returned to the makeshift studio, and Mr. Shelley then explained he'd need more time to add the 'children' and would drop off the final painting at Devonshire House later in the week. I could tell Georgiana was seemingly satisfied, and she said she'd bring the miniature painting to Blackheath the following week, where we could share it with Caroline in advance of our meeting with the Astronomer Royal.

The story of that strange and evolving frontispiece was not, however, to end there.

WHEN THE UNVEILING FINALLY HAPPENED, Caroline burst into such hysterical laughter that I feared there might be something wrong with her. Georgiana looked at her, annoyed. "What is wrong with you, Caroline?" she hissed at her.

Caroline, ever 'unfiltered,' came back at once. "Margaret, bless her— she looks like an old cow about to be milked. But as for the 'children,' I love the 'children.' They are brilliant!"

At this, Georgiana softened a little and admitted that maybe she'd gone a little too far. "I'll have the engraver take off a few pounds and change the hair."

I decided to pipe in at that point and said, "I do so love it in general, but when Mr. Shelley added the 'children,' he repositioned the globe where I was resting my hand, so it now appears as if I am trying to touch one of the children's breasts." Being a scientist, I was only trying to point out what would be clearly obvious to any studious observer of the painting to be a mistake or an incongruence, but the others just broke into laughter, until Georgiana finally pulled herself together and said, "I can fix that, too."

The original miniature frontispiece painting to
A Compendious System of Astronomy. *Image courtesy of*
Herschel Museum of Astronomy—Bath Preservation Trust.

14

GEORGIANA ARRIVED EARLY TO BRYAN HOUSE on the day we had scheduled the meeting with the Astronomer Royal. I could overhear her talking to Elizabeth in the hallway.

"Lovely to see you, Elizabeth. Has Margaret told you all the mischief we have been up to? It is ridiculous the games women must play to achieve anything of their own in this world, but we are going to get Margaret published, whatever it takes."

"In here—I am in the drawing room with Mary," I shouted.

The two walked into the room to witness little Mary walking across the room with her head held straight, trying to keep a book balanced on her head.

"There, Mary, you are getting it," I encouraged her. "Now, put the book down and try to keep your head in the same position and walk towards the piano. Eyes looking straight at me; try to relax. Go on now."

Elizabeth started laughing. "It is a labour of love, Gee; a labour of love with our girls."

Georgiana looked touched. "Margaret, whatever is the matter with you? You are, indeed, a mother to these girls, as you are as well, Elizabeth. It brings a tear to my eye to watch," she said, pausing for a moment to take it all in before she changed the subject.

"Margaret, I apologise for coming early," she said, gesturing for me to come into the library. "I thought we could talk for a few minutes alone before we go and collect Caroline to meet with the Reverend Maskelyne. I think it best that I lead the conversation, but I wanted to make sure that wouldn't be offensive to you."

From your lips to God's ears. I have been nervous about this for a week.

"Please, that would be God-sent," I replied.

After she revealed her intended approach, I gathered my things, and we made our way across the heath to Montague House to collect Caroline. The three of us then walked across Greenwich Park to the Royal Observatory.

As we arrived, Reverend Maskelyne was kind enough to give us a brief tour of the observatory. He jokingly explained that when they'd built the original observatory, it was put in the wrong location, because the Crown was financing the project. Apparently, the king was too miserly to move the existing foundation. Georgiana gave me a look, which I translated immediately from her raised right eyebrow to mean, *Really? Daft 'royal' men can be put in charge of the budget for what we now know to be perhaps the singular most important strategic investment ever made, to enable the prowess of the British Navy and ultimately the British Empire, yet they won't let women write books about mathematics, simply because we were born with the wrong side of the plumbing fixture?* The nod of the received translation brought a smile to both of our faces, which we attempted to stifle, as Reverend Maskelyne extended his arm for us to enter his private library.

Much to my astonishment, when Georgiana began her speech about my work at Bryan House and my wish to publish the lessons for the benefit of my pupils, Reverend Maskelyne completely interrupted her and said, "Your Grace, I am aware of the prestige of Bryan House and the uniqueness of its curriculum. My wife and I were both hoping to enrol our own daughter at Bryan House when she is of age, if that's agreeable to Mrs. Bryan. My daughter shares the same interest in astronomy as me. She has assisted me in my observatory since she taught herself to crawl out of her cot."

A warm feeling came over me, thinking about how my uncle and I had worked together side by side for all those years. This was going far better than I had imagined. The reverend then turned to look directly at me, as if expecting a reply. I froze; not only was I nervous, but I also didn't want to disrupt Georgiana's plan.

Georgiana immediately stepped in, saying, "I'm delighted that my very dear and clever friend requires no further introduction. I am sure Margaret would be happy to accept your daughter into her school when you and your wife feel it's appropriate." She then took a breath and said, "I know you're an extremely busy gentleman, so can we change the subject and discuss Margaret's endeavours to publish her astronomy lessons under her own name?"

The inflection in Reverend Maskelyne's voice changed ever so slightly as he answered Georgiana, as if he didn't quite know how to say what he wanted to say without incurring our offence. "Ladies, I don't need to remind you how difficult it is for a woman to be recognised academically in the emerging fields of the sciences, let alone published. Most Fellows in the Royal Society think women have no business trying to understand such complex subjects as advanced mathematics. I want to be clear that I'm not one of these men, and that I respect no one more, in terms of her expertise in astronomy and mathematics, than my own dear friend Caroline Herschel."

He then paused for what seemed like an eternity before continuing. "I suggest, though, that if Margaret wants to be a published scientist in her own right, she needs to present herself in a less threatening manner than Miss Herschel does. The Royal Society would ignore Miss Herschel completely if they could. They only tolerate her because of her enormous talent, and they constantly torment her by giving her brother credit for everything she does. She certainly does herself no favours, however, in how aggressively she presents her opinions."

Georgiana smiled softly at him and said, "My dear Reverend, I couldn't agree with you more, but you don't need to fret about that issue in this case, because I'm in charge of Margaret's 'packaging.' We've commissioned an accomplished artist to create a frontispiece for the book that will include her beautiful image and that of two children. She and I also intend to write a humble dedication and preface together, explaining the very limited purpose of her publishing endeavours. By the time the reader gets to page five, it will be abundantly clear that Margaret's only intention in publishing her textbook is to preserve her astronomy lessons for her pupils for years to come—pupils like your own daughter will be. What we really need your help with is attracting financial subscribers, and your public endorsement of the work would be of great value to us in that regard."

I noticed the reverend relax a bit, and I saw a small smile flit across his face. "Why, yes then, Your Grace," he said. "I'd be more than delighted to endorse Margaret's book, and I think if the objective is to find financial subscribers, might I also suggest she send her manuscript to my dear friend Dr. Charles Hutton at the Royal Military Academy for his endorsement as well. No one has a larger address book, and he's also a professional fundraiser for such endeavours."

This seemed to satisfy Georgiana completely. As a keen politician, having accomplished what she'd come for, she politely excused us, thanked him again for his time and help, and let him know we'd have the manuscript delivered to Dr. Hutton as soon as reasonably possible.

When we finally left the observatory, I couldn't have been happier with the results of our meeting. Being asked if I'd consider accepting the Astronomer Royal's daughter as a student at Bryan House was astonishing. I was also starting to see the brilliance of Georgiana's 'packaging' strategy, even though I still believed the imaginary 'children' were a real problem. Albeit, when Georgiana had mentioned to Reverend Maskelyne that we were planning to include some children in the frontispiece, he seemed to think it a good idea. I was quite sure, however, that he probably hadn't connected the dots that the 'children' were intended to represent my nonexistent motherhood and wifehood credentials.

Despite my elation over the meeting, I couldn't help but reflect on the unkind words that had been spoken about Caroline Herschel. Despite her extensive expertise in astronomy, it was clear that the Royal Society expected her to not only grovel to be heard, but also to be satisfied simply that her work was being read at all, even if all the credit was accruing to her brother's reputation, and presumably his bank account. This balance of who women needed to be, or more importantly, needed not to be, in this strange world of powerful men was becoming increasingly obvious to me. 'Beautifully stupid' might be the goal, but they needed to be addressed separately to understand the true objective, which was not too much of either one—a sort of 'above-average-looking porcelain doll who plays the piano with some mastery, but doesn't speak unless spoken to.'

I kept my thoughts to myself, though. I knew Georgiana would tell me, "Margaret, when you're dealt a good hand, even if you adore your opponent, you must play it. It's the only way to win and the only way the game is played."

By the time I made it through the front door of Bryan House, I was completely exhausted. Elizabeth insisted that I give her a full update on all the day's events, though, before I finally escaped to bed. I dreamt of publishing my own book that night.

15

THE NEXT DAY, AS PROMISED, I sent a copy of my manuscript, *A Compendious System of Astronomy*, to Sir Charles Hutton at the Royal Military Academy. As we were waiting for a response from him, Georgiana pushed forward on finding a publisher and finalising the frontispiece of the book. Despite a very circuitous journey, including the removal of my right hand from one of the 'children's' breasts, the final engraved version, completed by a man called William Nutter, was, indeed, very beautiful.

MRS. BRYAN AND CHILDREN

The final frontispiece to A Compendious System of Astronomy.
World History Archive / Alamy Stock Photo.

It seemed like forever, even though Georgiana told me to stop worrying so much, but finally a late Christmas present arrived, and I could not have been more delighted. Sir Hutton used the word *ingenious* to describe my manuscript. Georgiana decided we would include a copy of his letter in the book. 'Marketing,' I think is what she had called it.

Woolwich, January 6, 1797

Madam,

I herewith return the ingenious MS. of Astronomical Lectures you favoured me with the sight of, which I have read over with great pleasure; and the more so, to find that even the learned and more difficult sciences are thus beginning to be successfully cultivated by the extraordinary and elegant talents of the female writers of the present day.

Should you, madam, give to your friends and to the public to benefit by the publication of these your learned and useful labours, I beg to have the honour of being considered one of the encouragers of so useful a work:

And am, with great respect,

Madam,

Your most obedient and most humble servant,

Charles Hutton

———

Sir Charles Hutton's written response to Margaret Bryan's original manuscript of A Compendious System of Astronomy.

Then came the task of writing the promised humble dedication and preface. Georgiana suggested some parameters. "Margaret, I think both the dedication and the preface should be all about your pupils. Your wish to publish your lessons is solely to allow them reflection on their education at Bryan House," she eloquently stated.

I wholeheartedly agreed with her, particularly with the imaginary 'children' problem in mind. To that end, I thought that maybe I could subtly suggest in the prose that the 'children' represented my own pupils, not my own children.

"I agree, Georgiana, it should be about my pupils. It would certainly be an accurate representation of how dearly I care for them. Why don't I draft something for your review so we have something to work with?" I then painstakingly wrote the draft of both the dedication and the preface and, rather nervously, presented it to Georgiana. She read both sections thoroughly, at least twice, and initially seemed pleased.

"Margaret, you have a great talent for writing; you should consider writing novels. They're far more financially lucrative, I'd imagine. Your writing has a keen authenticity and humility that will capture your audience immediately. The only thing I'd say, to be consistent with the frontispiece, would be to change the part where it says, 'I've added my portrait to these lectures,' to include 'along with my own dear children.'"

I couldn't help but groan. Why did that phrase, *my own dear children*, feel so dishonest?

Georgiana was clearly losing patience. "Margaret, this is important. You're not telling lies; your pupils are your own, for heaven's sake. They live with you, you take care of them, and you are, indeed, a mother away from home to them. If people perceive you as even moderately motherly, you'll be less threatening and more believable with respect to your publishing motives. This might not be fair, but it is fact. You need to put your best foot forwards. You do go on to say, 'Believe me, to be forgotten by you, my pupils, would inflict a severe pang on that heart, which feels for you almost parental tenderness.' I think that's compelling. Personally, I would leave out the word *almost*. Parental tenderness is binary, in my opinion: You either have it or you don't."

I sighed, but attempted to compromise by saying, "How about 'my two *dear* children,' rather than *own*, and *almost* is staying. And yes, I agree that you either have or don't have parental tenderness, but you need to be a parent before you can have it or not. *Almost* just implies almost parental."

That made her laugh out loud. "Perfect, Margaret, that would be perfect," which is how we ended the entire uncomfortable conversation.

BY THE LATE SPRING, Georgiana and Sir Hutton had amassed more than enough financial subscribers to publish the book and provide me with a handsome profit. Before the close of 1797, I was the published authouress of a scientific book that bore my own name. I was forty years old. Caroline threw a lovely party at Montague House to celebrate the occasion. It was, indeed, a historic moment for us. Halfway through the party, and several glasses of wine later, she threw her arms around me, kissed me directly on the mouth, and screeched, "Margaret, we did it; we really did it!"

"Yes, we did," I said, laughing along with her. "Yes, we did!"

The book would be published in two subsequent editions, in 1799 and 1805, providing even greater profitability for me and credibility for Bryan House, adding to my legitimacy within both the scientific and educational communities. I can't describe the humility I felt, or the gratefulness to my dear friends and, most particularly, Georgiana. Without this support, the publication of my first book would simply have never happened.

Having said that, as I should have expected, the book was met with a reproving response from the *Critical Review* publication. They found fault with everything, from the accuracy of the scientific content to the senseless attempt to educate young ladies on complex subjects they were incapable of understanding. The publication poorly articulated that I was attempting to turn young ladies into young men, as if to suggest that this was an aspirational objective, simply by definition. To add insult to injury, they also had a go at my religious inclinations. I was more than annoyed and provided a cursory response, one that I knew would fall on deaf ears regardless.

Georgiana brightened my spirits, though, by saying, "Margaret, they have given you nearly four and a half pages of disparaging rubbish, which will sell more books than any single paragraph of praise ever would. You should send them a thank-you letter," which did make me feel better.

THE ONLY THING THAT DAMPENED my joy that year was the passing of my auntie Anne. Thomas had written to let me know she was very poorly, so I went to stay with her for a weekend at Bryan House on Golden Lane. After the servant had let me in, I went to find her in her bedroom. Knocking on the door, I said, "Helloooo" as Thomas would have.

"Margaret, is that you? What a lovely surprise," I heard faintly from behind the door.

"It is, indeed, me," I replied, now opening the door slowly to peer in. She looked weak and she'd lost a lot of weight, but that smile was still on her face and those beautiful eyes of hers still twinkled bright blue.

"Margaret, what brings you to visit? A little birdie told me you have been very busy writing and publishing a book."

"Well, that same little birdie told me you were poorly, so here I am," I answered, which made her laugh as I reached down to kiss her on both cheeks.

Well, Auntie Anne's health was the last thing she wanted to talk about that afternoon. "Margaret, come sit; tell me all about your book."

"I don't have to tell you about it because I brought you a brand-new copy of your own," I said, reaching into my bag, pulling out the book and proudly handing it to her. At first, she didn't say anything. She just ran her fingers softly over the cover, like she used to do to the beautiful clocks my uncle and I built together. Then she slowly opened the cover, saw the frontispiece, and gasped audibly.

"Margaret, you look so beautiful, but who are the children?"

"It's a long story, and if anyone else asks, please just tell them they are my two favourite pupils," I answered sharply.

"All right," she said with a laugh, sensing I didn't want to talk about it. "Margaret, your parents and your uncle would be so very proud, but can you imagine what Mamie would be doing if she knew you'd written a maths book that bore your own name?"

"Cartwheels," I answered, starting to weep a little. "Mamie is doing cartwheels."

Auntie Anne died ten days later. We had said our goodbyes for now. I knew she was telling anybody in heaven who would listen to her all about my book, and Mamie was interrupting her when she didn't get it all right. Auntie Anne is buried with Mamie, my grandfather, my parents, and my uncle at the family plot at St. Luke's, Finsbury.

Bryan House on Golden Lane was released shortly after Aunt Anne's death. Thomas and Sarah found a new home in Chelsea, near the Royal Military Hospital, where Sarah would be closer to the other families whose men were enlisted with the Fifteenth Regiment, now better known just as the 'Fifteenth.' Auntie Anne's death was hard on Sarah as, like my mother, she'd now have to live mostly alone, waiting for her husband's hopefully safe but infrequent returns home. Thankfully, the Fifteenth had recently come home from the Continent and were now stationed at Windsor, so at least Thomas was in England for the time being. Elizabeth and I went to see Sarah in Chelsea often, and she'd come to stay with us at Bryan House in Blackheath, sometimes for weeks at a time.

We were all celebrating New Year's Eve together that year—because Thomas had only had a few days leave with us at Christmas—when

Elizabeth opened a bottle of champagne and raised her glass. "Here's to the distinguished scientific authouress, Margaret Bryan," she cheered. It certainly made the moment real. I embraced her and Sarah, as if they were both my 'own' sisters.

16

HENRY CAVENDISH, GEORGIANA'S UNCLE, was arguably one of the most prominent scientists of his day in Britain, and an important Fellow and contributor to the Royal Society. He was frequently published in their scientific journal, *Philosophical Transactions.* He was also a close friend of the Astronomer Royal and paid frequent visits to the Royal Observatory, often improving the accuracy of the instrumentation there at his own expense. By all accounts, he was a shy but generous man. I never met him, although I felt like I'd come to know him through Georgiana's constant praise of him, not to mention the generosity of his semipublic library in Bedford Square. Henry Cavendish was neither a political nor religious man, but simply a man with the most intense curiosity of understanding how the world works, solely through a mathematical lens. Whilst I was a regular visitor to his library at Bedford Square, I'd only been to his home in Clapham Common once, with Georgiana, to meet the painter for the original painting for the frontispiece of my book.

One afternoon, I was having lunch with Georgiana at Devonshire House when she began a conversation with me about her uncle's most recent work. "My uncle has just begun a new experiment at his home in Clapham Common, and the entire London scientific community is up in arms about it. There's been much discrepancy in the Royal Society for years regarding Isaac Newton's gravitational theory, and my uncle has now decided to physically prove his hypothesis one way or the other."

After taking a small sip of wine, Georgiana continued. "Apparently, the first part of the experiment requires the accurate weighing of planet

Earth, which, if you can believe, he's now attempting to do in his back garden. The neighbours are completely outraged, as the contraption he's built to conduct this 'weighing of the earth' is apparently circus-like and very dangerous. I feel so ignorant—I don't understand it, and therefore I can't talk about it. Will you come and observe it with me tomorrow morning and perhaps explain to me how it all works?"

What I learnt soon after was that Henry Cavendish was really trying to calculate the gravitational acceleration constant of the Earth, better known as g. As a student and teacher of Newtonian mechanics, I was very familiar with Newton's equation used to measure the mechanics of force acting on an object: the multiplication of the mass of the object with its acceleration ($F = ma$). I also knew that when the acceleration was limited to only that of the earth's gravitational force, then a simply became known as g. Isaac Newton had been the first to define g conceptually, but he'd stopped short of trying to calculate its actual empirical value. The subject had long been in discussion within the broad scientific community, even as far back as 1772 when the Royal Society had set up a committee to do exactly that: calculate g. The 'Committee of Attraction,' as it was called, ascertained an empirical value for g, which Henry Cavendish, himself part of the committee, disagreed with. His basic contention was that the underlying assumptions used at the beginning of the experiment were unsupportable. Now, at the age of sixty-seven, Henry Cavendish had decided to rectify this supposed miscalculation by conducting his own experiment in his back garden, and I was going to observe it the following day with Georgiana. I was giddy with excitement. I sent word to Elizabeth that I'd be staying the night in London with Georgiana, and the next day, the two of us made our way by carriage to Clapham Common.

"Margaret, I must warn you that I'm not exactly sure what to expect or how close we can get. My uncle won't even be there this morning, and as I mentioned, there have been multiple complaints lodged with the authorities over the entire spectacle."

"I can't but imagine, myself," I quietly answered as we turned the corner onto her uncle's street, panicking inside as to whether I'd even understand the experiment, let alone be able to explain it to Georgiana. As we slowly approached the house and went round the back, I couldn't believe my eyes. Up ahead were multiple huge lead balls, large and larger, arranged on a balancing contraption, all in perpetual motion in, as much as was possible, an otherwise completely controlled environment. I couldn't believe all this was happening in his back garden, and I must admit, I did feel some sympathy for the neighbours.

I also breathed a sigh of relief after about ten minutes of observation, because I now understood exactly what Henry Cavendish was attempting to do. He was trying to measure the differential force between the larger and smaller balls within the earth's gravitational force, from which he would then make an extrapolation to determine the earth's mass. Once he'd found a reasonably accurate value for the earth's mass, m, better known as *weight*, he'd be able to solve for the final unknown variable, g, earth's gravitational constant, in the rest of Newton's theoretical equation ($F = mg$).

I explained to Georgiana the maths her uncle would be trying to do, at least in theory, which she seemed to grasp as fast as I could get the words out of my mouth. The woman never ceased to amaze me. We stayed there together for another full hour, watching this repetitive experiment, with barely a word spoken between us. I'll never forget that day, that beautiful spring morning in Clapham Common, with Georgiana. Two women out of time and place, quietly enjoying our temporary dislocation from planet Earth, observing her uncle's peculiar science experiment.

As we were leaving, Georgiana grabbed my hand urgently and said to me, "My dear Margaret, thank you for such a magnificent day. It's just been unbelievable. I now feel completely prepared to drop jaws at Devonshire House as I explain how it all works to my political friends. I think, Margaret, had we been born in a different time and place, I'd be the prime minister and you'd be chairwoman of the Royal Society."

"Chairman would be fine. I wouldn't make them waste the money reprinting the stationery," I said, which made us both giggle. In that particularly glorious moment, all of that felt possible.

Henry Cavendish did, indeed, recalculate g, the earth's gravitational constant in Newtonian mechanics. He published his defence of it in a thesis of fifty-seven pages addressed to the Royal Society a little less than a year later. The man was thorough, for sure, and his work withstood the test of scrutiny. He was eventually credited as being the first man to accurately determine the empirical value of g, and Georgiana and I had been there to watch it all.

I apologise, I digress—but I find great humour in the fact that the gravitational constant force of planet Earth will be forever known as g. I can think of nothing more appropriate than this legacy to my beloved and dear friend Gee, who was as large a gravitational force on planet Earth than perhaps any other mortal being who has ever inhabited it. With all due respect, of course, to whatever Sir Isaac Newton and Sir Henry Cavendish could have described in a series of mathematical equations that have unquestionably changed the world in which we live forevermore.

17

W E ' D B E E N A T B R Y A N H O U S E, Blackheath, for nearly five years, and we had achieved a prominent reputation as a top boarding school for young ladies—albeit there were precious few to begin with. Margaret Maskelyne did become a pupil of ours, in 1798, and, like myself, I believe her disposition to understand complex mathematical concepts was at least partially innate and inherited from her very talented father. She was also a very diligent and hardworking student in her own right. In general, our pupils came from well-to-do families, although we also provided accommodation for those young women who demonstrated talent but whose families didn't have the resources to afford the tuition. Both Georgiana and Caroline were generous contributors to these scholarship opportunities.

In addition to our work at Bryan House, Elizabeth and I had also become involved with an orphanage being run out of Pagoda House, just across the other side of the heath from Bryan House. Caroline had been the orphanage's sponsor since her adoption of Edwardina Kent. The Duke of Kent had taken respite at Montague House after a serious war injury, and had regretfully, in late 1797, impregnated one of Caroline's servants. Clearly, he hadn't been completely incapacitated. Whilst the duke took little responsibility for the whole affair, Caroline made sure the young lady's reputation was somewhat repaired, gave her a sizeable sum of money, and promised her that she would take care of the baby. It was in such circumstances that Caroline was, indeed, at her best, helping those in need, especially young children.

Edwardina filled a huge void for Caroline, given the growing absence of her own daughter, Princess Charlotte. So, shortly after adopting

Edwardina, Caroline decided to surround herself with the love of many children, even if they weren't of her own womb.

"Margaret, I have been thinking," she said to me one day whilst feeding Edwardina on the kitchen floor of Montague House, baby between the folds of her skirts, legs spread on the bare wooden floor.

"I think I should like to start an orphanage to do something more useful in my life. This little one has inspired me," she said, looking down at baby Edwardina, now cooing at her. "I don't know if you know of Pagoda House. It is a beautiful but peculiar building right here in Blackheath, and I have just learnt that it is part of my estate. I was wondering if you and Elizabeth would help me run it; I don't think I can manage it on my own. Could we go over there tomorrow and see if it might be suitable for an orphanage? I have been told there are a great many bedrooms on the second floor."

So, the following day, Caroline, Elizabeth, and I walked to Pagoda House for the inspection. Caroline had understated how beautiful the building really was. It looked like something one might see in a Japanese tea garden: a sculpted roof and the entire building covered in black lacquer, like some of the clocks I used to build with my uncle. Without much effort, we all concluded that we could make it work and began making plans as to how to make it happen. Elizabeth and I had already agreed as we were leaving Bryan House to collect Caroline that we'd both like to be part of the orphanage.

"Count us in" was the last thing Elizabeth said as Caroline locked the door behind us. Funny, Pagoda House was later fashioned by the press to be Caroline's 'summer residence,' which seemed ridiculous, as you could almost see it from Montague House. This, however, proved to be a strategically suitable title for the new orphanage when we were forced to entertain menacing questions from some intrusive neighbours about what was going on there. At the end of the day, there was very little anyone could do about it. Caroline owned the rights to the property, and she was still the Princess of Wales, much to her husband's dismay.

By November 1799, we had nine children in our care at Pagoda House: five girls and four boys. I'd hired a live-in childminder, and we all spent as much time over there as we could. Caroline would bundle up little Edwardina to cross the heath and, whenever she could, bring Princess Charlotte with her. Caroline would sit on the floor and play with the children, often for hours. Some of the children learnt how to speak a little bit of German from the games Caroline taught them.

I will say that those were some of the happiest moments I had at Blackheath, helping to provide a beautiful and loving sanctuary for innocent children who'd done nothing wrong other than to have been born poor, or worse, to parents who simply didn't want them. I also realised in those moments, though, the irony of helping to care for these unwanted children and the bittersweetness of never being able to have children of my own.

18

IN THE LATE SPRING OF 1800, Georgiana invited me to attend a party at Chiswick House, just outside London. Chiswick House was Georgiana and her husband's summer residence—a beautiful neo-Palladian villa with rolling gardens of indescribable beauty. Georgiana referred to it as her earthly paradise, which I thought was an understatement. I was more than delighted when I received the formal invitation. I was also a bit curious when I noticed Georgiana's additional handwritten note.

> *Margaret,*
>
> *I'm so ever hopeful that you'll be able to attend the party at Chiswick. If possible, I was hoping you'd also be able to have dinner with me and stay the night at Devonshire House afterwards. I have something of a private nature that I wish to discuss with you. If you can't make the party, maybe we could arrange to meet another time?*
>
> *Gee*

With her courier still on the steps, I scribbled a reply.

> *Georgiana,*
>
> *It would be my pleasure to attend the party and have dinner with you afterwards. I'm looking forward to it already.*
>
> *Lovingly,*
> *Margaret*

I often asked Elizabeth to attend these social events with me, but she always politely declined. She simply had no interest in milling around with the British aristocracy when the rest of the country was suffering so much financially due to the heavy price of the wars in France. She reminded me of Papa that way. Whilst she was close with both Georgiana and Caroline, as she knew them so well, everybody else from that elite class she just put in the same bucket as 'no time for.' 'Empty-headed and frivolous' I think is how she put it.

I must say, I wasn't much interested in the pomp and circumstance of the British gentry, either. I never turned down an invitation from Georgiana, though, for fear of offending her. On this occasion, however, I was very much looking forward to it, and I was particularly curious as to the 'something of a private nature' she wished to discuss with me afterwards.

I arrived at the afternoon party on time, which meant nobody else was there yet. It was a wonderful opportunity to drink in the beauty of the place and the glorious afternoon. The main building was rather unassuming in comparison to Devonshire House, but it had a presence nonetheless. It was the grounds, though, that created the majestic splendour of the place: acres of rolling grasses and a small, winding river running through the middle of it, all littered with tiny footpaths and bridges and covered in the most exotic flowers I have ever seen.

There was no sign of Georgiana yet, not that I was surprised. Not only was she expecting hundreds of people at the party; she was also preparing for her eldest daughter's coming out as a debutante. This would likely employ all her time until the appropriate husband had been identified and the final dowry deal brokered. It made me laugh to think I hoped her daughter was a little less nervous than I was at my publishing coming-out party, and at least, unlike mine, she wouldn't have to deal with the imaginary 'children' as uninvited guests on the invitation.

The day seemed to go on forever, and the shoes I'd misguidedly worn were becoming more unbearable. I let Georgiana's lady-in-waiting know that I was retiring to Devonshire House until the duchess was ready to receive me. I then took a waiting carriage back to Devonshire House, where I quickly took a bath and went to the drawing room to wait for Georgiana. True to form, she arrived about an hour later, like a ball of fire, having ordered a private dinner for us in her bedroom suite. When the meal was served and she'd dismissed the servants, after taking a large gulp of wine, she looked at me with a seemingly heavy heart.

"Margaret, we have a problem that I need your help with. I hesitate to ask such a burden of you, but I know of no other whom I trust as I trust you."

I was lost for words, just as I was when we had first met and she told me how much she envied my life. I was also confused as to who 'we' was.

"Georgiana, you're like a sister to me," I said. "I'd do anything to be of assistance in your hour of need."

She smiled a little then, and said, "Margaret, I'm touched by your kind words, but it's my own sister, Harriet, who most needs your help."

"Your sister?" I interrupted her, now puzzled.

"Yes, let me try to explain. Perhaps you know that my only sister, Harriet, is married to Lord Bessborough. Well, she now finds herself pregnant with a child that is not only not his but mathematically impossible to be his. I have told you already that I myself have also made this error of judgement, and was punished brutally for it by my husband. Not only was I forced to give up my daughter, but I was banished to the Continent for years and separated from my other children. I fear my sister's punishment from Bessborough will be even worse, and more permanent, if she is found out."

Georgiana started to get visibly upset at this point, and I wasn't quite sure what to say, so I just reached for her hand.

"I'd like to ask you, Margaret," she said, tears now welling up in her eyes, "if you and Elizabeth would consider being this child's foster parents? It would all be done privately, and we could say the baby came to the orphanage at Pagoda House anonymously and that you've always wanted a child of your own." She had to stop for a moment to pull herself together before she continued. "Most importantly, this child, and particularly if the child is female, will have an unprecedented education in your care. Surely that would give her a better chance in this judgemental world, having been born illegitimate through no fault of her own. Take your time, Margaret; I know this is a lot to take in." She then reached up to wipe her tears with a lace handkerchief.

I looked at her in sheer disbelief, the words still spinning in my head like an unhinged door in a storm. I could hardly breathe. "I don't know, Georgiana. This is not without risk to Elizabeth and me, and the school we have worked so hard for. Can I ask you who else knows, or will know, about this pregnancy? And what power do you have to protect your sister and her child, as well as our school and our reputation, if this is exposed?"

Georgiana sighed audibly. "Harriet and I are still trying to work all this out, and I'll do everything in my power to protect those concerned. The only other person who knows of this pregnancy now is the child's father, Lord Granville Leveson-Gower." She paused for what seemed like an eternity. "Margaret, I know this is a lot to ask, especially as you and Elizabeth must also be comfortable with just being foster parents. Harriet doesn't want to give the baby up for adoption, and both she and Granville intend to maintain a relationship with the child. Of course, that implies that they will both be contributing the necessary financial support for the child's upbringing."

The money was the last thing on my mind. I could hear Thomas's voice in my head, banging away, telling me what a terrible idea this was. *It was a chance, though, a chance to be a maman, even if only a foster maman.* I trusted Georgiana with my life, so I took a very deep breath and said, "Georgiana, let me talk to Elizabeth tomorrow. If she is agreeable, we will find a way to make this work."

Georgiana was clearly relieved. She leaned in towards me and took my other hand in hers. "Oh, Margaret, I knew I could count on you. Would you like me to come with you to talk to Elizabeth?"

"No, I don't think that would be fair to her. Let me do that on my own." We both stood up, and I embraced Georgiana closely in a surreal moment that seemingly bound us together forever.

The journey back to Blackheath seemed endless. When I finally arrived home, Elizabeth was in the drawing room reading the Sunday paper. I just barged in.

"Elizabeth, do you remember me mentioning that Georgiana had something private to discuss with me?"

"How could I forget, Margaret? It's all you've been talking about for weeks. So, what was it then? What was so 'private' about what she wanted to talk to you about?" she said, smiling and putting down the newspaper.

"Georgiana's sister, Harriet, is pregnant with an illegitimate baby, and she wants us to foster the child for her, and I'm hoping you'll agree."

"What?" she exclaimed, followed by complete silence. A short while later, she seemed to finally find her voice. "Margaret, what are you talking about?"

"That's about it. Her sister is pregnant with a child who doesn't nor couldn't belong to her husband. The child needs a family, and Georgiana has asked us, and I think we should say yes. If not us, who? The baby could end up in an orphanage if no one else wants to touch that dirty laundry." I regretted the last words as soon as they came out. I certainly didn't mean to imply the baby was dirty laundry. He or she had nothing to do with the bad behaviour that had led up to their conception.

Elizabeth understandably looked worried. "Margaret, you know that Thomas would say that this is a terrible idea, and not without good reason. This is a significant risk to the reputation of our school."

"I don't want to talk to Thomas about it," I spat at her. "Sorry, that was rude. Let me leave you to your thoughts. I understand it is a big decision. I will understand and respect whatever decision you make. I am not daft enough to think I can do this without you."

I left her and retreated to my library, where I sat motionless in the wingback chair and waited. About an hour later, she knocked on the door.

"Margaret," she said, poking her head in the door. I stood up immediately, as almost to attention; I am not even sure why. "This may be our only chance, so . . . yes, count me in."

I started to cry and embraced her tightly until I heard her gasp for breath as I did so. As with my apprenticeship, the school, and my book, in a seemingly random moment from heaven, my life was again about to change forever, this time with a newborn baby we could call our 'own.' I could hardly breathe myself. Both Elizabeth and I agreed that we would tell no one until something happened, to be sure this baby miracle was real.

We also learnt several weeks later that Sarah and Thomas were expecting their first child. Neither Elizabeth nor I had breathed a word about our secret baby, but I lived vicariously through Sarah's pregnancy. I'm sure I was completely annoying, worrying her with the most inappropriate questions, particularly as it was her first pregnancy. I was just consumed to have our 'own' pregnancy to follow, as unimaginable as that had once seemed.

$$19$$

THE NEXT SIX MONTHS OF our lives seemed to hang entirely in the balance of our secret pregnancy. I did, however, do as much research as I could on the baby's biological parents during this time, given that we'd all need to figure out how to get along. Not that I was particularly impressed with either one of them, but Georgiana's sister, Harriet, had a particularly colourful past. Granville Leveson-Gower certainly wasn't the first extracurricular activity in her marriage to Lord Bessborough, although it was public knowledge that the man was regularly abusive to his wife.

One particularly noteworthy ex-paramour of Harriet's was Richard Brinsley Sheridan, the Irish playwright and owner of the Drury Lane Theatre. Harriet's husband had apparently caught the two of them fornicating in his own bed. He'd immediately filed for divorce, and certainly would have succeeded in her total demise if not for the intervention of Georgiana's brother and husband. Harriet had also been arrested once and held overnight in the Newgate prison because she'd been unable to pay her outrageous gambling debts. Not exactly the gold standard for motherhood, but let beggars not be choosers, I felt. I was just eternally grateful at any chance to be a maman, even if it was just a foster maman.

The baby's father, Granville Leveson-Gower, was a young bachelor and a Whig MP who came from Staffordshire gentry. He was twelve years younger than Harriet. Apparently, the couple had met in Naples, Italy, on holiday in 1794, with Leveson-Gower being immediately besotted with Harriet. According to Georgiana, they'd become lovers shortly thereafter.

I did wonder how Harriet's husband hadn't suspected anything of the affair, as it wasn't apparently conducted with any sort of discretion—even before the concealed pregnancy. I tried to put all that negativity out of mind, though, and just reassure myself that Georgiana would protect us all from injury.

When the day finally arrived, I gave Mr. Murphy the details I'd been given by a messenger in the middle of the night, which was simply an address. I was disappointed that there wasn't a reference to the sex of the child, but I understood why and just hoped he or she was healthy. I didn't know what to expect when we finally arrived at our destination after what seemed like a trip round the world. As we approached the house, at the end of a very long driveway, I saw the front door open and a woman come out, cradling a swaddled bundle. I opened the carriage door and took the child into my arms. The only words the woman said were "It's a girl; her name is Harriet. Please take care of her."

I held the baby in silence all the way back to Bryan House, in a seemingly straightforwards military operation to secure the safe passage of an infant child from point A to point B. It wasn't until I arrived home with her, with Mrs. Murphy and Elizabeth anxiously awaiting our arrival, and after Mr. Murphy had safely secured the carriage step, that I presented our collective daughter to her new family.

"Her name is Harriet," I said, and then I wept uncontrollably. At forty-three years old, I was now officially a maman, even if just a foster maman.

Once Little Harriet arrived, it was hard to find time for anything else beyond our usual Bryan House responsibilities. Mrs. Murphy was particularly helpful with the baby, as she came from a large Irish family. She was forever reassuring Elizabeth and me that we couldn't 'break' her. Less than two weeks after Little Harriet's birth, Sarah delivered a healthy baby girl. She and Thomas named her Elizabeth Jekyll Bryan, after Mamie. We would also learn just a few months later that Sarah was pregnant again, and on September 9, 1801, George Bryan arrived into this earthly world.

Despite our newfound parental responsibilities and running Bryan House, we still managed to make sure we had enough time to help Caroline keep the orphanage going. It was a couple of years after Little Harriet's arrival, when Elizabeth was minding the children there, that she heard a knock at the door. Convinced it was a menacing neighbour trying to spy on us, she was hesitant to open the door at first.

"Yes, who is at the door? How can I help you?" she said from behind the locked door.

"I need help; please help me," she faintly heard from behind the other side of the door. "Please help me; I'm having a baby."

Whether the orphanage's reputation for also accepting babies was now getting around, I don't know, as we'd certainly inferred that was where Little Harriet had come from, but we were ill-prepared for delivering babies there. Elizabeth flung open the door to find a young woman, now squatting to the ground in piercing pain, who was clearly about to deliver a child.

Elizabeth turned to the childminder, who lived at Pagoda House with the children, with a calmness that only she could have had in such a moment. "Claire, you need to go and get Mrs. Murphy as fast as your legs can carry you. You need to tell her what is happening and that she needs to bring supplies. Now! Find Margaret after that."

Claire nodded, looking petrified and racing towards the door. By the time I arrived with Mrs. Murphy and Claire in tow less than an hour later, the baby's arrival was imminent. Mrs. Murphy took over from there, and a beautiful baby girl came into the world a few minutes later. When mother and daughter were announced healthy, Mrs. Murphy put the child on her mother's breast, and the world seemed to stop turning for a minute. It was certainly the most heavenly thing I had ever witnessed, this miracle of life. The afterbirth not yet finished, the young lady turned to Elizabeth and said, "I have no home for her—will you take care of her? It is known you are kind to unwanted children here."

"Yes, of course, but you must name your baby first," Elizabeth said, holding her hand.

"What is your name?" the young girl asked her.

"Elizabeth," I answered for her, seeing now that the whole chain of events of the day was finally starting to get to her.

"My name is Lucy," the young girl said, still looking at Elizabeth. "We brought this baby into the world together, so her name will be Lucy Elizabeth."

Lucy Elizabeth's mother stayed with us a few days after the birth, but she left of her own volition without letting us know. Elizabeth had already tucked a sizeable sum of money into her bag to make sure she could at least get back to wherever she might call home. Elizabeth then carried the newborn back to Bryan House, swaddled at her breast. Little Harriet now had a baby sister who completely amused her and who she tortured to no end.

I remember one day being in the kitchen when I overheard Elizabeth talking to Little Harriet in the music room. "Harriet, why does Lucy's face look like a chimney sweep? She's not old enough to have done that to herself."

She's not going to try to reason with her, is she? I looked on, amused, eavesdropping from the crack in the door.

"No, Maman, I did that. I lost my cat, so now Lucy's my cat."

What do you say to that? Perhaps she'd make a good barrister one day—if she was allowed to be one. I couldn't help but barge in. Little Harriet looked up immediately and hesitated, no doubt to consider whether punitive action was coming her way. When Elizabeth and I started laughing, she happily joined in, finishing off, "Lucy cat's name is Black," which made us all laugh even harder.

I apologise; I digress. Eavesdropping is one of my worst sins, despite knowing it's unchristian and rude. It's an acquired talent from sneaking around my uncle's shop for so many years—one that I've never really found a good reason, nor the discipline, to get rid of.

Not long after Lucy Elizabeth's unexpected arrival, Caroline, too, experienced a similar event at Montague House. A woman by the name of Sophia Austin came to Caroline's back door. At first, it seemed like she just wanted Caroline's assistance in getting work for her husband. Shortly afterwards, though, she asked Caroline to adopt her infant son, William Austin, for a small amount of money. Caroline had immediately obliged her.

Despite all the joy our 'own' babies now gave us, it saddened me to think about all the unwanted babies in this cruel world who didn't have any place to call home. It made me grateful to be helping even just a little bit through our work at the Pagoda House orphanage.

20

I T WAS SOMETIME IN THE SPRING of 1804, when Caroline was throwing one of her infamous Montague House parties, that I had the pleasure of meeting her brother-in-law, Prince Augustus Frederick of the Royal House of Hanover, more commonly tailored as the Duke of Sussex. I was fortunate enough to be seated next to him at dinner, which, with the benefit of hindsight, I now think was by the calculated design of Georgiana.

"Mrs. Bryan, Gee has told me a little bit about you. I must admit, I'm most intrigued," he said as the starter was being served. "I'm a student of natural philosophy and mathematics myself and have many connections within the Royal Society."

"You're very kind, Your Royal Highness, but I'm afraid what I do isn't that intriguing at all. The most rewarding part of my work is the teaching, and the success of that investment is often measured in the repetition of the instruction, which can be quite laborious," I replied.

"I'm sure you vastly underestimate your talents, Mrs. Bryan, and please, don't call me Your Royal Highness."

"And please don't call me Mrs. Bryan," I interrupted, which made him laugh, and that started to put me at ease.

Almost immediately after dinner, Georgiana pulled me aside with that mischievous giggle of hers, which implied she'd had either too much to drink, a bit of good gossip, or both.

"Margaret, I think the Duke of Sussex fancies you," she said. "I caught him looking your way more than once during the opening reception, and he's been inquiring of me and others about your affairs."

I felt my face flush and found myself at a complete loss for words. It wasn't that I wasn't flattered, but I'd never in my life found myself having this sort of conversation about a man with anyone before. I'd deliberately avoided potential suitors all my life, despite my uncle's valiant attempts before I became his apprentice. After a certain age, though, if you're female and unmarried, even by choice, one achieves the very official, government-endorsed status of 'spinster.' The title clearly requires no elaboration if you've gained such a miserable label in life, other than to state the obvious: that you don't spend much time daydreaming about meeting a handsome prince. It occurred to me, though, that Georgiana was completely blind to this condition, having been bred—and I use that word respectfully—to attract the attention of men since her very birth. I considered her kind, then, when I realised she was simply trying to pay me a compliment. Of course, what she was suggesting was absurd.

Georgiana continued, "Don't think your age is an issue for him; his ex-wife is our age, and I'm certain you're far more beautiful and agreeable than she. Maybe he just likes older women. Trust me, Margaret, he's a perfect gentleman—not a *beast* like the rest of the Hanoverian band of brothers. Don't be such a prude, I beg of you—what a waste of such an alluring and intelligent creature."

I didn't quite know if she was referring to me or him as an 'alluring and intelligent creature,' but I wasn't about to ask for clarification. "Georgiana, you're very kind, but that's a ridiculous thought," I said, and was delighted to be interrupted by Caroline, who was now very drunk and starting to undress herself.

"We will see, Margaret. I am seldom wrong when it comes to matters of the heart," Georgiana replied as she gently attempted to remove a toy monkey from Caroline's now nearly bare breast. When Georgiana was finally successful in removing the offensive object without tearing Caroline's garments, the toy animal then sprang a very large erection as a result of Caroline having pulled some sort of string out of its bottom. Caroline was delighted with herself on this new development, even if Georgiana and I were not the least bit amused.

"Really, Caroline, stop. It's rude," Georgiana scolded her.

I was about to go outside for a bit of fresh air; with all of Caroline's antics and the discussion regarding the duke, I was beginning to feel a bit short of breath. Just then, I felt Georgiana touch my elbow and whisper in my ear, "Margaret, what on earth is going on over there?" She pointed discreetly across the room to the shadows of a quiet corner. "Is that Lady Charlotte Douglas and Sir Sydney Smith? Am I wrong? She is almost kissing him on the lips, and he has his hand on the small of her back. Wherever is her husband?"

"I think you are right. It is them," I said, squinting a bit to get a better look at the dark corner. "I don't know much about Sir Sydney Smith, but I can tell you I don't care for Lady Douglas. I don't think she has Caroline's best interests in her heart when she pretends to call her *friend*. She hangs about Montague House a lot.

"I just worry she is too close to the Prince of Wales and can't be trusted. I realise that isn't nice, but I would never reach such a conclusion without reasonable observation and evidence," I finished.

Georgiana looked pensive, and I am sure her lips pursed. "You do know that Lady Charlotte is wife to the Duke of Sussex's equerry, Sir John Douglas, who is also his gentleman of the bedchamber?" she replied. "Sir Sydney Smith is a decorated naval officer who lives with them in Greenwich Village. It is rumoured that Sir Sydney is one of Caroline's many lovers, but perhaps he also has affections for Lady Douglas, as perhaps she does for him. Don't tell Caroline that, though. That would cause serious trouble. Watch that one for me, however. I agree she could be dangerous."

I wasn't much interested in the 'gossip du jour' other than looking out for Caroline, but when Georgiana brought the Duke of Sussex into the conversation again, he began to occupy my thoughts. As I was gathering up my things to leave, I heard his voice directly behind me and realised he was addressing me.

"Margaret, would you allow me the pleasure of walking you home tonight? I understand your school is just across the heath, near town, and I could well do with a bit of fresh air after such a large meal," he said, laughing and patting his belly.

I completely froze. I was ever so grateful to be staring directly into the cloakroom, so he couldn't see my face. Between the wine and now this encounter with the duke, I was sure I was as red as a tomato. I could feel the heat burning my cheeks.

"Why, yes, yes, that would be lovely. By the way, what should I call you, if not Your Royal Highness?" I said, finally turning around to face him, my coat in my hand.

"Augustus," he said with another laugh as he helped me into my coat. "Just Augustus would be fine. I'll let Gee know I am taking you home."

I can only imagine how delighted she'll be to receive that bit of news, I thought, still smiling at him.

The time he was absent finding Georgiana did, however, give me a couple of minutes to try and relax. I was ever so grateful for all the wine at this point.

"Shall we?" he said when he returned.

"We shall," I reciprocated, as I took his arm.

We walked out of Montague House into a beautiful, spring breeze and began to make our way across the heath to Bryan House. After a short period of welcomed silence, Augustus suddenly turned to me and said, "Margaret, could I be so bold as to ask you how or where a woman like you would acquire the vast scientific knowledge you've so clearly and competently mastered?"

The darkness was almost black, so I was sure he couldn't see the small grin spreading across my face. Georgiana, Caroline, Elizabeth, and I had made a pact just before we published my book never to reveal the true origins of my scientific education, for obvious reasons. I'd never worried about anyone from the old Finsbury neighbourhood blowing my cover. That world and the one in which I currently lived were galaxies apart. When anybody asked this question, however, which happened quite often, we all had the same well-rehearsed reply. In this case, however, my grin was more derived from the assumption that Augustus had already asked Georgiana this question, and she had presumably given him the standard response. Now he was asking the same question again, directly, and no doubt hoping for a different answer. *The cheek of him.*

"I had a very kind benefactor who provided me with a very expensive education, but it was contingent upon the details remaining private, and him anonymous," I said mechanically, having read and said the lines so many times before. "And, by the way, what do you mean by *a woman like me?*"

"I told you that I thought you were intriguing; that's all I meant by *a woman like you.* And I apologise for my rudeness in asking about your education. I won't enquire of it again," he said, with a slight edge in his otherwise emotionless voice. This, too, felt rehearsed, but I could feel my face getting warm again, regardless.

"Could I change the subject then," he went on to say, "and ask how you feel about a woman's right to vote? There are starting to be small movements all over the world calling for it, and it certainly has the attention of some members of parliament."

"And my opinion on such a sensitive subject isn't also a very private matter?" I answered pretentiously without even glancing at him. Fearing I might have offended him, though, I didn't wait for his response and rushed on. "I try to avoid having any public opinion on politics, as I never know where my pupils' fathers stand on such issues. Having said that, why shouldn't women have the vote? In fact, I think everyone should have the vote, man or woman, lord or peasant, black or white. If I were a member of parliament, though, it would be the millions of men who still can't vote that I'd be worried about. Unfortunately, most women don't have the expectation, but the men are angry, and they have arms. Look at the French and American Revolutions. People don't like being treated like animals, and if they're treated as such for long enough, they'll eventually begin to behave like them."

"I couldn't agree with you more, Margaret," Augustus replied, "and that's before you get to the institution of slavery, which defines our African brothers and sisters as animals."

By now we had arrived at the front door of Bryan House. After getting my key in the door, I turned around to thank him and suddenly realised how awkward he looked: a bit like a very large schoolboy who didn't quite know what he should do next. He didn't say anything else, then fumbled a bit to kiss my hand, bowed politely, turned around, and disappeared into the dark of night.

"Thank you," I called out to the darkness, which I regretted instantly, bristling at myself as I was closing the door behind me.

Georgiana came by the following week for lunch. After Mrs. Murphy had laid out sandwiches and tea in the formal dining room and closed the door behind her, I turned to her, trying to sound as casual as possible. "Georgiana, what do you know of the Duke of Sussex's past? He seems like a kind man but a little bit lost in this world."

"That is a good way to put it. I don't really know that much about him. He just sort of showed up in London a couple of years ago. He married a woman in Rome years ago, but the king didn't recognise their marriage under the Royal Marriages Act. They had two children together. The Crown forced him to separate from his wife several years ago if he wanted to inherit his dukedom and gain the implied financial benefits therein. So, that is what he did. He now maintains a residence at Kensington Palace. He is rumoured to be an intellectual man, which is generally not true of most royals. I've heard his library at Kensington Palace is four times that of my uncle's in Bedford Square."

Georgiana then started to giggle. "Margaret, why, however, do you have a reason to ask? Did I not tell you that the Duke of Sussex would spark your fancy? That's all I'm going to say. Well, no, I'll say this, too: I'm never wrong on matters of the heart—never." This was all delivered with the hugest of grins as she walked off to pour herself a drink, skipping the sandwiches and the tea service altogether.

I shrank in my chair and said sheepishly, "You can pour me one as well," which made her laugh and say, "I told you so," at least one more time.

21

AUGUSTUS CAME TO VISIT CAROLINE at Montague House regularly over the next couple of years, often with the intention of trying to get her more access to her daughter and his niece, Princess Charlotte, whom he loved very dearly. Caroline would then bring Augustus and the princess to Bryan House to listen to the music lessons, and particularly to one talented music instructor who also performed regularly at the London Opera House. Augustus would often join in the music himself. He had a voice that could match any baritone I'd ever heard, professionally or otherwise.

He eventually started visiting us at Bryan House on his own, sometimes when he was also visiting Montague House, and sometimes just when he was in the vicinity. I'd learn on one of these more private visits that, as well as having a scientific mind, he was also a very religious man.

"Margaret, I don't think I've ever asked you what your religious inclinations are?" Augustus blurted out one afternoon whilst we were sitting in the drawing room at Bryan House.

"None of your business, Your Royal Highness," Elizabeth answered, giggling as she did so, all whilst carrying a tea service on a trolley behind her.

"I didn't ask you," Augustus said jokingly, lifting his teacup in the air to be filled. "No, really, Margaret, I'm asking you because you're a scientist in its purest form. There are many people, scientists included, who don't think it is possible to reconcile believing in the fundamentals of both."

"There is certainly tension building between the two sides and likely to escalate, as science is moving forwards at an unprecedented pace, making particularly the Catholic Church very nervous," I started to reply. "They see themselves losing power and money, so they demonise the scientists. I am of Huguenot descent, so I believe in a very direct and personal relationship with God. There is nobody trying to grab any power in the middle. So, I don't see or feel the conflict as real as perhaps someone who was raised a Roman Catholic."

"I agree, and I would say the same for the Church of England and in some ways the monarchy itself. I think they're all ancient and antiquated institutions desperately trying to hang on to power they have long since abused. I haven't told you that I almost became a theological minister when I was younger. I also speak fluent Hebrew, painstakingly learnt as part of my desire to read the ancient scriptures directly, without interpretation. Like you, though, I find no conflict in my relationship with God and the enquiry into the sciences."

I didn't quite know how to respond, as he had hit a chord in my heart that I might not have ever heard before. It felt like *tick-tock, tick-tock*. He made my thoughts seem thoughtful, not *odd*, not *vixen-like*, as my inebriated uncle's colleague had called me on that strange but fateful day in his library.

Elizabeth interrupted us by replacing the tea trolley with a decanter of whiskey. "Enough of the seriousness, you two. Would anybody like a real drink?"

"Why, I could never refuse you, Elizabeth, nor ever a whiskey, so yes, that would be lovely," Augustus responded.

Like Georgiana, Augustus was also smitten with my private laboratory. We often spent hours up there, exchanging the ideas of the day being discussed amongst the Fellows of the Royal Society. I remember one conversation we had in the laboratory regarding the emerging science of electricity.

"Augustus, what do you know of the concept of electrical energy?" I asked one day when he was trying out one of my most recently acquired telescopes. "I've started a new book and I'm writing lessons about it, based on my research at the Cavendish library. I've studied Henry Cavendish, as well as Franklin and Williamson, but I'm curious as to what has been presented to the Royal Society in more recent years. I'm starting to believe that this emerging field may change the way we live our daily lives. The secret seems to lie in how we harness this thing called *electricity*, and, perhaps more importantly, how we store it." I stopped as he put down the telescope.

"I think there's hope for its limited potential in very controlled circumstances," he said, "but I'm far less optimistic than you about its broader applications. I think you're right about our current inability to control it, and therein lies the problem. My understanding is that the resistance of investors to put up large sums of money for research is because they believe it's deadly dangerous. There are, of course, some quacks who think electricity is the devil incarnate himself, which, of course, is ridiculous, but there are certainly material dangers. We see this regularly in the destructive power of lightning. The Great Fire is never far from the minds of people, particularly the London financial community."

I loved the banter of these conversations in my laboratory. In terms of agreement, we always seemed to end up somewhere in the middle at the end of the day. I think most of the time he conceded to me when he was hungry, or ready for a drink and a cigar.

I don't remember when, but I also learnt sometime shortly after meeting Augustus that, like me, he suffered from lungs that didn't work properly. This apparently had cost him a military post in the war effort abroad—one that most of his other brothers had been granted. It was obvious he was angry about that and still trying to figure out his purpose in life. It seemed cruel to me that such an intelligent and thoughtful man had, in reality, very little to do.

I would also come to learn over time that Augustus had a keen sense of humour. He reminded me of Mamie in that way, the quintessential prankster. Like my first introduction to him, when Augustus had first met Elizabeth, he had immediately insisted that she call him by his

Christian name. Elizabeth just couldn't get used to this lack of protocol and always insisted on calling him Your Royal Highness. So, he then started referring to her as "Your Royal Highness, the only Queen of Bryan House." This was obviously intended to annoy me. Well, that made Elizabeth blush and laugh at the same time, particularly when he'd then accompany it with a backbreaking curtsy. I pretended to ignore them, which just egged the two of them on even more.

22

IT WAS AN UNUSUALLY QUIET AFTERNOON at Bryan House in the early summer of 1804 when our pupils were preparing for their year-end examinations. There was a sort of pins-and-needles feeling about the entire place as the girls moved quietly through the house, not wanting to disturb anyone else. You can imagine our surprise, then, when Caroline burst through the front door.

"Margaret," she cried out. "I must speak with you immediately!"

I raced into the hallway with my finger to my lips, hoping to silence her.

"Caroline, whatever is the matter? Let us go out into the garden to talk privately. The girls are studying for their examinations, so it is a bit like a morgue in here, and they need their peace and quiet," I said, reaching out for her hand and taking her outside. "Now, Caroline, please tell me whatever is troubling you so much. I've never seen you this agitated."

"Margaret, I need your very large brain to think for me. I've done something terrible, and I may be in a lot of trouble—like off-with-her-head trouble. I'm certain I will fall further from grace with the Crown and the Prince of Wales and lose even more access to Princess Charlotte if I'm found out. You must help me."

It wouldn't be an honest account if I didn't mention I nearly had to hold my breath to imagine what Caroline might have done that she deemed had crossed the line of appropriateness. It was certainly no secret that Caroline's parties were very strange affairs, and she was rumoured to have had many lovers. Not that I blamed her—her vile husband seemed to have a new mistress by the day.

My first assumption was that she was pregnant. Georgiana had warned Caroline on multiple occasions that the rules were different for women and told her about the great personal cost she'd paid herself for having an illegitimate child. Caroline had told both of us that she knew an unaccounted pregnancy, however much she loved children, would send her to the gallows. She also told us that she wasn't stupid enough to let that happen and that her illicit relationships with men were, for the most part, just for the sheer amusement of the chase, not for the physical consummation of an intimacy she'd never find in the arms of her otherwise silly men.

Let me be clear—she didn't say it quite like that, but that would be a kind interpretation of what I believed was her intent. Georgiana and I had taken her answer at face value, but now I feared that it might have been puffery, and she was now pregnant, by who knows whom.

Caroline immediately read the pained expression on my face and quickly said, "No, Margaret, I'm not with child. No, no, no. I promise you I'm not. I have, however, greatly offended the Douglases, and I've just learnt that Sir John Douglas is now equerry and gentleman of the bedchamber to the Duke of Sussex. I'm afraid Sir John will speak unfavourably of me to the duke, and he'll then feel obliged to pass such information on to the Prince of Wales, or, worse, the king himself."

"All right," I responded cautiously. "So what exactly did you do that could have caused such a rift amongst otherwise amiable friends?" I'd come to know the Douglases as regular visitors to Montague House in recent years. As I had told Georgiana at the Montague House party, I didn't have much time for Lady Charlotte Douglas. In fact, she made the hair on the back of my neck stand up every time she opened her mouth. I hadn't, however, heard of any discourse between the parties heretofore.

"Well, you know I regard the Douglases' friend Sir Sydney Smith with the greatest of affections," Caroline continued, "and, well, I'll just say it—I caught him shagging Lady Douglas in the round tower on my grounds. I was so cross that I drew two pictures of them engaged in *it*, and I sent them to her husband, Sir John Douglas."

I winced. "You did what?" My initial and rather naive feeling to her alarming disclosure, however, was to feel relieved. I wasn't quite sure whether to believe Caroline's story. Not that I thought she was lying, as such, because Georgiana and I had both seen some rather curious affections exchanged between Sir Sydney and Lady Douglas at the Montague House party earlier in the year. Whatever Caroline had seen or not, though, didn't really matter. I was just grateful it hadn't been Lady Charlotte Douglas who had caught Caroline shagging Sir Sydney Smith in the round tower—or anyplace else, for that matter. What I was relieved about was that it would not be Caroline's inappropriate behaviour under scrutiny if any of this got out. I was also confident that if this were ever mentioned to Augustus, he would find a way to quietly make it go away.

Though I had some sense of relief now that I understood the situation, it was certainly not an enviable position she'd put herself in, given the other problems she had with the Crown.

"How lewd were the drawings you sent?" I asked her.

"Lewd . . . I don't know this word," she replied, looking confused.

"Vulgar," I almost spat back at her.

"Oh, vulgar . . . yes, they were very vulgar. There was a very large penis involved in the pictures," she replied.

"It wasn't Sir Sydney's penis though," she then clarified, as if that mattered materially.

I groaned and stared up at the sky, thinking of what to do. "I think you should send a letter, or even better, present yourself to the Douglases in person. Tell them none of it is true—that you'd had too much to drink. Tell them it was an error in judgement, and you hope, from the bottom of your heart, that they can forgive you for such a cruel and thoughtless act of unkindness."

Caroline flatly refused to do any of this.

"Caroline, this is not the hill you want to die on. It will cost you nothing to apologise, and you risk everything if you don't," I pleaded with her.

"Margaret, I am apologising to no one—not now, not ever," she replied and then stormed off in the same huff as she had arrived. I shook my head, hoping this unfortunate incident wasn't going to be the end of her. I was preparing to visit friends in London for a few days when the examination period had finished, so I decided I would just let her settle down and talk to her when I got back.

23

VEN AFTER AUNT ANNE'S DEATH and Bryan House on Golden Lane had been released, I kept close ties to Finsbury, where I'd lived for so many years with my aunt and uncle. It was during that trip back to visit friends that I had the pleasure of being introduced to a woman by the name of Jane Marcet (née Haldimand). We had both been invited to afternoon tea by a mutual friend. Like me, but for different reasons, Jane had been blessed with an education well beyond what most other British women had access to, including that of the sciences. She'd come from a wealthy Genevan family, and her father was a well-respected London banker. Jane had married a fellow Genevan scientist and doctor by the name of Alexander Marcet.

With her husband's encouragement, Jane eventually developed an interest in writing books about the sciences. Like me, her intent was to publish scientific textbooks targeted at the education of young ladies. As you can imagine, I felt like I'd met a kindred spirit. It wasn't long before she was asking me how I'd achieved my publishing objectives. My guard went up then. I engaged with her but avoided any specific details, particularly regarding the ancillary husband and children. I liked this woman, though, a lot, and I wanted to help her.

Maybe I will tell her another time, I thought to myself as I was getting into my phaeton to drive back to Bryan House.

When I arrived back in Blackheath, I found a letter from Caroline waiting for me.

Margaret,

    I just wanted to thank you for listening last week. I have not apologised to anyone in any way, shape, or form, and I will not, but I have, however, sent a letter to Sir Sydney Smith stating that I hadn't meant to create any dissension between us and that I hoped we could all put the matter behind us. I have heard nothing back. I know you are visiting friends in London. Will you come by for a visit as soon as you return?

Caroline

I would learn a few days later that the Duke of Kent, Augustus's brother, had also been informed of the existence of the lewd pictures and had also advised everyone to move on, as there had been no injury incurred. I sincerely hoped all parties would heed this sound advice.

JANE MARCET AND I, INDEED, became fast friends over the coming months, and on one beautiful autumn day when we were strolling through the gardens in Hyde Park, I decided to tell her the whole truth about how I got published.

"Jane, it's quite a funny story. If I could indulge you, though, please keep this in the strictest of confidences and not even tell your husband," I almost pleaded, so desperately wanting to help her publish, as Georgiana had done for me. I knew that by telling her, though, I was breaking a pact of seven years, but in that moment, it all seemed worth it. I was also sure the others wouldn't mind. After all, it was mostly my own reputation that I was putting at risk.

"Of course, Margaret. Any secret of yours is safe with me. I must admit, though, I'm intrigued as to how a textbook on astronomy lessons could have anything enigmatic about it," she said, which made me smile, remembering Georgiana and all her 'packaging' antics. I then went on to tell Jane the entire story about the misleading frontispiece of 'Mrs. Bryan and Children,' followed by how I'd also benefited by Reverend Maskelyne's and Sir Charles Hutton's assistance.

"Margaret, that is some story," Jane said, laughing. "You're very lucky to have such a kind and important friend as the Duchess of Devonshire. All the papers ever want to talk about is where she goes and what she's wearing. It certainly sounds like you couldn't have done it without her."

"Indeed, I could not have, but that is what it comes down to, Jane, is whether you care about publishing under your own name or not. That's the difficult part—not the subject matter of the book, no matter how controversial. It'll be your sex that's the obstacle. I've no doubt that the content of the book will sell itself. Mine did. I've had a subsequent edition of my book published at higher volumes than the initial publication. It will simply be easier for you to get published anonymously, or with a male pseudonym," I said.

"Yes, regarding whether to publish my book under my own name, I've thought about this issue a great deal already." Her posture then subtly shifted as she leaned in towards me, and her voice got a little softer. "Margaret, unlike you, I have a husband and one who's a scientist himself, who wants to be published and ultimately wants to become a Fellow of the Royal Society. Neither he, nor the general public, would appreciate his wife trying to trump him in his own occupational space, even if my intended audience is only young ladies. It is for this reason, and this alone, that I wish to publish my scientific textbooks anonymously. I hope you can respect me for that."

I paused before answering her. I guess I hadn't expected that. "Of course, I respect your decision, Jane. In fact, I admire it, and I understand how our situations are different. It will make your publishing efforts more straightforward. Maybe you could publish anonymously but reveal that you're female. That might be important to the audience that you're trying to attract, if for no other reason than to prove to them that not only can a woman understand the subject matter, but she can teach and write about it as well." I reached for her hand, which was now trembling ever so slightly.

I remember reflecting on how fortunate I was not to have had to make such a difficult choice in my own life. Also, despite what I'd said to Jane, I did have mixed emotions as to whether to admire her for being so respectful of her husband's career to the clear long-term detriment of her own. I was torn between thinking whether she was doing it to be subservient to him—in which case, shame on her. Conversely, though, if she'd truly found a man who allowed her the freedom to be so willingly selfless, well, shame on me. I suppose I'll never know the answer to that question, and nor should I.

24

THE YEAR 1804 WAS ALSO the year I was asked to put my name to a popular astronomy board game called Science in Sport, or the Pleasures of Astronomy. It was very cleverly done by a man called John Wallis and based on the Royal Observatory in Greenwich Park. Elizabeth used to relish regularly beating me at the game, if for no other reason than to remind me that there were, indeed, two female educators who ran Bryan House, and that only one of them had the title of 'Queen,' should such fame and fortune ever start to go to my head.

As exciting as the year had been, though, we were ill-prepared for the encore. The Murphys and all our pupils had gone home for the Christmas holidays, so Bryan House was eerily quiet, although Elizabeth and I both welcomed the break. It was Christmas Eve, and the children were asleep, or at least in bed. Little Harriet was now four, so Father Christmas and sugarplum fairies had been solidly dancing in her head for at least a month. Elizabeth and I had lit a roaring fire and opened a bottle of wine, then sat down to play a game of Science in Sport.

"All right, Lizzie, I am going to best you this time," I said, scrunching up my face, throwing my fist to the air, and taking a large gulp of wine.

"Not a chance," she replied.

Suddenly I thought I heard something outside, and I put my finger to my lips to stop her. "Did you hear someone at the door?"

"I can't imagine who would be out on Christmas Eve, let alone when it's so dreadful outside," she said. It had been softly snowing all day, and it was bitterly cold.

"Let me just check. Maybe it's the wind," I answered, getting up from my chair and heading for the front door. When I opened the door, wind whipping the snow, I almost intuitively looked down to see a newborn baby in a makeshift manger on the step. She wasn't crying or making any noise, and I feared she might have died from the cold. There was no sight of any other person, so I immediately called out to Elizabeth.

"My God, Lizzie, it's a baby! Come quickly, she doesn't look well," I screamed to make sure she heard me.

When I picked up the child, however, she was as warm as the fire inside. She opened her eyes, looked straight at me, and cooed. As I lifted her up from the makeshift manger, I saw a piece of paper beneath her blanket. I slowly unfolded it.

HER NAME IS JESSY;

PLEASE TAKE CARE OF HER.

I gasped, as these were the same words the woman had said when she'd put Little Harriet into my arms: "Her name is Harriet; please take care of her."

Elizabeth began boiling water immediately. We didn't even discuss whether we'd keep her. And so it was that another miracle baby had come our way, and, indeed, a miracle Christmas baby. We named her Jessy Anne that Christmas Eve after my auntie Anne, and we thanked God for her blessed arrival. When we showed up for Christmas dinner at Thomas and Sarah's the next day with a third child in tow, I am sure they thought we had gone stone mad—that is, before we had to explain her to Little Harriet and Lucy. There was just no way to explain to Little Harriet that Father Christmas hadn't delivered her himself.

We did promise ourselves that this was truly the last one; any other stray babies that came our way we would need to find another home for. We were also delighted that Christmas to learn that Sarah was pregnant again, which filled the whole house with great hope and joy for the pending new year.

25

THE YEAR OF OUR LORD 1805 would, indeed, hold many surprises for us, good and bad. It was the year Jane Marcet published the first of many successful scientific textbooks—all anonymously, but by a 'female authouress' nevertheless, until long after her husband had died. Her first book was called *Conversations on Chemistry*, where she explained complicated chemistry lessons through everyday conversations between a female teacher and two young girls.

I remember the day I was helping Jane finish her very humble and anonymous female preface to *Conversations on Chemistry*, she surprised me by saying, "Margaret, you've been so helpful to me in my publishing efforts that I wish to offer something back, which hopefully might be of some small use to you. I'm going to name the female educator in my book Mrs. B after you. As an anonymous female authour with a character by the name of Mrs. B, maybe some will assume that it's you who are the authouress. That would make me far happier than a random rogue taking credit for it, particularly if that random rogue was a man."

I was surprised and almost didn't know what to say. I knew this book was going to be a success, and now my lovely new friend was offering to attach my name to it, even if just implicitly. "I don't know, Jane. I am certainly very flattered, but what's wrong with Mrs. M, or even Mrs. J? Wouldn't that make more sense?"

"Maybe, Margaret. But if people think you're the authouress, it may turn out to be more profitable for both of us—if it helps me sell more books and raises your tuition fees at Bryan House," Jane said, then laughed out loud.

This made me laugh, too, and think of Georgiana, the quintessential political and commercial negotiator. "You are, indeed, a banker's daughter, Jane. That is very kind, and I'm most flattered. Thank you so much." We then gently embraced.

I can't explain how humbled I was by this generous gesture of support from my fellow authouress of scientific books. Whilst I've, indeed, been credited for her book many times over, I've also become forevermore known by most of my pupils and even some of my friends as simply Mrs. B. It would be remiss not to mention, however, that despite the enormous success of Jane Marcet's books around the world, particularly *Conversations on Chemistry*, because she published anonymously, many male rogues indeed plagiarised her work for decades. She certainly only ever received a small fraction of the royalties she was entitled to.

King George III also made Caroline the Ranger of Greenwich Park in the early spring, giving her control of the tenant allowances for anyone leasing a home from the Crown. Caroline viewed this as the perfect opportunity for a very measured retaliation against Lady Charlotte Douglas. Upon receiving the rangership, she immediately began legal proceedings to permanently evict the Douglas family and Sir Sydney Smith from their Greenwich village home. It was then that I realised this was not to be the end of this dreadful *lewd pictures* matter after all. A favourite expression of Georgiana's, as both a political strategist and an avid card player, was now crystal clear: Caroline had completely overplayed her hand.

MY RELATIONSHIP WITH AUGUSTUS STARTED to get more complicated that year of 1805 as well. Complicated, I mean, in a good way. He started to visit more frequently, and he began to feel *familiar* to me, for lack of a better word. I also started to miss him if there were long distances between his visits. I remember one day coming home from

Montague House and seeing his horse tied up outside. I immediately felt my heart start to beat faster, and I even felt myself pick up the pace to get home.

"Lizzie, is Augustus here?" I said, almost out of breath, charging through the back door.

"Yes, Margaret," I heard. "We are in the drawing room with the children."

When I walked into the drawing room, Augustus was down on the floor with Harriet and Lucy riding on his back as if he were a horse. They were both bobbling around as if they might fall off at any moment and giggling at the same time. It was such a precious scene. It made me stop and think what it would have been like to have my own husband, with my own children—no disrespect to Elizabeth.

I bristled at myself. *You made a choice, Margaret. Don't think about that; you can't have everything.*

26

PERHAPS THE MOST INTERESTING EVENT of 1805, though, was attempting to get our children christened without incident. Little Harriet was now nearly five, Lucy Elizabeth nearly three, and Jessy Anne but a few months old when Elizabeth poked her head out from behind the Sunday newspaper at the breakfast table to say, "Margaret, I've been thinking. We really need to get the girls baptised. Little Harriet will be five in August. It doesn't seem right to delay, especially for her."

The thought had occurred to me more than once, but I always hesitated when it came to Little Harriet. The thought of putting any record of her or her birth date on a formal piece of paper gave me indigestion, if not nausea. I'd also have to ask both of her parents' permission, which gave me nausea for sure. Even though her parents had initially been clear about wanting a relationship with their daughter, up to now they'd managed that exclusively through written correspondence. Neither of them had ever suggested a visit to the Bryan House school, which had certainly made our lives simpler. I knew I'd have to extend a personal invitation to her christening, though, and I wasn't sure how they'd respond. Anyway, we couldn't baptise the other two children without including Little Harriet, and the children needed to be baptised, so I replied by saying, "I totally agree. I just worry about Little Harriet. I've been thinking about this recently, though. I think Thomas can help us, although I am sure he'll hate the idea."

George Valerian Wellesley had just been appointed the new rector of St. Luke's in Chelsea, where Thomas and Sarah attended services, and Thomas was also the church warden. Thomas knew Wellesley's brother, Arthur, well from the European battlefields. He was argu-ably Britain's greatest Napoleonic war general and would eventually become the 1st Duke of Wellington, just before the infamous Battle of Waterloo in 1815.

Upon Reverend Wellesley's appointment to St. Luke's, he'd asked Thomas to take on additional responsibilities within the parish, as both the overseer of the Chelsea Workhouse and the parish clerk, as well as his existing responsibilities as the church warden. Surely, I had surmised, with such seniority and those specific responsibilities, particularly the parish clerk role, Thomas would have the access needed to get three innocent girls christened without any questions being asked. I knew, however, as I'd said to Elizabeth, that he'd hate the idea because of Little Harriet's parental situation.

Thomas and Sarah were the only two people Elizabeth and I had shared Little Harriet's biological parentage with. Not that I intended to burden anyone else with the responsibility of that information, but I had felt the need to confide in them should something happen to Eliza-beth and me. When Little Harriet was a newborn, Elizabeth and I asked Thomas and Sarah if they'd take responsibility of her, and eventually for all three of our children, should some awful circumstance ever present itself that we could not.

I know it sounds callous, but sharing secrets about the other two just didn't matter. Lucy Elizabeth's mother left almost immediately after she was born, and we never knew who Jessy Anne's parents were. Not that we'd made enquiries, of course. We knew, however, that people would eventually come looking for Little Harriet, and we didn't think it fair to burden Thomas and Sarah with that responsibility without knowing her true identity.

Thomas, of course, was furious when he found out about Little Harriet's very gentrified and illegitimate lineage. Elizabeth and I went to Chelsea shortly after her birth, and almost immediately after the birth of their own daughter, Elizabeth Jekyll, to surprise them with the exciting news.

"Margaret, are you mad? Why would you get involved with a situation like this?" He was almost screaming at me at this point. "This could ruin your school and your reputation—before you get to the shaky ground you are on with the fabricated inferences in your book. What on earth were you thinking? If this is only a fostering relationship, then I suggest you give the child back. Right now."

His face was so red at this point I thought perhaps I should suggest we sit down. I glanced across the room and saw Sarah turn as white as a sheet, as if she might faint. I suddenly felt awful. I hadn't even thought about how she might feel. She'd only just given birth herself.

"Let me get Sarah some water," Elizabeth said. "And then we'll go and sit in the garden so you two can have some privacy," she added, as if she'd read my mind. Elizabeth then reached for Sarah's hand and walked her towards the kitchen.

I took a deep breath and turned back to Thomas with the calmest voice I could muster. "I was thinking that Elizabeth and I wanted to know what it was like to be parents." I gave him a moment to digest this, then added what I knew would sway him the most. "Someone was going to have her, so why shouldn't it be us? It'll be one less little girl to grow up in England without an education."

This point did seem to soften him slightly, and after a long and uncomfortable period of silence, he eventually said, "I don't approve of this at all, but this is the last I'll say about the matter." For him, at least, the conversation was over.

"I've one other thing to ask of you," I said, "which is not intended to infuriate you more; I promise you that. If, God forbid, something happens to Elizabeth and me, please tell me you'll take care of this child. I know it's an unlikely scenario, but it's one that happened to me. I don't know if her biological parents will want her or not. I'm sure it would depend on the circumstances. So, for now, I just need you to say that you'll do this for me and Elizabeth. She is Sarah's sister." I stopped abruptly and just looked him in his eyes, silently pleading with him.

Thomas paused. I knew he was angry. He was probably also tired. When he finally spoke, he simply said, "Yes, Margaret, I will do that. Sarah and I will take care of Little Harriet if it's ever needed. Hopefully none of us will see that day, but you have my word." He then turned his back on me and walked away, and the conversation was, indeed, finally over.

Now, nearly five year later, I was going to ask my brother to do something again that I knew would make him feel compromised. Before I could engage Thomas's assistance in the christening, though, I needed to get Harriet and Granville Leveson-Gower's permission, as her biological parents. I was almost certain Leveson-Gower wouldn't object or show up, but I didn't have an inkling as to what Harriet might do, apart from using it as an excuse to engage with her lover.

I decided that it was probably better to have Georgiana plant the seed of a christening in both their minds, and assuming they were both agreeable, Harriet and I could then discuss how it was going to get done. I wrote to Georgiana—discreetly, of course.

> *Dearest Georgiana,*
>
> *I hope this letter finds you in good health, and I pray we'll see each other soon. I'm writing to ask for your assistance in getting 'our' children baptised. Your contacts would be invaluable to me in this regard.*
>
> *Lovingly,*
> *Margaret*

As expected, Georgiana must have smoothed the path, as Harriet sent me an invitation to have lunch with her at Devonshire House a couple of weeks later. I drove myself there to meet her. The meeting was short, as she was clearly distracted planning for the marriage of her legitimate daughter, Lady Caroline Ponsonby, to the Honourable William Lamb, scheduled to take place a few weeks hence. Lady Caroline Ponsonby was Harriet's third (legitimate) child with her husband, Lord Bessborough, and their only daughter. She'd been born in Dorset in November 1785, which made her almost fifteen years older than her half sister, our Little Harriet. Realising I had a short window of time to speak to Harriet, I hurriedly brought up the subject of the girls' christening.

"Harriet, your daughter's wedding sounds lovely, but you must have a million things to do, so I'll be respectful of your time. I believe Georgiana has mentioned that Elizabeth and I would like to have Little Harriet christened along with our two adopted children, but obviously we'd need yours and Lord Granville Leveson-Gower's blessing." Harriet nodded.

"Yes, Gee did mention this, and Granville and I think it's a splendid idea. I'll leave the arrangements to you and Elizabeth, with a few stipulations: I'd like it to take place on my birthday, Sunday, June 16. I may or may not attend, depending on whether circumstances allow it, but I'd like there to be some discreet attachment to me in Little Harriet's christening documents."

I honestly was at a loss for words. I tried to finish my lunch without being sick and drove back to Bryan House like a raving lunatic. By the time I reached home and found Elizabeth, I just exploded.

"Lizzie, she wants it to happen on her birthday, she may or may not show up depending on whether circumstances allow, and she wants to be in the documentation. I mean, the disrespect was unbelievable, but I can get past that. It's the risk that she so callously takes with her own daughter's life that I don't understand. She might as well be handing us all a noose."

"She's stone mad," Elizabeth replied. "Stone mad."

"That is not helpful," I spat back, "and Thomas will have no part of this now."

"He will," Elizabeth countered. "I'll talk to him. He will, Margaret, I promise you."

Thankfully, that turned out to be true. On June 16, 1805, Big Harriet's forty-fourth birthday, Little Harriet, Lucy Elizabeth, and Jessy Anne were baptised at St. Luke's Church, Chelsea, by Reverend Wellesley. We bought little white dresses for Harriet and Lucy, and a beautiful lace christening gown for Jessy Anne. By the time we entered the church, the three of them looked like they'd just fallen from the heavens.

It seemed such a beautiful vision—until we were taking our seats at the front of the church and Elizabeth suddenly leaned over and quietly said, "Do not look, and do not look at Thomas for sure, or he'll never be able to get this done. Gee and H have just arrived, and it's nothing short of Shakespearean. The ostrich feather in H's hat won't clear the door frame. Someone's trying to adjust it as we speak, but he can't reach the tip. She's not very happy. . . . Oh, now she's waving her hands at him, as if she were swatting away a very large fly."

I couldn't help but turn and look, now seeing two cloaked, unrecognisable women dressed head to toe in veiled black gowns. The only thing I was grateful for in that dreadful moment was that at least Georgiana was there as well to supervise Harriet. I would later learn that they were meant to be mourning the loss of their husbands on the European battlefields and finding peace by witnessing the christening of God's children.

The poor greeter who'd finally been forced to remove the entire ostrich feather from Harriet's hat was now looking for any direction on what to do with the foul thing, no pun intended. Harriet still looked like she was going to assault him at any moment. I gratefully watched Georgiana, as discreetly as she could, reach across to try to restrain her. Elizabeth was wrong: It was better than Shakespeare. We should have sold tickets.

Thomas, as Elizabeth had promised, in his role as parish clerk, made sure the paperwork gave no hint of anything other than the baptismal record of three little girls he had sponsored and, because of this paternal mark, all bore only the Bryan surname. In the end, Thomas had been even more protective than Elizabeth and me when it came to concealing Little Harriet's real identity. I discovered this when I met with him in the rectory a couple of hours before the service to work out how we were going to fill out the documents.

"Margaret, I think we should marginally modify Little Harriet's birth date. We only need to change it by a few months. There are people who know the date of her birth and her name."

"I couldn't agree with you more. But tell me, Thomas, I know you're listed as the paternal father to all three girls, but who are you listing as the mother?" I asked.

"I thought we'd list Harriet as the mother of all three girls, so they'll be forever memorialised as legitimate sisters. That way, Harriet gets what she wants too. I also think that Jessy Anne should be christened something else, so as not to tie Little Harriet to such an unusual name. Maybe Jane Anne?"

"But Jessy is her name," I adamantly objected.

"Margaret, my most amiable big sister, might I remind you that this is putting my professional reputation at risk? This is not a battle worth having; she's a baby," he replied, at which point I kissed him, thanked him profusely for all his support, and went outside to find Elizabeth and the children. The girls were getting christened, after all, and that had been the objective.

When the beautiful service finally reached its natural conclusion, however, I began to panic inside. I'd not counted on Harriet showing up, as we'd not been given advance warning, and now I was unsure as to whether we'd be expected to socialise with them afterwards. I was also starting to regret that I hadn't prepared Little Harriet for this. Deep down, I'd been hoping that the two mourning widows would have discreetly slipped out before the ceremony ended, but much to my dismay, when I turned around to check, they were both belting out the final hymn. I looked at Elizabeth with such anxiety that she reached for my hand gently, as if to say, *Leave this to me.*

When the reverend gave the congregation leave to go, Elizabeth took Little Harriet's hand and gestured to Georgiana that she was taking her to the back of the church. I waited with the other two girls in the front pew as Elizabeth and Little Harriet had a brief exchange with the two cloaked women, and then they returned to the front of the church to collect the rest of us.

"How did that go?" I whispered to Elizabeth whilst we gathered our things.

"Fine," she said. "The only thing Little Harriet said, after she realised who Harriet was, was that her letters made her seem far prettier than she actually is."

"She did not," I said quietly, trying hard not to burst into laughter. "Tell me she actually didn't use those words?"

"She did, yes, and in fairness to the child, the woman looked like something out of a Lent carnival. I'm surprised she wasn't terrified."

And with that we left St. Luke's Church, headed to Thomas and Sarah's house for tea, having gotten our girls officially baptised. After all the fretting, with Thomas's help, our girls had now been blessed by the beloved Son of God and had forever been memorialised as sisters.

As the year came to its end, Elizabeth and I closed Bryan House for two weeks during the holidays, and we spent Christmas week with Thomas, Sarah, and family in Chelsea. They'd just welcomed a new baby girl, little Sarah, healthy and heaven-sent. There were now six children between the two families and a melody of first cousins. For the most part they adored each other, albeit poor George often found himself playing with dolls, maybe more than he cared for. We dragged the children all over the festive sites of London until their noses were red and their little hands were frozen.

I was trying to finish the final lessons of my second book, so once Christmas Day was over, I went back to Bryan House to do exactly that. Elizabeth and the children, however, stayed on in London for another week with Thomas, Sarah, and family. It was strange to be at Bryan House alone. Mr. and Mrs. Murphy had gone to Ireland for a fortnight's holiday to visit their own family. As I watched the night sky say goodbye to another year and the morning sunrise prepare to greet a new one, I felt accomplished and at peace. I had no idea, at this heavenly moment, that all was about to change.

27

I ATTENDED A GREAT BALL at Devonshire House in the early
spring of 1806. It was a spectacular affair, with the most delicious
delicacies from around the world I'd ever seen, let alone tasted. I
had attended the event in years past, but I was particularly looking forward to it on this occasion, as I hadn't seen Georgiana in months. She
had taken ill just after Christmas and been on ordered bedrest since.
I arrived early, hoping to get a bit of private time with her before the
crowds showed up. I spotted her immediately as I entered the ballroom,
and she caught my eye as well.

"Margaret, so lovely to see you. Happy New Year! It has been too
long," she said, walking over to me, then kissing me on both of my cheeks.

She didn't look well. Her skin was a sallow colour, and her eyes were
jaundiced. She didn't seem to be herself either, as though she was trying
too hard to be Gee. I tried to hide my concern, but I had a thorn in my
side with worry when I left and made a mental note to write to her the
next day, which I did. I received word back almost immediately, reassuring me that she was fine and just a bit tired. She became incapacitated
shortly afterwards, and by the third week of March, some of the papers
were hinting that her health was deteriorating rapidly.

When I saw Caroline's carriage arriving at Bryan House at half past
seven the following week, I knew something was terribly wrong. Caroline sometimes went to bed at that hour. My first instinct, as I looked
through the window and saw her approaching, was that maybe something awful had happened to Princess Charlotte. When I opened the
door, it was clear she'd been crying. I was quite certain I had never seen
her cry before, ever.

"Caroline," I gasped. "What on earth has happened? What is the matter?"

"Georgiana is dead. She died in the night, and it was said to have been very painful," she said, red-faced and trembling.

I stood there staring. I needed to sit down, or I feared I might collapse. I heard Elizabeth coming down the hallway.

"Who is it, Margaret?" she called out to me. "What's going on?"

"It's Georgiana," I somberly replied. "She is now with our Heavenly Father. Caroline is at the door, Lizzie. Can you look after her, please, and try to find out exactly what happened, and what we need to do? Please, if you don't mind, Lizzie, I just need to sit down for a minute." It was the last thing I remember telling her before I ran for the stairs.

What I would later learn is Georgiana died an excruciating death from an abscess in her liver. She entered the kingdom of heaven in the early hours of the morning of March 30, 1806. She was surrounded by her family, including her heavily pregnant eldest daughter, Little Gee. The country and, indeed, the world were in a state of shock and grief. Masses of people lined London's streets and left flowers and messages at Devonshire House. The *Bath Chronicle*, reporting her death, printed the following in her memory:

> Never a woman more exalted in every accomplishment of rapturous beauty, of elevated genius and of angelic temper, has met nor adorned the present age.

Georgiana was buried in the family vault in Derbyshire soon after, with a funeral procession that rivaled royalty. I felt a numbness and acute pain at the same time. The grief was nothing like anything I'd ever experienced before. I felt like I'd truly lost a soulmate. I hardly slept for weeks.

That hole in my heart has never healed. That's all I will say. I never even got to say goodbye.

28

S HORRIBLE AND SUDDEN AS Georgiana's death had been, we would only learn later that the Year of Our Lord 1806 would completely upend our lives. In early January, the prime minister, William Pitt, suddenly died. I won't go into all the moving parts of how that affected the country's politics or the power of parliament; I am sure there are many things that I'm quite sure I don't properly understand myself. Nevertheless, the resulting chess pieces left George IV, the Prince of Wales and Caroline's husband, with more influence and power than he'd ever had before. I wouldn't understand the grave implications of this changing of the guard for our own lives for months to come.

I hadn't heard from Big Harriet since Georgiana's passing, and I hadn't expected to, given the enormity of her loss and the short time since her sister's passing. In the middle of May, though, I received an invitation to meet Harriet at Devonshire House for lunch. I didn't think much about it, except being anxious about how to acknowledge the loss of her sister in a meaningful way so as not to compound her unimaginable pain.

When she arrived in the drawing room, she greeted me with such urgency that I started to feel like something else might be amiss. She then sat down and said without hesitation, "Margaret, I'm afraid I have more devastating news. I've just received word from the Prince of Wales himself that there's to be an imminent enquiry at Blackheath into the immoral behaviour of Caroline, the Princess of Wales. He is adamant to be finally rid of her. Apparently his brothers, the Duke of Sussex and the Duke of Kent, are now in agreement."

"I am sorry, Harriet, slow down; this is a lot to take in. What are you talking about and why hasn't Caroline been told of any of this? I was with her only yesterday."

"I think they intend to surprise her. We both know and have experienced some of her bizarre behaviour, but this feels different. I have been told by the Prince of Wales himself that he has plenty of evidence. I know my brother is involved, as is Spencer Perceval. Apparently, he has the support of all of parliament, too."

George Spencer, Harriet's brother, and Spencer Perceval were both members of parliament at the time. I felt my heart begin to pound, not understanding exactly where all this was going.

"It's all very secretive," she continued. "It is to be called the *Delicate Investigation*, but everyone is to be interviewed, with the focus of the enquiry being the biological parentage of all the children living in or around Blackheath."

Harriet was visibly upset and shaking by now. She finished by saying, "Margaret, I know I've put you in an awful situation, and after all you've done for us already. If we're found out, though, I fear we're all in ruins. My husband will certainly divorce me, and leave me without a penny. He's attempted to do that once already. Little Harriet's future will be irreparably injured, and I can't but imagine that your own personal reputation would also suffer material damage. I beg of you, Margaret, please tell me if you've uttered a word of Little Harriet's parentage to anyone else."

I couldn't breathe. The protection of Georgiana and her political prowess was gone forever, and my worst fears were now realised. The truth, of course, was that Elizabeth and I hadn't mentioned Little Harriet's parentage to anyone besides Thomas and Sarah, who would take such information to the grave. This aristocratic world Big Harriet lived in, however, was filled with loose, drunken lips and agendas of self-preservation. The thought crossed my mind that I had no idea who else might have knowledge of Little Harriet's parentage via 'Big' Harriet herself, which was now far more relevant than whomever I might have trusted with such a sacred confidence. *Maybe I should ask Harriet that question?* Instead, I breathed in all the air I could without choking on it. I realised that, for all the intellectual gifts the good Lord had bestowed upon me, I was now in this den of powerful men who thought nothing of destroying other people's lives to advance their own interests. Whatever respect I'd mustered up as a headmistress and a published authouress held neither currency nor protection for us in this colosseum of gladiators. I missed Georgiana so much in that moment. The queen of maneuvering such a male minefield, however, was gone forever.

I breathed again as my lungs tightened, and then suddenly, as if God himself had heard me, my mind became crystal clear. I had to make sure Big Harriet didn't panic, and who could I turn to, except maybe Augustus? She'd said he was in the know, but I couldn't believe he was part of this madness. I'd think about that tomorrow, though. For now, I had to silence Harriet from being her own and possibly all our own worst potential enemy.

"Harriet," I said, very calmly, "the most important thing now is to not create unnecessary alarm and not to mention this to anyone until we have more information."

I then tried to sip my tea without spilling it all over the who-knows-how-much-it-cost Devonshire House drawing room settee. Taking another belaboured breath, I continued. "Elizabeth and I know the Duke of Sussex quite well. We will contact him tomorrow to find out what he knows and how he can help. Please bear in mind that the Prince of Wales only wants to destroy Caroline; he doesn't care about anyone else."

I stayed on for another hour to make sure Harriet was more emotionally stable and that she understood the importance of holding her tongue with absolutely anyone else. By the time I left, I think I had reassured her that Little Harriet and, perhaps more importantly, she herself weren't in harm's way.

On the journey home, I tried to convince myself that this was indeed true. I was grateful to be alone, with only the soft rain outside to keep me company on that somber, late Saturday afternoon. Apart from my thoughts of Little Harriet's welfare and a general unwelcome enquiry into my past, my only attention was to the road beneath me and arriving home without incident.

I didn't share what Harriet had told me with Elizabeth until the following afternoon after we'd returned home from church.

"I've asked the Murphys to take the children to the heath for a couple of hours," I said to her, touching her forearm. "There is something important I need to talk to you about." I felt sick even as the words were coming out of my mouth.

"You'd best just get it out then," Elizabeth snapped back at me. "Your mood has been strange since yesterday. Are you ill?"

"Oh no, Lizzie, no, I'm not ill. This is far worse. I just learnt from Big Harriet that all hell is about to break loose in Blackheath. There is to be a government-sanctioned investigation into 'all' the illegitimate children of Blackheath. Now that the Prince of Wales is solidly in power and aligned with Parliament, he plans to destroy Caroline. We'll be dragged into this by association. Certainly, Edwardina and Willie, the Pagoda House orphanage, our children, and maybe even our school will be investigated."

It took Elizabeth a while to respond, but it was clear she understood the gravity of the situation. "Margaret, whatever's coming our way, I know we'll move forward as a family together like we always have. I know you trusted Georgiana to protect Little Harriet, but I've no doubt you'll manage that yourself now that she's gone. Let your anxiety not trouble you. It moves nothing forward for any of us. The only energy that should be spent is that which gets us to higher ground, for our children's sake. If I can offer any advice, though, I think you should speak to Augustus. Now, if you don't mind, I think I'd like to lie down for a few minutes. Clearer minds will prevail with some rest. Nothing is ever as good, or as bad, as it first seems."

I looked at her enviably as she calmly ascended the stairs.

Rest? Who can rest right now?

29

THE FOLLOWING MORNING, JUST AFTER DAWN, I sent word to Augustus that I wished to speak with him as soon as his schedule allowed. Whilst Elizabeth had taken the news in stride the day before, I noticed that she didn't allow the children out to play on the heath that day—a seemingly metaphorical attempt to shield them from whatever ugliness was coming our way.

I was relieved to hear from Augustus later that day, inviting me to his apartments at Kensington Palace the following afternoon. Normally that would have given me some anxiety, as I had never been there before. There was no room for any more anxiety in my body, though, full up to the brim as it was. Augustus met me personally on the doorstep to his apartments at Kensington Palace and led me into what appeared to be one of his many libraries.

"I apologise for the short notice, but I needed to speak to you urgently. I've just learnt that there's to be a formal investigation at Blackheath, specifically into the children of Blackheath. What do you know of this?" I asked, handing my hat and coat to a servant.

He looked surprised and certainly confused. "Margaret, let me dismiss the servants so we can talk more privately," he said, already shooing them away.

"Yes, of course," I said as he gestured for the last remaining maid to shut the door behind her, with which she hurriedly complied. I then took a deep breath. "Augustus, I fear that there will be scandal in Blackheath, and that it will affect my school."

Augustus offered me a chair. "I fear I may share some blame for this, but I don't understand how any investigation at Blackheath could affect your school." He paused and started to pace. "I'll tell you everything I know. When I spoke to both the king and the Prince of Wales on this subject, I didn't think there could be any broader implications."

He put his index finger to his mouth, as if he were looking for the right words to dictate the story. "My equerry, Sir John Douglas, and his wife, Charlotte, came to me with what appeared to be a legitimate claim: that the Princess of Wales had given birth to a male child called Willie Austin, and that she intended to proclaim he'd been fathered by the Prince of Wales, making him the rightful heir to the British throne. All I could think of was protecting my niece, Princess Charlotte, who would lose her succession to a male child. Whoever Willie Austin is, he's not of Hanoverian lineage. My brother hasn't laid a finger on Caroline since he threw her out ten years ago. There were letters and lewd pictures involved as well. The evidence was too substantial to ignore, with the princess's future and the Hanoverian succession at risk." He paused. "There, I've told you all that I know."

"So, you just believed this horrible tale, without additional enquiry?" I asked, trying hard not to raise my voice. I'd just suffered through Big Harriet's miserable and selfish excuses, and now I'd learnt that Augustus was at the heart of this potentially damning investigation—an investigation that could potentially ruin my family, my reputation, and my career. I felt an urge to smack him in the face but restrained myself.

"You're responsible for this?" I then spat at him, my voice now starting to shake. "You are so naive, Augustus, and you have been so played. Everyone in Blackheath knows that the Douglases were sent there by the Prince of Wales to discredit Caroline's reputation. You have no clue about the shrewdness of misguided women like Charlotte Douglas. I wouldn't believe a word that comes out of her mouth. If you want to know the truth, of which I've witnessed, it is she who games the attention of Sir Sydney Smith, not Caroline."

He looked uncomfortable at this point, putting his hand on the fireplace mantelpiece and tilting his head downwards towards the hearth, almost in shame.

"Did you not think to ask Caroline herself, or even me, about these awful allegations before you brought the entire political establishment of London upon us? Willie Austin was brought to Caroline's house by his birth mother because she couldn't feed him. A mother gave her own child to Caroline so he could live. Do you think that was an easy 'transaction' for her or for Caroline? Because your brother denies Caroline any access to her own daughter, she takes children off the street to try to be a mother to anyone else's. You're aware that we run an orphanage at Pagoda House. Well, now those children's lives are at risk, as well as the lives of my own children. You've no idea how much damage you've done!"

Augustus was now visibly upset and maybe even annoyed. "Margaret, I don't think I understand. I need to know exactly what's upsetting you and what and who you're trying to protect if I'm to help you. It would be easier if I had all the facts. I'm beginning to feel very responsible for this unfortunate situation, and I want to be diligent in its timely repair."

I looked down immediately, because I feared he would see my answer in my eyes. The truth was, I trusted no one beyond our tiny family when it came to the protection of Little Harriet, nor any of my other children, for that matter. Seemingly, though, I had no choice. I could hear Georgiana's voice then: *He's different, he's not a* beast *like the rest of them.*

"Little Harriet's biological parents are Granville Leveson-Gower and Lady Harriet Bessborough," I whispered, turning to look at him with tears in my eyes.

"Oh my," he said, now adjusting his posture awkwardly as if he wished he'd been sitting down to receive such unexpected news. He was quiet for several moments before he finally spoke. "I completely understand now what's at stake for you and your children. I'm not sure whether the Prince of Wales would care about that interesting gossip, but certainly King George, as an avid Tory, would yield great pleasure from the moral humility of any member of the Whig party. Leveson-Gower and Lord Bessborough would please him to no end."

Augustus sat down at this point and seemed to be gathering his thoughts before continuing. "It would very be helpful, then, Margaret, to be in possession of any evidence you have as to where we can find Willie Austin's biological mother. I'll make some enquiries to try to suppress, or at least narrowly limit, the scope of the pending investigation. I'll call on you in Blackheath by the beginning of next week." He paused, and a small shadow of a smile crossed his face. "We'll sort this out without injury to you or your family, or the rest of the children at Pagoda House, I promise you, Margaret. I so admire your compassion for all those children in Blackheath, and I know none are of your own womb. You make me think about the welfare of my own children, whom I don't see or enquire about often enough."

I relaxed a bit then and said, "I'm not sure what you know of Edwardina Kent's parentage, either. I don't know if Caroline will be able to protect her if this witch hunt is so determined in her complete demise."

The expression on his face changed again, and I feared I'd finally angered him. It was certainly time to go. Then I realised his face was just full of sorrow, and he said, "I promise you, Margaret, my niece will also come to no harm."

At this, he walked across the room and embraced me. It felt like Thomas's big and able body carrying me to my uncle's carriage after he had died. I breathed it in, not wanting to let go. Then I thought about my own children, and I slowly let my body retract back to its very controlled and familiar cavity again.

"Thank you, Augustus. I should be going then, before it gets dark. I look forward to hearing from you as soon as possible. It feels like there's an urgency to this situation. We're all on pins."

Augustus retrieved my hat and coat and walked me outside to my carriage, where Mr. Murphy was waiting to take me home. He assured me again that everything would be sorted out soon. In the carriage and still rather flustered, I realised I'd caught my skirts in the door. When I looked up from freeing them, I saw Augustus still on the step, staring at me. Our eyes locked, and he didn't turn away. But I did, as quickly as possible, so as not to imply any reciprocity. I turned and stared out of the other window and began to cry. I couldn't begin to think what that was all about, and I didn't even know if I cared. The only thing I knew for certain was that I was terrified for our little family, and I needed his help.

Elizabeth had put the children to bed by the time I arrived home, and was waiting for me in the kitchen. I'd made the decision on the way home that if she was agreeable and if this enquiry wasn't stopped immediately, it was probably time for us to leave Blackheath. This so-called *Delicate Investigation* might not so delicately ruin our entire lives and everything we'd worked so hard for, not to mention Little Harriet's general welfare. For sure the Prince of Wales would use the press, and specifically the *London Times*, to help persuade the British public that he was the injured party, and we needed to get well ahead of that.

I decided to talk to Thomas about our options—not that any parent, nor anyone at all for that matter, would believe we were leaving Blackheath for any other reason than that of the scandal happening at Montague House. It would, however, make the correspondence with the outside world more palatable if it appeared our move had been planned before all this gossip made its way into the newspapers.

I hadn't even begun to think about how this was going to affect Caroline. I would call on her first thing in the morning to at least let her know what I had learnt and that Augustus had agreed to help. I thought about what Georgiana would do. *Shoulder to shoulder, a line of one* seemed like the best plan—maybe the only one.

In my heart, I believed Augustus would help us. I could hear Thomas's voice in my head, though, saying that was a totally stupid idea given that Augustus had arguably instigated the entire crisis to begin with. He was, however, the only currency I had with any value in that long, sobering moment when we believe our children are in harm's way.

WHETHER AUGUSTUS HAD CONTACTED HIS brother after my visit the day before, I don't know, but when I arrived at Montague House the following morning to speak to Caroline, the Duke of Kent was already there, letting her know what was about to happen.

"The authorities are on their way as we speak. They've been given licence to interview your servants and anyone else in Blackheath they deem to be a person of interest," I overhead him telling her as I walked into the drawing room.

I gasped, having no idea what all that meant or why this was all happening so quickly. It was everything I could do to hold myself together, but when I glanced across at Caroline, she was calmly drinking a glass of wine, snorting tobacco snuff, and skimming through various foreign newspapers, all at the same time.

She looked up from the pile of papers and addressed the Duke of Kent. "All right, I think it's proper that you stay with me until they come and talk to whomever they want, as I wouldn't want anyone to accuse me of trying to influence anyone else's tongue. I've committed no crime, and I'm sure I'll be freed by the lack of evidence in this cruel inquisition my husband has brought upon me for no other reason than to divorce me and forever banish me from seeing my only child. If the Prince of Wales wants a fight, then he shall have one. You might remind him that, regardless of my sex, I'm far more German than he could ever hope to be on any battlefield, or anywhere else for that matter."

"Caroline, I'm so sorry," I interrupted, "but I think you need to take this more seriously and at least hire some counsel. The Prince of Wales obviously sees this as an opportunity to finally finish you off. Please think of Princess Charlotte . . ." I trailed off as she motioned with her hands for me to stop.

"Please, Margaret, I don't want to talk about this nonsense."

I visited with her for another couple of hours but left without any assurance of what she was or wasn't going to do and what that might mean for the rest of us.

30

CAROLINE DIDN'T BUDGE AT ALL in her resolve, at
least initially. She just let the whole investigation play itself
out, almost without any interference. The second round of
questioning of her servants went on into the early part of summer,
without Caroline being formally accused of anything other than her
husband despising her—and he was the Prince of Wales and therefore
had the power to do so. When it became clear from Sophia Austin's
testimony that she was indeed William Austin's biological mother and
that the Hanoverian succession to the throne of England was in no
danger, the investigation quickly pivoted to Caroline's alleged infidelities. The goal of destroying Caroline hadn't changed—just the means by
which to get there. The Prince of Wales was certainly Machiavellian
by nature. Despite Augustus's best efforts to squelch it, the so-called
Delicate Investigation had now developed a life of its own.

By early July, *The Times* was leaking some very juicy depositions,
including one from one of Caroline's footmen, who'd been quoted as saying, "The princess was fond of fucking." Let me be clear: Caroline hadn't
been able to see any of these depositions. She had no idea what crime
or crimes she was being charged with despite several appeals to King
George III, which went completely ignored. Finally, in early August, a
copy of the full report of the investigation, which was now being referred
to as 'The Book,' was begrudgingly delivered to Caroline by one of the
prime minister's servants. In the meantime, she'd been completely shut
off from the Palace and hadn't been allowed to see her daughter since the
initial investigation had begun in early spring.

That was the most painful thing to watch, but throughout the months of torture, Caroline just got tougher. She also began to realise her power with the press and the British public, particularly when she became bold enough to point out the Prince of Wales's hypocrisy regarding her alleged infidelities. At one point, she threatened to publish 'The Book' herself and promised there would be counter claims against *his* infidelities, accompanied by colourful testimony and graphic pictures. It all got very ugly, but at no point did I see her even flinch, let alone cry.

I, myself, was in tatters, and was just grateful in those summer months of 1806 that Bryan House had closed its doors for the holiday recess, and I wasn't fielding daily questions about the Montague House 'gossip du jour.' Elizabeth and I, in the meantime, were now anxiously preparing for a move to Margate. Thomas had been extremely helpful in making most of the arrangements, including managing the letting of Bryan House, Blackheath, and arranging the movement of our furniture and belongings. I'd feared that he'd be angry and say, "I told you so," when I went to him for help, but he did nothing of the sort.

"Margaret, I'm so sorry you're in this abominable situation, and I've seen the merits of the risks you and Elizabeth have taken. We'll get through this together, and Sarah and I will do whatever we can to help. I agree with you, though; you need to get out of Blackheath. I'm sure it's no secret at the Palace that you have a very personal relationship with the Princess of Wales. I don't think you'll be spared, regardless of what your duke says he can do for you. He simply yields no power to his brother's might."

We had decided to relocate to Margate for several reasons, the main one being that I still owned the large home my uncle had left to me in his will. It had been under lease for several years, but somehow Thomas managed to undo that and ensure that the house would be vacant for us by the late summer. We also decided we'd open a day school, as opposed to another boarding school, so we could adjust the curriculum to fit the educational needs of our own children. Attracting younger day students would be much easier than our previous efforts to open a boarding seminary in Margate more than a decade earlier. Thomas was also now stationed with the Fifteenth very near to Margate, so that would be an additional benefit. All told, it wasn't a bad plan, just one we felt we really hadn't been given much choice in.

PRESUMABLY FEELING GUILTY ABOUT HIS role in the *Delicate Investigation*, Augustus generously financed the entire publishing of my second book that summer of 1806, which I'd decided to call *Lectures on Natural Philosophy*. In addition to incurring all the publishing expenses, he also amassed hundreds of additional 'financial subscribers,' which translated into pure profits for me.

He also commissioned the engraving of a frontispiece of me to grace its cover. He personally supervised the entire project from start to finish. I remember him saying to me just before the unveiling, "Whilst I agree, Margaret, that the frontispiece to your first book is very beautiful, this one not only captures your physical beauty but all the other more interesting dimensions of you as well. I hope you don't mind that I was presumptive enough to drop the prefix 'Mrs.' I'm sure you don't need it anymore. Margaret Bryan stands firmly on her own two feet, wouldn't you agree?"

I looked at him with pure mystery—talk about the forgiveness of sins. I must admit, I thought the frontispiece was beautiful myself, and it brought a sophistication to my work that the first one had certainly lacked. I just smiled and said, "Augustus, it's just so beautiful. I have no words but *thank you*."

Elizabeth walked in as we were observing the little painting. "Oh, Margaret, it is so lovely. You look so accomplished in it. Who knows where that portrait might be hung? Perhaps the British Museum itself?" she said with a wink and a smile.

"I couldn't agree with you more," Augustus answered, reaching across and putting his arm around her shoulder. Then he kissed the top of her head and said again, "I couldn't agree with you more."

MARGARET BRYAN

The 1806 frontispiece to Lectures on Natural Philosophy *by Margaret Bryan.*
Chronicle / Alamy Stock Photo

As some attempt at retribution, Augustus also demanded that Sir John Douglas and Lady Charlotte Douglas sponsor my book, which I thought was very cheeky of him. When I thought this might anger Caroline, though, I asked her if she minded.

"Mind—why would I mind?" she said curtly. "'Lady Harlot' is now paying to read your boring book, and she no longer has a house in which to read it, at least not here in my village. She might be flat on her back, but I'm not, and there is no skin missing off mine."

This made Elizabeth blush, then giggle, putting her hand over her mouth all at the same time. I was, of course, very grateful to Augustus for his fundraising efforts. It was something I was terrible at—asking people for money, that is. I was also very grateful to finally put the problem of the 'children' to rest by including a reference to my 'own' dear children in the body of the preface, as well as at its conclusion, where I expressed how much 'I rejoice in the titles of Parent and Preceptress.' It was probably only me that saw the nuanced difference in the prose, but it felt very reconciling to try and finally put the fib to rest.

Augustus was also able to obtain the Prince of Wales's permission to dedicate my book to Princess Charlotte, which was particularly helpful in the highly polarised political environment that we now found ourselves drowning in. Thomas thankfully had been wrong about Augustus's inability to influence his brother, although admittedly, I didn't know the price that had been extracted for the favours. I was obviously respectful enough to ask Caroline for her permission also, which she gave me with all her blessings.

Augustus often apologised for his role in our now-pressing need to relocate. He offered that his assistance was the least he could do for us given the circumstances. Neither I nor Elizabeth ever did anything to correct him, not for one single minute. We did, however, always thank him profusely for his help. We certainly couldn't have landed on our feet without him, nor Thomas and Sarah.

As promised, Augustus also managed to spare anyone from Bryan House and the Pagoda orphanage from being interviewed by any of the authorities. The children from the orphanage had all been placed in foster homes, which I'm sure was accompanied by a generous financial donation from Augustus.

One afternoon, Elizabeth was quietly thanking him for his assistance in the dismantling of the orphanage when Augustus sheepishly brought his own daughter into the conversation.

"I can't thank you enough for helping us to place the orphanage's children in safe hands. It's hard enough leaving our life here, but knowing that those children are all in a safe place brings some redemption to this whole sordid mess," Elizabeth said, chatting with him in the dining room whilst packing up the crystal. "Life will also be easier with only our own children to take care of, and a much simpler operation to run in a day school. I must admit, I'm looking forward to a bit of relaxation by the sea as well, from time to time."

"Elizabeth, I have wanted to talk to you and Margaret about the new day school. My daughter, Emma, lives with her mother only a few miles from Margate, and I was hoping that you'd both consider admitting her into your new school."

Before he could finish whatever was left of his clearly prepared speech, Elizabeth cut him off. "Augustus, why do I feel like you're testing the water with me on this subject? Of course, we'd welcome your daughter at the new school. If it's Margaret you're worried about, I will talk to her on your behalf. She is not as gruff as you think. For future reference, though, your timing could have been more thoughtful."

"I am sorry, Elizabeth, and thank you," he said before I interrupted them to ask if anyone was ready for a break.

Augustus's daughter, Emma D'Este, indeed joined our new school in Margate later that year, where she almost became like another member of the family. She and Lucy Elizabeth fast became best friends, for what I assume will be the rest of their mortal lives. Perhaps everything does happen for a reason.

31

THE MOVE TO MARGATE WAS LARGELY without incident, and our new day school was open by the spring term
of 1807. We had twenty-two young girls as pupils, including Augustus's daughter, who often stayed overnight with us at Bryan
House, Margate. Augustus came to visit from London often. He and
Emma and Lucy Elizabeth would play the piano and sing songs together
for hours at a time. It was the happiest I'd seen him in all the time I'd
known him, and his daughter worshipped the ground he walked on.

Thomas, Sarah, and the children also came to visit us at Christmastide. By the early spring, we'd developed a new routine that was certainly
less stressful than the boarding school at Blackheath but also lacked its
sophistication and the demand for the breadth of subjects I could teach.
These are the trade-offs one makes, though, when the well-being of one's
children is the priority.

We learnt later that spring that parliament had decided to drop the
Delicate Investigation entirely, and Caroline was now being accepted
at Court again. She'd also moved into new apartments at Kensington
Palace, ironically right next door to Augustus. Caroline had prevailed
and more than shown her tenacity as an avid opponent to the Prince of
Wales. I couldn't have been prouder of her. When she finally returned to
Court to attend King George III's birthday celebrations, a tumultuous
applause broke out from the crowd, all but affirming whose side they
were on. The German princess had amassed her own cavalry from within
the British people and its press, and it was capital that she would save for
an even greater battle down the road.

Augustus also told me that spring he had been informed by his brother that the Prince of Wales had granted an annual pension of two hundred pounds to Lady Charlotte Douglas for her assistance in the not-so *Delicate Investigation* of his wife. The whole wretched affair still turns my stomach. The only saving grace was that there wasn't a hair on Little Harriet's head out of place.

On a very warm day in late July—particularly for the Kent coast—I received word from Augustus that he wished to call on us two days hence. My first instinct was to decline the invitation. Elizabeth had taken the children to visit Thomas and Sarah in London, as the school was in its summer recess. Protocol meant that we shouldn't meet alone, even if I was a forty-nine-year-old spinster. Not that any of this mattered to me, except that I could hear Thomas's voice banging in my head, saying I was playing with fire yet again. I decided to let Augustus know that Elizabeth and the children were in London in case he might wish to postpone the visit. I sent word back to him via his courier, who was still standing on the step, perspiring profusely in the relentless heat even after I'd given him a glass of water.

> *Augustus,*
>
> *So lovely to hear from you, but Elizabeth has taken the children to London for the week, as the school is in its summer recess. I've stayed back to reconcile my book's accounts. If you still wish to visit, I'd appreciate the company, but it may be better to postpone if you were hoping to spend time with Emma. I am not sure what brings you to Kent and how long you will be here.*
>
> *—Margaret*

I, too, was starting to perspire—not with the heat, but with the uncertainty of not knowing how my message might be received or interpreted. Whatever I was expecting, what happened the next day surprised me entirely.

Margaret,

> *I hadn't realised you were on your own. I've just leased a beautiful estate on the Broadstairs Cliffs and would very much like you to be my guest for dinner tomorrow evening. We can eat on the verandah overlooking the sea. If you would be so kind as to accept my invitation, I will send my coachman for you at five o'clock tomorrow, and he can bring you back the following morning. I look forward to your response.*
>
> *—Augustus*

When I finished reading the message, I was so visibly shaken that I had to turn my back on his courier. I hadn't even known that Augustus had taken accommodation in Margate at all. What frazzled me the most, though, was that it was crystal clear he wanted me to *sleep* there. *Sleep* sounded like a strange kind of word to use in that context. I could feel my face flush. I knew if I didn't accept immediately, I'd talk myself out of it. I didn't even bother to write a response, as my hands were shaking so badly. I just politely told the messenger to tell the Duke of Sussex that his invitation was graciously accepted.

That night, I pulled out a book Georgiana had once given me about the *Pleasure Gardens of London*. She'd also given me a signed copy of her book *The Sylph* the same afternoon. At the time, I'd thought the *Pleasure Gardens* book was vulgar and told her so, but that night I read it like a hungry teenager, searching for knowledge of a world I now yearned to know. I yearned for Georgiana as well that night and wondered what it would have been like to be able to talk to her about Augustus. Her extinguished light still burned so fresh in my chest. I sometimes felt like it might catch fire at any moment.

Sadly, I didn't have anyone to talk to about the feelings I now had for Augustus and my desire to know him as a man. I wasn't even sure what a naked man might look like. Of course, I'd seen pictures in medical textbooks, but it was hard to determine the scale and what it might look like in real life—or perhaps more importantly, how it all worked. After perusing the book for a couple of hours, I finally went to sleep dreaming about Augustus and what the following evening might bring.

I awoke at sunrise, not knowing how long I'd slept. As I'd mentioned to Augustus, I'd intended in Elizabeth and the children's absence to reconcile my latest book's accounts. I always reconciled my own accounts. I'd heard nightmares of women being taken advantage of with regards to the management of their money by seemingly agreeable and honest men. The task took the entire morning and the better part of the early afternoon to accomplish. Thanks to Augustus, the profits were handsome, and already exceeded those of all three editions of my first book. Indeed, I could retire on my own merits, but I wouldn't do that, nor would I have wanted to.

I tried to turn off the clock hands in my head and took a long, hot bath, imagining myself as beautiful, as Augustus's invitation had made me feel. I chose a simple blue summer dress and hat to wear and less sensible shoes than I normally would, and at a quarter to five by my uncle's watch, Augustus's coachman was knocking on the front door. Just before I left, I scribbled a letter for Elizabeth explaining where I'd gone, should she come home unexpectedly early. Even whilst writing it, I was thinking about destroying it upon my safe arrival home the following morning.

The estate at Broadstairs was magnificent, with panoramic views of the sea, and by the grace of God, the oppressive humidity had lifted with a soft afternoon rain. As promised, we had dinner on the outside terrace. It was a half-crescent moon, and the sky was lit up by the stars, covering me like a soft blanket. I'd already decided that I wanted to be Augustus's lover the minute I had received his lovely invitation, but probably for a long time before that as well.

On a purely lusty level, I didn't have much interest in the simple physical pleasures of the flesh that only seemed to get Georgiana and her friends into so much trouble. Albeit that was clearly their only currency in the misogynist social circles they were so begrudgingly confined to.

It wasn't even a moral compass that had held my carnal curiosities at bay. I'd already convinced myself that Augustus wasn't really a married man, although, admittedly, by a rather weak technicality. I apologise, I digress, but the Bible is very clear that the relationship between a man and a woman who live together as husband and wife is to be respected at all costs. The notion, however, that sexual intercourse between two consenting adults is offensive to God is absurd. How would the human species survive without copulation? The entire animal kingdom plays by those rules.

The reason for my hesitancy, then, in resisting Augustus's not-so-subtle advances was that I was scared I was falling in love with him. I think it was Shakespeare who said that to consummate love is to make it mortal, and that terrified me. How I'd fallen in love with Augustus isn't as obvious as it might seem, as it had little to do with the abundance of kindness he had shown me. Nor did his demeanour remind me of my uncle or Thomas, who'd certainly been the most influential men in my life after my papa and grandpapa died. That is long before the fact that I was more than fifteen years older than him, and we'd been born into different galaxies.

No, my love for him was born of the shared belief that God and science can peacefully exist together and take us to a kinder place, where all mankind could live in some sort of reasonable prosperity. Augustus and I constantly challenged the ridiculously self-serving excuses touted by the crumbling institutions on both sides of the argument that God and science could not coexist compatibly. Not only could they coexist, but they could be completely at harmony with each other. The entire world wanted them to be mutually exclusive, to suit their own agendas and protect their own power bases. The Church believed the scientists were heretics, and the scientists believed the Church was corrupt.

That was the lust of my love for him and the fuel that fed my desire to know him as a mortal man in the biblical sense. So, on that beautiful night on the Broadstairs Cliffs, at the end of dinner as we were finishing our dessert, I very quietly said to him, "Augustus, do you know that I've never known a man in the biblical sense?"

I'd clearly caught him off guard, as he at once reached for his drink, which went down in one go. I cringed, wishing I could take the sterile words back. "No, Margaret, I was not aware of that fact," he finally answered. "At the risk of being presumptuous, could I ask why you're providing me with such private information at this moment? You've always been so guarded in your privacy. I would not be humoured to be just another science experiment for you."

My heart caved. "Oh no, Augustus, that was not my intention—and so rude and so awkward. I apologise."

"Margaret, I'm serious. I've thought about this moment for a long time, but I'm not here to satisfy your curiosity. I'm already starting to feel inadequate. I have nothing to offer you but my heart."

"Oh no, Augustus, no, of course not. It is I who should be feeling embarrassed and inadequate. This is getting awkward fast." I could feel my face becoming flushed, and I was starting to feel dizzy and a little sick.

"Margaret, this doesn't have to be awkward, but you do have to be able to trust me if you want to understand physical love from a man who loves you in every way possible. Can you do that? Trust me to be in control? I am certain that's the only way that I can trust you."

I think, somehow, as awkward as that moment was, we both decided to tear down the protective walls we'd so mightily built around each other for entirely different reasons. For years I had fought for the independence to pursue my own occupation, and now I had found the freedom to be vulnerable to love on my own terms. I felt myself completely surrender to him. I held my breath, looked across at him, and nodded my head. He reached for my hand and entwined his fingers in mine, then led me inside the house and up the grand staircase to the most magnificent bedroom I had ever seen.

The details of that night cannot properly be expressed in words, nor should they. Except to say that, however unlikely the union of a forty-nine-year-old virgin and a thirty-four-year-old royal prince was, it seemed that night as if we had known each other in another lifetime. Because I hadn't had anyone to ask, I'd not really known what to expect when it was all over, either. I mean physically over, for clarification. Augustus must have sensed my uneasiness, as he pulled me closer to him and just whispered, "Margaret, you are like your night sky: full of heavenly surprises. Will you stay with me another night?"

I felt so loved in that moment that I just closed my eyes and went to sleep. I dreamt of Georgiana that night and somehow expected her to be proud of me, as ridiculous as I am sure that sounds. I was laughing out loud for thinking such a peculiar thought when the maid knocked on the door, at who knows what hour of the morning, to let me know breakfast was being served. Augustus had clearly crept out sometime in the middle of the night, presumably to protect me from idle gossip. The thought did cross my mind, however, just how practised he might be at that very gentlemanlike tactic.

The weekend flew, as if it were just a dream. I could already see, though, that our relationship was forever changed. There were certainly unfamiliar periods of discomfort, at least for me, as I had no idea what I was doing having an intimate relationship with any man, let alone a royal prince.

It was in one such moment, when we were walking the Broadstairs Cliffs on Sunday morning, that Augustus started telling me about parliament finally passing the Abolition of Slavery Act. This was different from previous efforts to abolish the heinous industry. This time, parliament had finally put some real financing behind it. Whilst I knew of the slave ship atrocities reported in the papers, I felt physically sick when Augustus described the conditions of a slave vessel he'd personally boarded.

He then went on to tell me a story about a negro woman called Dido Belle and her ancestral connection to the slave trade in the West Indies. "I have firsthand accounts of the conditions in which they keep slaves in the British West Indies. My wife's cousin Dido Belle is the daughter of a slave. She was born into slavery, before her father brought her to England. Her father was a British Navy officer in the Caribbean, and he's also related to Chief Justice Lord Mansfield, by whom she was raised."

Chief Justice Lord Mansfield had apparently been instrumental in getting the new anti-slave-trading law passed in parliament. Augustus then went on to say, "Dido Belle was married on the same day as I was, at St. George's in London, and by the same vicar."

I thought I'd like to meet this woman, Dido Belle; even her name meant *beautiful*. I was also a bit at a loss for words, and more than a bit uncomfortable after the words *marriage* and *wife* had entered the conversation. He must have sensed that he'd offended me, as he then quickly changed the subject, oddly enough, to that of his mother, better known as Queen Charlotte, the Queen of England!

"My mother once told me that she has African descent in her lineage, along a Portuguese line of some sort. You can see it in her features up close. Amusingly, the Palace hires painters who paint those features out. They don't think 'lily white' England can deal with a mulatto queen. I must say, I think they're beautiful. Funny enough, they don't seem to show up much in her children. I'm sure, though, Margaret, you'd attest to me being all German, stitch to stitch," he finished off with a laugh.

I had no idea what to say. It seemed completely inappropriate to be talking about the Queen of England's negro features, even if with her own son. I was also annoyed at his last comment, however he'd intended it. It had been received as rude, crude, and insensitive.

I curtly replied, "Augustus, as a scientist, I have no relevant specimen with whom to compare you to, so I can provide you no opinion on that subject. Speculation is the best I could do, and that would be unfair to you, don't you think?"

He immediately winced. "Margaret, I'm sorry. I seem to have made you cross. Please accept my apologies. I'm not new to love, but I am new to this love. We men can be naive, and I didn't have a great deal of time with my mother to learn the complexities of a woman's heart and mind.

Can we not just enjoy the day together? You will have other responsibilities that will take you away from me tomorrow."

I had to admit the apology seemed heartfelt. He'd also said the word *love* twice. He reached for my hand, and at first I said nothing, but after a few minutes I responded to him, trying to camouflage the hurt in my voice.

"I can't imagine what it must be like to have the Queen of England be your mother. I juggle my time between Bryan House, writing textbooks, and my children, but it's hard. I never feel like I'm doing it all right, or that I spend enough time with my children. But I only have three, and one school to run, whilst she has fifteen and is arguably second-in-command of the most powerful country in the world."

That made him laugh out loud. "Margaret, you certainly have a keen ability to paint the world as it is. To answer your question, it's not easy being royal." He paused for a minute to catch his breath. "I'm the queen's ninth child and her sixth son, so I've never spent much time with either of my parents. The king's health is really the limitation. For company, I rely more on my brothers and sisters. The hardest part for me, though, is that the Palace won't give me a real job because of my health issues. The focus of the family is the direct heirs to the throne, George and now Princess Charlotte, but at least my other brothers have respectable positions in the army. There are many days when I feel like I have very little purpose in my life. I'm also entirely dependent on my father and parliament for my very existence. I can't even get married without asking for permission."

I now felt I'd been crude and insensitive as I listened to him baring his soul to try to explain an innocent gaffe. I felt annoyed with myself for being so short-tempered. Georgiana was right: The man was sensitive and certainly no 'beast.'

"That must be hard, Augustus. It sounds a little bit like being a woman. Your life is already defined for you by someone else's rule book. Who knows, though, maybe you would have hated being a general? Maybe God chose your birth order for a reason. Maybe, if no one is paying attention to you, you can define your own path, on your own terms. I'd like to believe that's how I arrived at my own unique destination. You'll find your path, Augustus, and it'll be uniquely yours when you do."

"Can you tell me how you found your path, Margaret? I don't want to disrespect your privacy, but surely things are different between us now," he said softly.

My heart filled to the brim with emotion. "Yes, I will. It's not a story without pain, but it's certainly not one without magic, either. I don't think I've ever told it in its entirety to any human being before, not even Elizabeth."

He kissed me on top of my head and squeezed my hand, almost to the point of pain. "I'd love that, Margaret, but let me hear it without distraction over a private lunch. I want to hear every detail. Thank you for trusting me, Margaret."

We walked back to the main house mainly in silence, hand in hand. He ordered a private lunch on the verandah, and I told my story from start to finish—from Ipswich to Margate, and everything in between.

I left to go back to Margate later that Sunday afternoon. Augustus insisted on making the short trip back into town with me. I was grateful, or maybe relieved, when I finally arrived home. I was also completely exhausted. I was now in love with this man, this HRH, this royal prince, who now simply referred to me as 'Margaret, my love.'

It was only a few days later, though, when Elizabeth and the children arrived home, that the whole weekend began to seem like a celestial illusion.

32

I ENJOYED THE YEARS WE SPENT in Margate when our children were little. Those formative years after they lose their 'babyness' is the time in a child's life when parenting starts to become more interesting. The truth is, no matter where your children come from, biologically or otherwise, their personalities can quite literally come from anywhere. Even as parents to the same child, one can see totally different sides of them. I remember having an amusing conversation with Elizabeth on this very subject, one rainy Sunday afternoon, as we were watching our girls do a jigsaw puzzle together.

"Lizzie, do you think Little Harriet is the most like me out of the three of them, in terms of temperament? I think she's quiet, like me."

"*Quiet*, Margaret? That's the last adjective in the world I'd use to describe you. You speak to the world every day—with so much more than the words that come out of your mouth. And no, I think that Little Harriet is the least like you of all our children, my stargazer, and probably more like me: *practical*," she said with a smile on her face.

"We really are quite different, aren't we, Lizzie? Who would have thought that we'd be parents together to three little angels sent from heaven? I wonder if married couples ever think about how they'll influence their children, or if it's just all about their love for each other. And, by the way, what do you mean by *practical*? I think I'm very practical."

"I knew that would bother you," Elizabeth said with a laugh, disappearing into the kitchen to get the tea service.

When Augustus came by several weeks later for a visit in Margate, Elizabeth chose a moment to corner him on the subject. "Your Royal

Highness, we have been in an ongoing discussion regarding which of our children are most like each one of us. We are in complete disagreement, and now you must break the tie."

She had certainly caught him off guard; his panicked look my way would have surely been discovered if Elizabeth hadn't had her back to him, picking up toy dolls off the kitchen floor.

"Lizzie, that is not fair," I chimed in. "You can't put Augustus in such a position."

"No, no, that is all right. I am happy to entertain the question." He then winked at me and said, "The truth is, I see both of you in all your children, the good and the bad . . ."

Elizabeth didn't even let him finish. "Stop, you; you should have been a politician. Oh, you already are a politician," she said, laughing, and then I quickly changed the subject.

Several months later Elizabeth and I concluded that, from the cot, Lucy Elizabeth was a born performer, fascinated with art, music, and the fashion of the day. Like Georgiana, she was always in charge and was truly probably also from another planet. She could play both the violin and the piano with some mastery by the time she was six. She and Emma D'Este were always performing new plays, sometimes in perfect French, whenever Augustus came to visit. I know he lived for those moments and often joined in himself.

We also agreed that Jessy Anne was probably most like me: always in her books and somewhat uncomfortable in social situations. I remember her telling me once that she didn't want to go to one of Lucy Elizabeth's birthday parties.

"Jessy Anne, would you please hurry up? It's your sister's birthday. We need to leave now, or we're going to be late."

"I don't like birthday parties, Maman. They're *soooo* boring. The last time I went with Harriet to one, someone weed in her pants and then started to cry. Do I really have to go? Can I at least take some books with me?" she pleaded with me.

It was one of those moments that, as a parent, made me laugh out loud. I'd not given birth to this child, and yet I saw so much of myself in her. She was actually negotiating with me, much as I used to negotiate with my uncle whenever he tried to distract me with anything bar my mathematical education. I finally compromised and let her take two books with her. It wasn't as if Lucy Elizabeth was going to notice, which, of course, she didn't.

We also agreed that if Lucy Elizabeth and Jessy Anne were our extremes, Little Harriet was somewhere in the middle and the most like Elizabeth in temperament and personality. She was also the most selfless and loving of all my three children. She just went along to get along. I often marvel at the fact that Big Harriet could have given birth to such a sweet and tender child. Let me be crystal clear, though. Elizabeth gets all the credit for her warm and steady composure. All said, the girls got along well, and Emma just tucked in, as if a fourth leg of the stool. She and Lucy Elizabeth were totally inseparable, like twins separated at birth who had just rediscovered each other. There was less than a year between them in age.

We also got to see Thomas a lot more often in Margate, at least in the early years. He was stationed in Ramsgate, where Emma's mother lived, so we often went to visit him there. Whilst stationed in Ramsgate, Thomas often used to train on Spencer Square, which happened to be owned by Harriet and Georgiana's brother, George Spencer. The irony of bringing Little Harriet there was not lost on either of us. Sometimes I tried to imagine how different her life might have been had she been born into the 'legitimate' side of the Spencer family ledger.

Thomas's regiment, the Fifteenth, was a particularly important one to the British Army. It had been exercised in front of the royal family on more than one occasion, including once on Wimbledon Common, an event that Augustus had attended. Much to our disappointment, the Fifteenth was redeployed back to Spain in 1808. Thomas wrote to me immediately upon their arrival on foreign shores, and I decided to save his letter. Thomas rarely described the war in the letters he wrote, but this letter was an exception. I knew the winter was particularly bitter that year, but I could also read between the lines that my brother was losing his will to endure this war. I'd originally thought of throwing away the letter because it was so painful. I decided to keep it, though, as a reminder of all those men who'd sacrificed so much so the rest of Britain could maintain its way of life without fear of their children speaking French as their first language. No disrespect to any of my Huguenot ancestors, of course.

> *My dearest Margaret,*
>
> *I hope this letter finds you well, and that you have been able to find time to visit Sarah and the children. I'm missing them terribly. It is bitterly cold here. Some of the men have frostbite and are losing their limbs without medicine. It's impossible to sleep at night for fear of the cold and the angel of death. I have the Lord's courage, but I must admit, my faith is waning.*
>
> *Yesterday, we were outmanned, two to one, by the French, and under attack all day. We had to hide with the horses in the freezing river to wait for the enemy to pass so we could come from behind and take them by surprise. I couldn't feel my fingers or toes all day. By the grace of God, we somehow prevailed. We lost many men and several horses, though. I'm tired, and I'm also having trouble eating anything. I'm desperately hoping to be back on English soil soon.*
>
> *Please pray for my safe return.*
>
> *Love to Elizabeth and the children,*
> *Thomas*

This business of war was a deadly, dangerous one. I was genuinely grateful to have very little knowledge of the day-to-day details, and I deliberately avoided reading about them in the papers. Reading the names of the dead just reminded me of how close Thomas was to the kingdom of heaven every day he fought for our country and our way of life on foreign soil.

Our years in Margate passed quickly, with Elizabeth and I rearing and educating our three small children to the best of our ability, as well as looking after our day school. We very much enjoyed the city of Margate. It had become a popular seaside resort, with funny little bathing machines on its beaches. The beaches were randomly scattered with the rich and the poor from London, intermingling often for the first time— as if, for a moment, on that beautiful sandy beach of the Lord's creation, class distinction didn't seem to matter much at all. The sunshine and the refreshing saltwater were simply free for all to indulge in, and everyone got an 'equal' allocation of both.

An added benefit of Margate was that the air was better for my lungs. There was also a specialised hospital near the port, where I received some new experimental treatments for my episodic dyspnea, a very technical term for my inability to breathe comfortably at times. All said, we'd made a good choice in Margate, despite it feeling like it had been thrust upon us. I did, however, miss the prestige of Bryan House, Blackheath, and the convenient access to the great libraries of London. For the time being, though, our lives felt full and, welcomingly, very ordinary.

33

THE YEAR 1811 TURNED OUT to be a sad and tumultuous one in many ways. At Spencer Perceval's recommendation (now the prime minister), parliament finally declared King George III unfit to rule because of his failing mental health. Following his father's incapacitation, the Prince of Wales then became Prince Regent, which meant he ascended and performed all duties of the king. Whilst that ordinarily would have made sense, in this case it seemed to me that a well-intentioned king with a feeble mind, surrounded by a few good advisors, would have been a better answer to a malintent regent with no brains at all, in the company of fools. Clearly, though, neither I nor the British public were consulted on such a decision.

Momentarily, Prince George IV's accession to the throne did bring some hope to the Whig Party that the new Prince Regent would be more supportive of some of their liberal social policies, as he'd always been an avid Whig Party supporter in the past. This, however, was not to be the case, as he did an about-face almost immediately after gaining his new title. He feared that if his father, a staunch Tory supporter, ever reclaimed his health and took back the Throne, he'd punish his son for supporting the liberal views of his opposition. Unlike his wife, Caroline, George IV was a coward to the core. I've often wondered whether, if he'd supported the implementation of some basic reforms and wage protection for workers, the public uprisings like the Luddite riots and the Battle of Peterloo could have been avoided entirely.

I would be remiss not to mention that whilst the entire financing of the Napoleonic Wars was falling on the backs of the British working class, the Prince Regent was still building golden palaces like nobody's business. The party he threw after his regent appointment—entirely at the taxpayers' expense—would have been considered extravagant in peaceful times, but with ordinary men and women starving to finance the war, it was nothing short of vulgar.

Our concern regarding the political unrest in the nation was to pale in comparison, though, to the pain of a permanent fracture that was about to occur in our tiny little family. The news, of course, came completely out of the blue.

> *My dearest Margaret,*
>
> *I hope you are all well. I apologise for the short notice, but I was hoping to come to visit you in Margate next weekend if that would be convenient for you. There's something I wish to discuss with you privately, so I'm hoping you could suggest a restaurant where we can have lunch.*
>
> *I look forward to my visit.*
>
> *—Harriet*

As soon as I read the message, my heart sank. I knew that no good news could possibly come out of this conversation. I gave the message to Elizabeth immediately and hesitantly asked her, "What do you think of this?"

Elizabeth read it and didn't say anything for at least a minute. Then she looked at me and said, "I think she wants her back, Margaret; that's what I think," as the tears started to swell in her eyes. "This is not going to be like running away from Blackheath. There's no power that can save us from this, not even Augustus." She took a deep breath. "We should remind ourselves, though, that we knew this would be a possibility from day one. What we need to do now is try to negotiate."

That was not the answer I'd hoped for, and I felt defensive. "Lizzie, we don't know that yet. There could be dozens of other things that she wants to discuss with us. Let's not come to any premature conclusions before I have it from Harriet herself. I'll just accept the invitation. Let's try not to speculate until then."

Elizabeth just stared at me and walked away. I sent word to Harriet that I'd be delighted to meet her for lunch the following Saturday afternoon. I then did exactly what I'd told Elizabeth not to do, and worried constantly about every dreadful thing that might come out of Harriet's mouth until, finally, the day of the meeting.

"Margaret, you look well," Harriet announced upon my arrival at the tavern. "The seaside air really suits you. I should spend more time away from the black soot of London myself."

I didn't understand how I could look well. I hadn't slept properly since receiving her letter, and it was a miserable, rainy day, so I was soaked to the skin and completely annoyed with myself for not letting Mr. Murphy bring me in the carriage.

"You're so kind," I almost bristled. "You're looking well yourself" was all I could say as I eased myself into my seat, trying to squeeze some of the water out of my skirts at the same time.

After the waiter had assisted Harriet into her own chair and then departed, she went on to say, "I won't waste anybody's time, Margaret, in getting to the subject with which I wish to speak to you about. My apologies for having been so vague in my correspondence. First and foremost, Lord Granville and I want to thank you immensely for all that you and Elizabeth have done for Little Harriet. She's such a lovely and well-mannered young lady."

Please, just get to the point. I began to feel sick and became worried about whether I would be able to eat anything without public embarrassment.

She continued, "Her father, however, is now married, and we believe this would be an appropriate time for Little Harriet to join his family at Tixall Hall in Staffordshire, where they'll soon be taking up residence."

She said much more, but that's all I heard. The word *appropriate* nearly sent me over the edge, and my mind shut down. I just couldn't listen. All I could hear were Elizabeth's words, and I desperately wished we'd talked more about what *negotiation* might look like. I was now thinking on my own two feet without the benefit of her very big and very *practical* brain.

Big Harriet must have sensed my shock, if not total paralysis, as she looked at me and said, "I know this must be a big surprise, so please take a minute, Margaret. May I offer you a glass of wine?"

I nodded. "Yes, that would be lovely, thank you. And yes, I'd like to take a minute. I'm going to excuse myself now for a minute, if you'll oblige me?" I wasn't sure if I was going to make it, but I did manage to reach the water closet, and by the grace of God, it was unoccupied. I vomited immediately once inside whilst also trying to hold back the tears. I must have been in there for a full ten minutes before throwing cold water over my face and managing to pull myself together. By the time I got back to the table, there were two glasses of wine waiting, and Harriet was looking extremely pensive, which didn't help anything.

"Harriet, I'm obviously not happy about this," I said, trying to keep calm and remembering Elizabeth's words as I did so. I breathed heavily and continued. "Having said that, I trust you and her father have put a great deal of thought into this decision, and it would be inappropriate for me to enquire as to how such a decision was made. I will ask, however, if Elizabeth and I can continue to have access to Little Harriet, along with her sisters, and whether we could discuss a reasonable transition plan." I took another deep breath. That was all I could get out.

"Yes, of course, Margaret. That would only be fair to everyone, including Little Harriet. And you can write to and visit her as often as you wish," she said, trying to smile at me.

That, thankfully, through no doing of Big Harriet's, did indeed turn out to be true.

The whole thing was done atrociously, though, as everything Big Harriet ever did was. I nearly lost my mind when she initially explained that the new parenting arrangement was only to be on a temporary basis to see if Leveson-Gower's new wife would accept Little Harriet as a member of their family. I couldn't help but think that these people treated their dogs with more affection and respect. I also learnt from Big Harriet, shortly after our meeting in Margate, that her illegitimate daughter, 'our' sweet little girl, was never to know who her true biological parents were. She and Leveson-Gower would always be as they always had been—her 'special benefactors.' This made trying to explain all of this to Little Harriet even harder.

"Maman, but I don't want to live any place else, and I don't want to leave my mamans and my sisters. This is my home, where I belong," she said, then started to cry.

Trying hard not to do the same, I just said, "Darling, I know this is a big surprise for all of us. Your new home is like a beautiful castle, though, and your new family loves you very much."

"But, Maman, I thought *this* family loved me very much." I could think of nothing else to say to ease her or my own excruciating pain. I just held her tightly, and we both wept. We had no way to explain to any of the children why this was happening, and there was no path to ease Lucy Elizabeth's and Jessy Anne's anxieties that they, too, wouldn't be reassigned.

It made me feel like an imaginary parent for the first time since fostering Little Harriet. I remember Georgiana telling me the pain of being separated from her own children after she'd given birth to an illegitimate daughter. I was nauseous all day, every day. I pretended I was just sending her away to a boarding school, whilst trying to ease the separation fears of my other two children. It was an awful period in all our lives. It is a wound in my heart that has never healed.

The good news, though, as bizarre as it sounds, was that Leveson-Gower was now married to Georgiana's second-eldest daughter, also called Harriet but better known as Harryo. *Thank goodness.* I was running out of qualifiers for all the women in the Spencer family named Harriet, and most of them had red hair. I began corresponding with

Harryo immediately and was pleased to soon learn that she was nothing like her aunt, Big Harriet. In all honesty, she was nothing like her own mother, Georgiana, either. Her sensibilities and temperament were, indeed, far closer to that of Elizabeth's and Little Harriet's.

> *Dear Lady Leveson-Gower,*
>
> *You may not remember me, but I was a dear friend of your maman's, which is how we became foster parents to Little Harriet. Your aunt has informed me of your pending move to Tixall Hall and the new parenting arrangement with Little Harriet. I was hoping we could start a correspondence to make the transition easier on everyone involved. I look forward to hearing from you.*
>
> *Respectfully,*
> *Margaret Bryan*

It was only a couple of days until I heard back, which gave me some sense of relief in and of itself, but the actual letter started to make me feel a little better about the awful situation we now found ourselves drowning in.

> *My dearest Margaret,*
>
> *Yes, of course I remember Maman talking about you. We couldn't have hoped for a better guardian for Little Harriet. You may have read recently in the newspapers that my father died and that my brother, who is now the 6th Duke of Devonshire, has very generously offered us accommodation at Tixall Hall. We thought it the right time to bring Little Harriet and her younger brother, George, to come and live with us there as a family. I realise this must be painful and disruptive for you and Elizabeth. I promise to make this as easy as possible on everybody. An ongoing dialogue between us would be a very good*

start. I will be in Margate next week. Is there a chance we could meet for tea?

Most kindest regards,
Harryo

I remember thinking, *George? Who is George? Could Harriet have concealed a second pregnancy from Lord Bessborough?* Unbelievable that she hadn't mentioned this at our lunch meeting. I would have no idea how to explain that to Little Harriet. *Maybe I will let Harryo do that*, I thought to myself.

Little Harriet's move to Tixall Hall did, however, give the rest of us an opportunity to reevaluate where we might want to live in the future. We'd come to Margate, after all, to shelter us all, but particularly Little Harriet, from the *Delicate Investigation* in Blackheath. Whilst we enjoyed the sunshine and the seaside, I craved the vast libraries of London and greater access to its scientific community. When I mentioned a move to London to Elizabeth, she seemed open to the idea.

"I'd be excited about London," she said, "but what about Lucy and Emma? I imagine they'd be devastated to be separated, and being ten years old next year, they're approaching such an important age."

An idea struck me then, and I suggested that if we were opening a new school in London, maybe we could take Emma with us. "Her education needs to continue," I said, "and what better place than Bryan House, London? There will be few educational opportunities left for her here in Margate, if we aren't here."

As soon as the words were out of my mouth, though, I felt her mother's pain. Augustus's former wife, Lady Augusta Murray, had been so agreeable to Emma attending our school in Margate. She'd never made a fuss, either, about how much time Emma spent with us, nor about the endless back-and-forth from Ramsgate. Letting us take her daughter to London was entirely different, though. I knew all too well the pain a daughter's 'reassignment' could cause to a family.

I decided to send word to Augustus that we were contemplating a move back to London and asked him if he could help us find a suitable residence. As I think I've already mentioned, a commercial negotiator I am not. Once in London, Elizabeth and I wanted to reestablish a boarding school, where I could resume my scientific lessons with a more mature audience of young ladies. A new start seemed like a good idea, and I'd be far closer to Chelsea, and to Thomas and Sarah. We could surely find a way to make it work for Lucy and Emma, and I decided that I would speak with Augustus about that in person.

Almost immediately, I got word from Augustus that he was coming to Margate two days hence. I'd been vague in my message; I hadn't wanted to mention anything about Little Harriet's move until I saw him in person. Upon his arrival in Margate, Augustus sent a courier to Bryan House with an invitation for me to meet him the following evening at his leased estate in Broadstairs. With Little Harriet's pending move to Tixall Hall rapidly approaching, the last thing I was contemplating was gaiety and intimacy with Augustus whilst everyone else was miserable. I was also sure that Elizabeth would disapprove of me accepting his invitation, given the circumstances. My other two children were also anxiously looking for other clues as to what other life-altering changes might be coming their way, so I thought it misguided to suggest he visit us, as we couldn't openly communicate without fear of being overheard. I will admit, given how awful and scared I felt, I also yearned to feel his big arms wrapped around me.

34

I THINK ELIZABETH HAD KNOWN FOR YEARS that Augustus and I were lovers, although we had never discussed it. She certainly supported and encouraged all the time we spent together, but always left my privacy intact, never asking questions, never prying. There were things she kept close to her chest that she didn't like to talk about, and I think she just respected this was one of mine.

I'd thought about talking to her about it more than once, but I never got up the nerve. It wasn't talking about the affair itself that would have made me uncomfortable; it was more embarrassment over the age gap. Augustus was far closer in age to Elizabeth than he was to me. I knew if I was to talk to Elizabeth about my affair with Augustus, I'd end up asking her what she thought about the age difference. I knew, theoretically, I would want the uncontaminated truth, but I was also almost sure that I probably wouldn't cope well with whatever her answer would be. I inevitably would read between the lines, and I didn't want anything to tarnish the feelings I had for Augustus, so the only way to avoid the inevitable age gap discussion was to never have the conversation at all. So that's what I did.

In responding to Augustus's invitation to Broadstairs, I attempted a compromise, telling Elizabeth that I'd go, but that I wouldn't be staying the night. Elizabeth interrupted me and said, "Margaret, you should absolutely stay. Our lives are in turmoil, and you deserve a distraction. I can see the pressure you are putting on yourself. Please, we will be fine for a night. Go!"

I looked at her. After all the chaos I had brought to this lovely woman's life, all she cared about in this moment was that I might have another taste of physical love with a man. I sent word back to Augustus that I'd be delighted to accept his invitation. I drove my own phaeton to Broadstairs, where Augustus had clearly been waiting for me. Suddenly alone with him, I felt the enormity of the pending loss of Little Harriet, and it hit me like a tidal wave. I was grateful I was sitting down when I told him what was happening. Had I been standing, I've no doubt I would have collapsed. He let me cry in his arms for what seemed like ages. I sensed his frustration that, even as one of the most powerful men in Britain, he couldn't repair this for me. He'd also have to explain to his own daughter, Emma, why Harriet Bryan didn't live with 'Mrs. B' anymore.

I then proceeded to get very inebriated—I mean *shattered*—and he taught me how to play cards into the wee hours of the morning. I'd never demonstrated such a lack of control around him before, and whilst he felt the weight of my pain, he was also amused by my intoxication. At some point I must have passed out, as when I woke up the next morning, alone and fully dressed, I surmised that Augustus must have carried me to bed. I should have felt embarrassed, but my head was thumping so hard I couldn't feel anything else.

Someone must have heard me stirring, as soon there was a knock on the door. I asked for a minute, disrobed quickly, found my dressing gown, and crawled back into the bed. I then called to the young lady to come in. She brought breakfast in on a tray for me and offered to draw me a hot bath. When I'd finished my bath and changed my clothes, I made my way downstairs to find that Augustus was also, apparently, still in bed. I decided to take a walk to clear my very foggy head. I secretly hoped that the fact that Augustus was still in bed was some indication that he, too, had been in a compromised state of mind the night before. I don't know why that mattered so much to me, except that I'd feel far worse if I'd gotten so drunk all by myself.

When I returned to the house, Augustus was on the verandah, still in his dressing gown, with a drink and a cigar in hand. I'd have laughed out loud had I not felt so awful.

"Margaret, did you sleep well, my love?" was all he said. I sensed that was his way of removing any embarrassment I might have had regarding the night before, and, indeed, it worked. We ate lunch on the verandah, and he convinced me to have a glass of wine, which did make me feel better. We then engaged in the strangest of conversations, which, for the first time since I'd learnt of Little Harriet's pending departure to Tixall Hall, brought some warmth back into my heart.

It began with Augustus asking me, "Margaret, how well do you know William Herschel?" He took a puff of his cigar, whilst not looking directly at me.

"William Herschel, as in astronomer Caroline Herschel's brother?" I replied. "I met him once at his observatory in Slough, by the kind invitation of Sir Charles Hutton when he was fundraising for my first book. Why do you ask?"

"I happened to be visiting him several weeks ago, also at Slough, on business for the Royal Society. When he invited me into his study, your portrait was on his desk," he answered, still not looking at me.

I was speechless, and my head was still pounding from all the drink of the night before. I was more grateful than ever for the glass of wine, so I politely asked for another. I almost started to giggle, now realising that Augustus was jealous. I'd never experienced this before: a man being jealous of another man's affections towards me, if indeed that is what it was. It felt powerful and silly, all at the same time, and between Augustus's emotions and the wine, I was starting to feel a lot better.

"I think it's best if you ask Mr. Herschel about the portrait, not me. It was on display when I met him there with Sir Hutton, but it certainly surprises me to learn it's still there. That was nearly fifteen years ago. Perhaps he's just showing support for female astronomers, given that it's also his sister's profession."

Augustus started to sound annoyed. "Margaret, it's not the picture of you with the imaginary 'children'; it's the portrait I had commissioned for your second book, published in 1806."

Then I did nearly giggle out loud, and I was now really enjoying myself when I said, "Oh my, Your Royal Highness, are you really jealous of an old man gazing at a stargazing old woman?"

It was clear I hurt his feelings, and I regretted my last remark altogether.

"I'm not sure that's fair. I just wasn't expecting it. You do look so beautiful and clever in it, and by the way, any man with able eyesight would never call you old," he said quietly, now resting his finished drink on the table.

I gently reached for his hand, and we went inside. We made love all afternoon, with the enormous French doors open to spectacular views of the Atlantic Ocean. I went to sleep afterwards and didn't wake up until nearly dinner time. Whilst Augustus couldn't resolve anything when it came to Little Harriet, he had made me feel human again.

When I did finally wake, I immediately thought about how strange it was for William Herschel to have a copy of my 1806 book's frontispiece proudly displayed in his study. I also wondered how many other people had seen it. His laboratories at Slough were a frequent destination of many of the Royal Society's most important Fellows. I wanted to ask Augustus what else was said about me in his meeting with William Herschel, but I dared not. If I'd learnt anything from Georgiana, it was that these men had egos that were easily bruised, and that was neither my desire nor my intent. I did make a mental note, though, to write to Mr. Herschel when we were installed in our new residence in London. He would be a perfect reintroduction to the London scientific community for me. I all but assumed he would engage in correspondence with me, if, indeed, my most recent portrait was on prominent display in his study.

The move to London was going to be a big transition, though, and I'd wait until the children were settled—my now two children were settled, that is. The other one I'd just have to hope and pray would be settled in her new home, without me in it. The only saving grace was that I didn't have to deal with Big Harriet anymore, and I did trust Harryo with Little Harriet's well-being. After all, I had no choice.

When I finally went back downstairs, in preparation for dinner, I found Augustus relaxing in the drawing room. "Margaret, I've been thinking about a residence for you and Elizabeth in London. Why don't you just take the apartments in Portman Square? They're unoccupied, and it would mean no expense for you. You could always move later if you wanted to, and it would be just one less thing to worry about now."

The Portman Square apartments—or more specifically No. 1 Gloucester Place, Portman Square—were a leased and furnished accommodation that Augustus kept for guests whilst they were visiting him in London. I'd used it as my 'official' London address for the past few years when I was negotiating new printings of my books.

Whilst I appreciated his very kind offer, the Portman Square apartments were only a stone's throw from Kensington Palace, Augustus's London home, which I assumed was by design. In fact, they were only separated by a short walk across the top corner of Hyde Park. That started to give me some indigestion. I had no intention of giving up any of my independence in London. In fact, I was seeking more. I certainly wasn't going to have the encumbrance of a pseudo-husband without also being the recipient of all the other derived benefits therein. I admonished myself for being so paranoid, after all the kindness Augustus had bestowed on us.

That is just Thomas's barking at me, I told myself. Thomas trusted very few people in general, and when it came to the safety and protection of his family, he simply assumed everyone had ulterior motives. I pushed Thomas out of my head and decided to accept Augustus's very generous offer, with the nonnegotiable condition that Elizabeth and I would pay a fair market rent for the apartments. As Augustus had pointed out, if we weren't happy, we could always move out at a later date, if the apartment or location wasn't to our liking. I stayed another night with Augustus, thankfully without repeating the drunken debauchery from the night before.

It was just before we were ready to retire that Augustus finally brought up the subject of Emma and how a separation from Lucy Elizabeth and our family might affect her.

"Margaret, I realise this is the least of your concerns right now, but can I ask for your help on how to talk to Emma about this move to London? I assume she doesn't know yet, but I'm certain she'll be devastated to see your entire family leave Margate," he said ever so softly.

This touched my heart, as I'd seen how close Augustus and Emma had become since our move to Margate. He was now talking about her well-being almost like a mother would, as unfair as that might sound. It certainly felt as if we'd been able to give something back to him by giving him greater access to his daughter.

"Elizabeth and I have been in bits about this issue. We could promise the girls that we'd commit to them seeing each other several times a year," I said, "or Emma could come to London with us." Then I just kept going. "Her education will have to continue somewhere, and neither Ramsgate nor Margate will have much to offer her once we're gone. At the risk of stating the obvious, you, too, would have greater access to Emma if she was in London."

Augustus didn't disagree. In fact, all he said was that he would talk to her mother and see what he could do. He seemed pensive, and I sensed that he was distressed about the whole London move in general. I had the distinct feeling that he would have been quite happy with the status quo: that of Bryan House remaining safely tucked away in Margate on the Kent coast.

35

I DROVE MYSELF BACK TO MARGATE later that afternoon. I was delighted to have a bit of good news for Elizabeth on the apartment front. My head, which had finally recovered from its hangover, was now completely engaged in planning our move to London.

Augustus came by three days hence, unannounced and in complete jubilation, to inform us that Lady Murray had agreed to let Emma join us in London at the new boarding school. She was going to find secondary accommodation in London and would divide her time between there and Ramsgate. Emma's brother was already at a boarding school in London, so it made more sense than not.

Whilst I'm sure Augustus was paying handsomely to accommodate such an arrangement, it would be remiss of me not to mention the enormous respect I had for Lady Murray in making what must have been a very painful decision. After all, Emma was not yet ten. Whilst obviously being the benefactors of this parenting arrangement, we were all acutely aware that there were no celebrations to be had in the shadow of Little Harriet's pending departure for Tixall Hall. There were just two very happy young girls holding hands in the music room when it was quietly announced that Emma D'Este would be safely on board the coach bound for London.

We had decided that everyone would say their goodbyes in Margate, but when the day finally came, it was hard to bear. The two carriages waiting outside were poignant physical reminders that this little family was about to travel in different directions. When I walked into the drawing room to observe the girls saying their goodbyes to one another, I succumbed to all the emotions I was feeling. I was almost physically sick. It was Harryo who came to the rescue by taking me by the hand and walking me out to her carriage to wait whilst Elizabeth got the other girls safely into the other one before Harryo returned with only Little Harriet in hand. Little Harriet entered the carriage red-faced, put her head in my lap, and wept.

With that dreadful goodbye, we were off. Elizabeth took Lucy Elizabeth, Jessy Anne, and Emma to London, where Augustus had promised to be waiting for them, whilst I took Little Harriet to Tixall Hall and stayed on for a few days to ease whatever anxieties she might have. Harryo had graciously offered to collect us in her own carriage, so the three of us could get to know one another a little bit better on the journey. This turned out to be a Georgiana-style brilliant idea. Harryo mentioned how fond Georgiana had been of Little Harriet, even though she'd only known her as a very little girl. Little Harriet, indeed, remembered Georgiana, even if just a little bit. After all, who could forget her?

By the time we arrived at Tixall Hall, Little Harriet seemed almost at ease and excited to explore the 'castle' she was about to call home. Harryo had also given birth to a little girl, called Susan Georgiana, the year before, so Little Harriet was already playing big sister to her.

Baa, baa, black sheep, have you any wool? Yes, merry have I, three bags full, I thought to myself, thinking back on my own days as big sister to baby Thomas. Little Harriet would have only been a little younger than I was when I came to live with my aunt and uncle at Bryan House on Golden Lane after Papa died—although I'd come to my new home with my maman, not to be presented with a new one.

Harryo was gracious enough to point out what a marvellous job Elizabeth and I had done in raising Little Harriet and how impeccable her manners were. I sincerely appreciated her graciousness in that otherwise dreadful moment called 'the exchange.' Funny, I thought, when Little Harriet had come to us, she'd known no other mother, so the *exchange* was simply the passing of an infant child into the safe and capable hands of a mother, or in this case mothers, who could take care of her. That had seemed so admirable and noble at the time, as if heaven-sent, for the good of an innocent child. This *exchange*, however, felt sinister, more like a *maman exchange*, in which I was somehow complicit because I didn't want her anymore. Of course, I knew that wasn't true, but I still felt the searing pain of what Little Harriet must be thinking. Nevertheless, I tried to stay brave and fought back the tears.

Whether Harryo sensed my sorrow or not, I was eternally grateful when she changed the subject. "My aunt Harriet's other daughter, Lady Caroline Lamb, is nothing like our Little Harriet. You wouldn't know they came from the same mother. It was one of the reasons why there was some hesitation at first about bringing Little Harriet to Tixall Hall. I couldn't cope with having the equivalent of her half sister here. I like to think our Little Harriet is all Leveson-Gower," Harryo concluded.

That lifted my spirits a little bit, given that Big Harriet was Harryo's own aunt, making Harryo and Little Harriet something of first cousins biologically. In virtually any other set of circumstances, I'd probably have found this comment very funny. It was certainly representative of how incestuous the British aristocracy was. This wasn't a time for humour, though, and this, unfortunately, wasn't to be the last conversation I'd have with Harryo regarding her aunt's legitimate daughter, Lady Caroline Lamb (née Ponsonby). I spent a few more days with Little Harriet at Tixall Hall, soaking up my last few minutes with 'our' little girl. I had never really thought about the possibility of losing her, even though we had all agreed to the 'foster' relationship. In that moment, I was glad that I hadn't thought about it. I think if I had considered the pain, maybe I wouldn't have said yes, and then we would have never had her at all. I wanted to make it as easy on her as possible, so I just kissed her on the top of her head and promised her I would be back to visit her before she knew I was gone. Harryo also promised to bring her to visit whenever the Leveson-Gowers were in London, which, indeed, turned out to be quite often.

By the time I finally arrived at our new apartments in Portman Square, Elizabeth had everything in good order. Augustus had also found a potential boarding school location in Cadogan Place in Chelsea, literally around the corner from Thomas and Sarah. It felt like a good new start for all of us, and I was delighted to be back in London.

Once we were settled in our new apartments, that autumn of 1811, I did, indeed, write to William Herschel.

October 3rd, 1811,
Portman Square, London

Dear Mr. Herschel,

> *I once had the honour of being introduced to you by my friend Dr Hutton, who was most delightfully and politely entertained by you at Slough, and I was particularly gratified by perceiving that you had afforded me the distinction of placing my portrait in your study. I mention this circumstance that you might recollect who I am. I avail myself of the obliging attention I then received to solicit your kindness for the results of your observations on the present Comet, so far as it relates to its apparent path and its situation in respect to the Sun and our Earth. I have been for some time past tracking its right ascension and declination, and by comparing them, with the same of the Sun, I conceive it is departing the Sun and the Earth. But I am not supplied by the means of more accurate information. I would be most grateful for your assistance.*

Most Respectfully,
Margaret Bryan

Funny, he never returned my correspondence, which initially hurt my feelings. I decided, though, to give him a pardon, for no other reason than that which my cheeky imagination might conjecture. Maybe Augustus had asked him too many questions about me. Maybe William Herschel even suspected that we were lovers, which made me giggle out loud.

I ALSO WENT TO VISIT Caroline at Kensington Palace as soon I returned to London. Seeing my old friend was lovely, as was returning to the bustling world of the city, but along with those joys came the drama of the political world we'd been spared by being tucked away in Margate on the coast.

Caroline was in a desperate state, as her husband's appointment to Prince Regent had now given him total power over the Royal Court—and most of parliament, for that matter.

"Oh, Margaret, of all the good fortune I've experienced since we both left Blackheath, it has all but disappeared with my husband's appointment as regent. His father has gone completely mad and is incapable of understanding, let alone responding to, my pleas for help. I have, again, been banned from the Royal Court, and the only person who will entertain a dinner invitation from me is my dear brother-in-law, Augustus, next door. I'm sorry to complain, Margaret, but I'm ever so grateful you're back in London. I've absolutely no one else I can trust in this dreadful place. I've sent my entire staff back to Blackheath, and I'm considering going back there myself."

I kissed her on both cheeks. "Oh, Caroline, I am so sorry. I'm so glad to be back in London, and I'm so looking forward to the pleasure of your company again on a regular basis. We're still trying to sort out our new lives here as well. The city has changed significantly in the years since we've been gone. It's also strange for Georgiana not to be here. I drive past Devonshire House and still expect to see her blowing kisses from the balcony."

I was obviously successful in distracting her by mentioning Georgiana, as she now moved on to filling me in on the latest Ton gossip.

"Yes, it's hard, like a lot of things I can't change. I try not to think about such things. But speaking of Gee, I've been told by people close to the Palace that her sister, Harriet, has become my husband's latest paramour. She spent the entire summer in Brighton at the Pavilion with him. Oh, I have so much more to tell you. One gets it right from the source when you live here—at the Palace, that is," she replied, audible excitement building in her voice.

I ignored the nauseating reference to Harriet's affair with Caroline's husband. I'd always marveled at the way Caroline ignored all his viciously public affairs, as if to say to whomever his next victim might be, "Go ahead. The only night I had with him, he went to sleep, but I did produce the only legitimate heir to the British throne in one go, so it wasn't completely a lost cause."

Caroline told me herself that she'd only had physical relations with her husband on their wedding night, and that he was so drunk she didn't think he'd properly finished the job. Apparently, she woke up to find him sleeping on top of a fire grate, and she believes that Princess Charlotte was really the product of a divine conception.

"Wouldn't that be the last laugh for the Brunswick clan over the Hanoverian dynasty?" she had gloated.

Seeing her again and experiencing her unfiltered sense of humour made me realise how much I'd missed seeing her regularly. I'd almost forgotten the infectious levity she brought to my otherwise serious soul. At the end of our visit, we both made a commitment to a standing lunch every Wednesday, which we kept to almost without exception. I always looked forward to those Wednesday luncheons with Caroline with great expectations. No matter how much I prepared myself about the current events of the day, I was never fully prepared for some of the subject matter that would inevitably come up. Elizabeth once asked me if she thought it would be rude if I took notes. I told her if she wanted to hear what was being said, she had to come and hear it for herself.

36

WHILE 1811 HAD BEEN a difficult transition year for us, by Christmastide we had reestablished a new routine for our lives in London. The new boarding school at Cadogan Place was up and running, which, without much imagination, we'd called Bryan House, London. Augustus and I were enjoying spending a lot more time together, and we also got to spend more time with Little Harriet than perhaps we had originally thought possible.

Then suddenly, tragedy struck again. Thomas and Sarah's eldest child, Elizabeth Jekyll, died of consumption in early January 1812. She was just eleven years old. No parent should ever experience the death of a child, but for one who'd been nurtured nearly to maturity to be ripped from her mother's arms is indescribable. And to have to bear witness to that small coffin, knowing what's inside it and the hopes and dreams that will never be. As painful as the separation from Little Harriet had been, I couldn't imagine the thought of having to bury her. Thomas was never the same after Elizabeth Jekyll died, and he never forgave himself for not being there, or maybe being able to save her if he had been. He was able to come home for a short leave afterwards, but was back with the Fifteenth, honestly, as soon as he possibly could. However, if we saw an altered state in Thomas's disposition after Elizabeth's death, Sarah was unrecognisable.

After the funeral, and after Thomas had gone back to the war, I brought George and Little Sarah back to the Portman Square apartments so Elizabeth could stay with her sister on Church Street in Chelsea. There Sarah confided to Elizabeth that she was pregnant again and was experiencing terrible all-day sickness. "I don't think I've the strength in me to bear this child. I just want to close my eyes and go to sleep" were the words she said as she was shooing Elizabeth away. It reminded me of the death of my own maman. It was as if Sarah had already died, except the cavity of her was still here, trying to bear new life without the required ingredients. The birth, seven months later, was a very difficult one. Sarah was now forty-three, so it wouldn't have been a straightforward delivery in the best of circumstances.

I know I shouldn't have blamed Thomas, but certainly he should have known that Sarah couldn't manage this pregnancy so soon after her daughter's death. When Sarah almost bled out during the birth, I didn't have to.

"This is my punishment," he screamed at the top of his lungs, tears streaming down his face. "This is my punishment for fighting for my country, for not being there for my dying daughter, and now I've killed my wife!"

It was scary to watch, and he was unhinged for sure.

"Thomas, stop," Elizabeth screamed back at him. "This is not about you! This is not helpful. Margaret, please take him outside, anywhere, but just not here!"

I reached out for Thomas's hand, which he unbelievably allowed me to take. The battlefields of Europe had indeed done a number on him. Even if the scars weren't evident, the pain was omnipresent. Together, we walked outside to the back garden in silence—the same garden where Elizabeth had taken Sarah when I was trying to explain Little Harriet's parentage to him. Thomas crouched on the ground, put both of his hands over his face, and cried like a child. I put my arm gently around his shoulder and said nothing. After all, what was there to say?

By the grace of God, Sarah eventually pulled through, and Little Thomas Bryan, a healthy baby boy, finally arrived on the 20th of December in the Year of Our Lord 1812.

I was so grateful he was a boy, as I thought that would be easier on Sarah and, indeed, on Thomas. That, unfortunately, turned out not to be the case. There was also a palpable distance within Thomas and Sarah's relationship forevermore. It was uncomfortable to be around them; the banter between them was just gone, and Sarah seldom seemed engaged in conversation at all. This rock-solid family, who had always been there for us in all our turmoil, seemed now completely fractured in a single, devastating moment.

37

B Y T H E A U T U M N O F 1 8 1 2 , we were near capacity at the new boarding school. Lucy Elizabeth and Emma D'Este were both students there and boarded together in the same room, if not the same bed, on most nights. We had hired two full-time teachers, a housekeeper, and a cook, so Elizabeth and I could split our time between the school and the rest of our lives. It was a sort of cross between the two schools we'd supervised in Blackheath and Margate.

Elizabeth, Jessy Anne, and I resided at the apartments in Portman Square. We had worried that this new living arrangement would upset Jessy Anne, but she hardly seemed to notice that the others weren't there. It was certainly a new chapter in all our lives. Jessy Anne, being only seven years old, was too young and, honestly, a bit too immature to even go to the boarding school, so Elizabeth continued her education from our new apartments.

The new schedule also gave me some time to start research for my third book. The move to London had made the loss of Little Harriet somewhat more palatable, although there wasn't a single day when I didn't think about her or wonder what she might be doing. We all wrote regularly, and I went to visit her as often as I could. Harryo also brought her to London whenever she visited, which initially was often. She'd just given birth to her second child, though, and had been unable to travel comfortably for several months prior to the birth and was now in her confinement period.

I always tried to read between the lines in Little Harriet's letters, trying to understand whether she was happy or sad, hungry or cold, even though Elizabeth encouraged me not to do so. It was one such letter, in

which she mentioned that Harriet and her daughter had come to visit
Tixall Hall, that literally made my stomach turn.

> *Dearest Mamans,*
>
> *We have recently been blessed with a visit from Lady
> Bessborough and her daughter, Lady Caroline Lamb. They call
> her 'Caro' for short. She was most kind to me but enquired a
> great deal about our family. I wondered how well you know her.
> It felt a bit awkward; that's the only reason I mention it.*
>
> *I am so looking forward to visiting everyone next month.
> You'll be very proud of me. I have been working very hard on
> my studies. Lady Leveson-Gower says my French is almost as
> good as her maman's was. There can be no greater compliment. I
> should like you to tell me more about her maman, when I see you
> all. She speaks of her often.*
>
> *Tout mon amour,*
> *Harriet*

I immediately remembered Harryo telling me, when I had first taken
Little Harriet to Tixall Hall, that her cousin, Lady Caroline Lamb,
had a peculiar disposition. My concern, in that moment, though, was
that 'Caro' had recently engaged in a very public extramarital affair with
the well-known poet Lord Byron. According to the papers, Caro, also the
wife of the Honourable Lord Melbourne, had called Byron 'mad, bad,
and dangerous to know.' She had also, apparently, gloated about sending him a lock of her pubic hair as a memento of their sexual trysts.
It made me shudder to think that Caro shared the same biological
mother as my daughter and shudder again to think about her being
engaged in any kind of intimate conversation with our Little Harriet
about anything.

It was also known that Caro was a frequent publisher of cruel and
gossipy literature about real people's lives and problems—often at the

expense of her own friends and family, without any regard to shame nor privacy. I started to seethe after reading the letter. Elizabeth immediately reminded me that causing any trouble might limit our access to Little Harriet altogether. She said very logically, "Margaret, Caro and Harryo are cousins, and Caro isn't the first woman in either of their families to succumb to the advances of a powerful and provocative man. I can't imagine why Caro would have any interest in our Little Harriet's affairs, particularly when she seems to make the front page of the newspapers on a regular basis, all on her own devices." I wanted to disagree with her for a million reasons, but I did not, as I was beginning to wonder if I was going mad with grief, jealousy, or both.

I let the matter rest until a few months later, when one of my former students, Emily Stuart, was kind enough to send me a copy of a recently published children's book called *The Little English Girl: A Tale for Children* by the authour of *The Fortunate Visit*. Both books unsurprisingly turned out to have been published anonymously. The reason Emily had been kind enough to send me the book to begin with was that the story opened with an orphan who'd received an education with us at Bryan House, Blackheath. I was mentioned quite favourably in the first chapter. I was neither flattered nor amused, however, and read on in fervor. I can't explain, after I'd finished the short book, how the hairs on the back of my neck stood up, except to say that I was certain Lady Caroline Lamb had written it, and that it was a semi-fictional account of her half sister's, our Little Harriet's, childhood.

I was now officially manufacturing maman venom, as I started to imagine that this twentysomething-year-old harlot not only had written a book about my twelve-year-old daughter's childhood, which was no business of hers to begin with, but could also be discussing the pleasures of the flesh with her. That last part, I willingly admit, would support my hypothesis that I had gone at least partially mad at this point.

With a moderately clearer mind, however, it was reasonable to conclude that Caro accurately suspected Little Harriet's true parentage, so who knew what a sequel to the book might look like? Certainly Harryo knew all about her aunt's affair with Leveson-Gower, so how could Caro, her own daughter, not know? If Little Harriet were to learn who her biological parents were from a book—or even worse, from Caro herself—I was sure she'd feel betrayed by Elizabeth and me, and now by Harryo and her father. Then who would she trust in the future? I thought about what to do and went to find Elizabeth.

After reading the short book herself, Elizabeth also shared my concerns about Caro. "Margaret, this can be no coincidence, and I, unlike many, always give others the benefit of the doubt. If Little Harriet's parentage is exposed in such a public way, she will be devastated. It would also be unfair to the Leveson-Gowers. I think you should go to Tixall Hall immediately and share this news with them in person. Surely Lord Granville has the power to put Caro in her place?"

I booked a coach to Staffordshire the following day. I'd planned to visit Little Harriet the following month anyway, so I sent word to Harryo to let her know I'd be visiting a few weeks early. When I arrived at Tixall Hall, Harryo greeted me with a tiny newborn swaddled at her breast, and an infant girl clinging to the bottom of her skirts.

"Margaret, you look well. Please come in; you must be exhausted," she said as she closed the front door of the 'castle' behind her. Little Harriet was delighted to see me, as Harryo had kept it all as a lovely surprise. I couldn't believe how much she'd grown since the last time I'd seen her.

After Little Harriet had gone to bed, I picked a strategic moment, when Harryo's husband was responding to a courier, to bring up my concerns privately with her.

"My apologies for arriving early and the sudden change of plans. There is actually something of grave concern regarding Little Harriet that I would like to speak to you about privately."

She looked concerned and put down her teacup to give me her complete attention. She looked so like her maman in that moment.

"Yes, of course, Margaret, please speak freely with me."

"A book has been brought to my attention that I believe may have been written and published by your cousin, Lady Caroline Lamb, about Little Harriet's childhood and her illegitimate beginnings. Bryan House is named in the first chapter."

I needn't have gone any further. She turned white as a sheet, and I saw her bury her fingernails in the palms of her hands.

"Margaret, this would not be the first time Caro has betrayed her own family in vicious prose, but I never expected her to victimise her little sister. I will say that she is stone mad and probably shouldn't be in the unchaperoned presence of children."

I was a bit shocked and angry. If that's how she felt, why was she letting Little Harriet be anywhere near Caro to begin with? But I kept my own counsel and excused myself early for the night. Not, however, before giving Harryo my only copy of *The Little English Girl* for her evening perusal.

When I came downstairs the following morning, it was clear Harryo and her husband had discussed the matter, as they asked me to join them for breakfast in their private dining room.

"Good morning, Margaret," Leveson-Gower said as a servant showed me in. Clearly, both he and Harryo had been waiting for my arrival, hopefully not for too long. Much to my surprise, as soon as I was seated, Leveson-Gower launched into speech.

"Harryo has brought to my attention this matter of Caro and our Little Harriet. First, I'd like to thank you for sharing this with us in such a timely matter, and at great expense to yourself, in terms of time and money." He paused to take a few mouthfuls of food, swallowed, and went on. "I want to assure you that from this point forward, Caro won't have any access to Little Harriet in any manner at all. I don't know what can be done about the book, but I will speak to her mother about it—without referring to you, of course. I should mention, though, that Caro is also now very physically ill, so perhaps some of her strange behaviour is a thing of the past. At least, we can only hope so." He finished the entire conversation without Harryo or me saying a single word.

Do they eat breakfast like this every day? I wondered. It was so calm and measured, like a church service, as compared with the bedlam that took place at our kitchen table in the morning. It made me wonder if Little Harriet missed our morning chaos—*the breakfast bedlam, that is.* I quickly dismissed the painful thought, though, as soon as it arrived. Lord and Lady Leveson-Gower could not have dignified my concerns with more respect, but the moment lacked any luster I may have anticipated from such a victory.

I watched from my carriage window as everyone waved goodbye from the front door of the 'castle,' Little Harriet's other hand solidly entwined in Harryo's. I saw clearly now that Harryo was now Little Harriet's mother, and that my little girl was in safe and capable hands. It was just hard to accept that they weren't *my* safe and capable hands anymore.

I'd known she was meant to be ours but for a moment in time. Upon reflection, I suppose all of one's children are only ever ours for a moment in time. I just wished that my moment with Little Harriet had been a longer moment. My trip home to London from Tixall Hall was long, lonely, and cold. I reflected on the fact that I couldn't have been more fortunate in having such a powerful ally in the safekeeping of my daughter, but I knew that I had to let Little Harriet go, and the pain was indescribable. I cried until there were simply no more tears. In the morosity of the seemingly endless journey, there was even a fleeting moment when I felt sorry for Big Harriet. Not only had she now lost her lover but also her two 'love' children to another woman, even if that woman was her very own niece. It was certainly crystal clear that Big Harriet wouldn't have any say in the affairs of the Leveson-Gower family going forward, and that, I'm sure, she hadn't intended. Having said that, I was also sure she'd conveniently forgotten any responsibility for the creation of such a strange and incestuous situation to begin with.

After my return from Tixall Hall, I clung to Jessy Anne as if she was an infant, including sleeping in her room at night—that is, until Elizabeth insisted it was unhealthy and that I had to stop. Elizabeth is far more measured than I am in her emotions, especially when it comes to our children. It's one of her many character traits I love and admire.

It was on one of those nights, when I wasn't supposed to be sleeping in Jessy Anne's room, that she asked me a question I'd been expecting for years, ever since we'd first fostered Little Harriet.

"Maman," Jessy Anne said, "who is my papa?"

The other two girls had never even remotely tiptoed around this question. It helped, of course, that their peer group was mostly Bryan House pupils, who often came from aristocratic families with *issues*—Emma D'Este being a prime example. I'm sure from Jessy's perspective, though, at least Emma had a father. I thought about saying that her uncle Thomas was like a father, because he'd sponsored her at her christening. But being a bright, precocious child, she probably wouldn't buy that for an instant.

Thinking about how Elizabeth and I had been concerned about Little Harriet learning about her biological parents from somebody else, I decided just to be honest with Jessy.

"I don't know who your father is, Jessy, my little angel; you were a gift from God. Someone who loved you very much brought you to us to take care of. It's God himself, though, who sent that person to our doorstep."

She seemed to be satisfied with this answer, and I felt relieved. But just as I was about to blow out the candle, she asked me the dreaded follow-up question.

"Maman, do you know who Harriet or Lucy Elizabeth's papas are, or are they gifts from God as well?"

I bit my lip to stop myself from laughing and then said, "Yes, darling, they're gifts from God as well. Now, it's time for bed."

"Well, I've thought about it a bit," she continued stubbornly. "You see, some people think it's strange that I have two mamans and no papa.

I'm not sure I'd want a papa if I'd had to give up one maman, but I am sure that I'd rather have two mamans than two papas."

"Very wise choice, Jessy Anne. I couldn't agree with you more," I answered, glad that, in the darkness, she couldn't see me smiling. She was, indeed, my little scientist. We said our prayers, and one of us went to sleep.

38

WHILST THE FIFTEENTH HAD BEEN stationed at Hounslow since 1809, they were called back to the Continent in 1813, where they were now under the Duke of Wellington's command. With a decisive British victory at Vittoria, Sicily, they were then easily able to access the French border, facing little resistance. Napoleon's armies were now surrounded and falling fast. Whilst intense fighting continued throughout 1814, by the end of the year, Napoleon had surrendered and had been exiled to the island of Elba. The Fifteenth returned home to London victorious, and the entire nation was cautiously celebrating the end of the war with France.

After over two decades of conflict, peace finally seemed like an imminent reality. For Caroline, it was also the end of a nightmare. She'd been waiting patiently for years to return to the Continent so she could live in some sort of privacy and peace. It seemed that, with victory over Napoleon finally in sight, that dream might finally come true.

It was on one of our Wednesday lunches that she brought the topic up again. "Margaret, I'm so torn over this issue of returning to my home on the Continent. I've been dead set on it for so many years, and now it seems possible. I'm not sure what will be left, though, when I finally get there. Princess Charlotte is also completely opposed to my leaving England as well, which makes me feel sad and guilty for wanting to go. It will just be increasingly difficult for her to have any relationship with me going forward because of her beastly father. This will only get worse, as she prepares to marry and assume her royal duties. So, I think I'm just going to go and see what happens. I can always come back. Of course,

Willie will go with me, but I'm also hoping that I can take Edwardina as well. It would be very helpful to me if you could talk to the Duke of Sussex in that regard before I approach the Duke of Kent—to test the waters with him, if you will. I've no idea how her father will feel about Edwardina leaving England."

I reached out for her hand. "Caroline, I can't but imagine how hard it would be for you to leave Princess Charlotte. You should think about this. It's a big decision and perhaps an irreversible one. Of course I'll talk to Augustus about Edwardina. I'm sure he'll be happy to speak to his brother. I cannot imagine why the duke would have any objections to Edwardina going with you. But you should think about all this some more."

Caroline said nothing at first but then suddenly looked relieved, as if maybe she'd just made her final decision at that moment.

"I'll make sure there's always a path back to England for me, but Charlotte doesn't belong to me; she never has. Surely there's a place for happiness in my own life? I've decided, then—I'm going home."

When I arrived back at our apartments that afternoon, Augustus had already sent an invitation for me to have dinner with him at his home the following evening. I immediately accepted his invitation. When I reached Kensington Palace the following night, after a beautiful walk across Hyde Park, I found Augustus in great spirits, deep in a pile of German newspapers. He was clearly excited about what the end of war might mean for Britain.

"Margaret, my brother won't have any issue with letting Edwardina go to the Continent with Caroline. He is not as 'beastly' as everyone thinks. More importantly, he has no home to provide for her here. I promise you, my love, I'll get that done. You can let Caroline know tomorrow if I don't see her myself first. You've raised a topic, though, that I've wished to talk to you about for some time. So, here goes."

What is going on here? I thought as I watched Augustus sort of squirm in his chair and clear his throat, not looking directly at me.

"I have an illegitimate daughter of my own, for whom I'd like to take some responsibility. I'd also like to ask you to help me provide an education for her."

I couldn't breathe. I instantly felt betrayed, whilst thinking that I'd no right to feel so. It brought me back to the harsh reality of that conversation we'd had on the Broadstairs Cliffs about his wife.

Maybe I should ask him how old this illegitimate daughter is?

He'd already read my mind. "Margaret, I know you're not going to be happy about this, but I need to tell you the truth. Several years ago—four to be exact—I attended a party, had too much to drink, and got a young lady from Tunbridge Wells pregnant. The child is in the care of her mother's kin at an inn near Windsor Castle. She's three now." He was now poking the fire, with his back to me.

"Augustus, I can hardly hear you," I said, trying not to give away any emotion in my voice.

"Sorry," he said, now turning to face me. "You're aware, I know, that the Crown prevents me from having any kind of normal relationship with a woman, so forgive me this transgression. Having said that, you're always sending me mixed messages. You can be as untouchable as the shooting stars you follow, always coming and going as you please. I've never objected to that, despite having loved you probably since the first time I saw you."

Well, he's never said that before. He's really piling it on.

He paused to catch his breath. "Your independence and confidence are two of the many qualities that I admire about you, but sometimes that is hard for a man to deal with. I don't know the word . . . maybe *boldness* is close. I've always managed to get past your *boldness*, and I've also always been there for you, Margaret, when you've needed my help," he said, now looking directly at me, reaching for my hand. "Now, I'm asking for yours. She's a little girl and, through no fault of her own, was born the daughter of a prince yet is still nothing but a bastard child in the eyes of the world. I've two other children who bear that shame already, but at least they have their own financial resources. I'd like my other daughter to have the same education as Emma and that of my son."

Finally he paused and sat down again. "What I'm saying to you is, I don't want my thoughtless indiscretion to be a lifetime penance for her. Will you help me educate her, Margaret?"

I didn't know what to say. I was hurt, and perhaps angry. But Augustus was showing the strength of his character, which made him the man I'd fallen in love with. It reminded me of that begging conversation I'd had with Thomas after Little Harriet had come to us. It was a hard argument to win when there was an innocent child involved. I wanted to ask Augustus whether he felt love for this woman with whom he'd sired another child—surely they must still have a relationship—but I didn't. I didn't want to know the answer anyway.

Instead, I asked for a glass of wine. I didn't say anything for a long time, and neither did he. He returned with the wine, gave me a glass, and then proceeded to stoke the fire again. I finally ended the deafening silence, with as much composure as I could muster.

"Augustus, of course I'll help make sure your daughter is provided a proper education. Just give me a couple of days to digest this. I'm sure you understand; it's a bit of a shock. What's her name?"

"Her name is Lucy, which I know won't help matters. Lucy Tranter. Her Christian name was her mother's choice; I learnt of it after her birth. Thank you, Margaret, for thinking about this. Shall we put the topic on hold then and try to enjoy the rest of our evening? There's so much to celebrate tonight—in Britain, I mean."

"Yes, that would be lovely, and indeed, there's much to celebrate tonight in Britain." I got out of my chair, walked over to him, and kissed him on the forehead. The conversation was over, at least for now. When the meal ended, Augustus walked me home through Hyde Park, then came inside to have another drink with us. The door had barely closed behind him when I felt the need to share his confession with Elizabeth.

"Lizzie, Augustus told me this evening that he has an illegitimate daughter and that he'd like us to help him educate her. Her name is Lucy, which really bothered me. But of course, I said we'd be happy to help. I was more than a little disappointed in him, though, as it appears to have been nothing more than a loose and drunken affair. At least Harriet had a relationship with Leveson-Gower."

Elizabeth paused, and I saw her furrow her brow like she was looking for the right words.

"Margaret, I've never been privy to the nature of your relationship with Augustus, and I am not sure I want to be. I'm sure, though, you're absolutely delighted that it was merely a loose and drunken affair, and that you hope that he has no emotional connection to this child's mother. Whatever your feelings, though, Margaret, you've never had any real exposure to men and—how can I put it—their urges? They're not built like us, and they don't seem to have the same control over their bodies as women do, particularly when they drink. You're in territory you simply don't understand. Jealousy also doesn't become you, Margaret. Please don't get in the way of any man willing to finance a little girl's education in this misogynist country. Augustus is a good man, and he's done a great deal for us. I say, let this be; you can't change anything about it now." She then got out of her chair, blew out one of the candles, and headed for the stairs. "Good night, Margaret, and please try to put this behind you."

Well, I felt like I was in a tragic play at the Drury Lane Theatre—one where I was the villain. It was clear that Elizabeth was going to side with Augustus on this one. I also got the instinctive sense that she may already have known about Augustus's love child. Regardless of whether she'd known or not, I knew she was right, and she'd just shown me how right she was. So, I just decided to let it be.

39

WHILST WE CONTINUED TO FIND our new footing in London, the greater world, too, rolled along. The planets moved in their orbits, the earth still spun on its axis, and the royals continued to publicly air all their salacious drama on the world's stage.

The lead-up to Caroline's decision to leave England for the Continent had been long and difficult for her. Life had been getting progressively worse for her in England since her husband's appointment as Prince Regent in 1811. He'd also further restricted her access to Princess Charlotte by essentially imprisoning his young daughter in Windsor Castle. All of this resulted in an enormous public outcry in support of the Princess of Wales, but Caroline still felt alone and defeated. Even the writer Jane Austen weighed in by saying, "Poor woman, I support her as long as I can, because she is a woman, and because I hate her husband." All this public commentary enraged the Prince Regent, but it did nothing to soften his position with respect to allowing Caroline more access to her daughter. Caroline wasn't winning that argument—full stop.

Caroline finally left Britain's shores for a more peaceful life on the Continent on August 8, 1814, without even being allowed a single farewell meeting with her only child. Augustus had arranged a little going-away party for her at his apartments the week before she left, which Elizabeth and I both attended. He'd chosen the menu himself to include all of Caroline's favourite German food. It was really a lovely touch. Caroline wanted no morosity, though, on the occasion and entertained us all evening with jokes in German. Augustus had to translate them back into English for everyone else, which then made no sense to the rest of us at all, all of which completely amused Caroline, who kept repeating the punch line in German, again and again. Caroline and Augustus both got very drunk and loud towards the end of the evening, and I was eternally grateful that there were no anatomically correct toy monkeys produced as the encore.

Elizabeth and I went to see Caroline off the day she left. We met her down on the docks on a terrible, blustery London morning. There was some discussion as to whether it was safe enough to sail, but we did get the final go-ahead from the captain, who looked like he was at least a hundred years old. Caroline was stoic by then and gave me a brief embrace and a kiss, saying, "I am the rightful Queen Consort to the Throne of Great Britain. I promise you: I will return to England."

I reached out and put both arms around her and gave her the biggest squeeze I could muster. With tears in my eyes, I said, "I've no doubt you will. Please be careful in the meantime." Then she was gone, like a star flying across the horizon, to a place I prayed she could call home again.

Whilst everyone had thought that 1814 would see the end of the French wars, Napoleon made one last attempt to rally any remaining loyalty left in his troops. He was, however, soon bitterly defeated by the Duke of Wellington the following year. Thomas and the Fifteenth had also returned to the Continent under Wellington's leadership and were amongst the victorious on that now very famous Belgium battlefield better known as Waterloo.

Whilst Britain's war with her foreign enemies had finally been won, a potentially more dangerous domestic threat to the country's peace was silently gaining momentum. That threat was Britain's own working class, who were sick and tired of having to live like animals whilst the entitled men they worked for lived lives of privileged indulgence. Protestors were commonplace in the streets of London, men and women alike. Liberal newspapers were also being privately funded and secretly distributed amongst the masses, calling for massive parliamentary reform or revolution.

In the midst of this brewing domestic unrest, though, 1816 provided the welcome distraction of a royal wedding. Despite years of the Prince Regent's self-serving machinations regarding who his daughter should marry, Princess Charlotte, by her own choosing, became engaged to Prince Leopold of Saxe-Coburg-Saalfeld. The couple were madly in love, and the British people were intoxicated by the authenticity of their fairy-tale relationship. As soon as I heard of the engagement announcement, I wrote to Caroline to see if she was coming back to England for the wedding.

> *My dearest Caroline,*
>
> *I hope you are well. I trust that Princess Charlotte has been able to reach you with her exiting news. I'm hoping that you're coming home for the wedding. Please send word of what your travel arrangements are, and how Elizabeth and I can be of assistance. There is always accommodation here with us, if you would like more privacy. Do please send word of your plans when you have a moment.*
>
> *Margaret*

I had to ask Augustus where she was living now. She'd started her travels in Germany and then Switzerland but had apparently bought a villa on a lake near Milan. Initially, he hadn't known where to find her, either. When he enquired at the Palace, however, he'd immediately been given the address: Nuova Villa d'Este, Lake Como. I sent my letter to Caroline as soon as I received the details from Augustus. I received a short reply from her several weeks later, which concerned me.

> *Margaret,*
>
> *It's so nice to hear from you. I apologise for not having written in so long and for being so brief. I have much to tell you. I will not, however, be returning to England for the wedding. I've already been told by the Palace that I won't be allowed to*

attend. I don't want to put any more pressure on Princess Char-
lotte, so I'll think on her from afar. Please save all the newspaper
clippings for me. I should also tell you that I don't think it's safe
for me to even return to London right now. I'm not safe here,
either, but I'm moving soon to a more private and remote loca-
tion. I'll write again when I can.

Caroline

I showed it to Augustus, and he grimaced. "I know what that feels
like. They were spying on me the whole time I was in Portugal and
Rome. I was constantly looking over my shoulder. Personally, I think it's
a good thing that she's not coming to the wedding. It would put more
pressure on Princess Charlotte. I'm not going to give my dear brother
the benefit of that information, though. It'll be fun to see him sweat a
bit, wondering if she's going to turn up and embarrass him. I do hope
Caroline is all right, though, and has some company to amuse her."

On the 2nd of May, 1816, Princess Charlotte married Prince Leopold of Saxe-Coburg-Saalfeld. The wedding was, indeed, a moment
of peace and celebration, uniting the entire nation around hopes for a
bright and prosperous future. Elizabeth and I took Lucy Elizabeth and
Jessy Anne, now fourteen and almost twelve, to see the marriage procession from Carlton House to Buckingham Palace. Whilst the procession
was filled with pomp and circumstance, including carriages made of
gold, they spent the entire day talking about Princess Charlotte's dress,
which apparently had been made by a famous London dressmaker at a
staggering cost of more than ten thousand pounds.

Unfortunately, Princess Charlotte suffered a miscarriage shortly after
the marriage, but by the spring of 1817, she was pregnant again. The
entire nation held their breath, waiting for the birth of the next heir to
the British throne. However, tragically, just months later, the fairy tale
ended. Both Princess Charlotte and her child died in childbirth in early
November, and Britain, as did the world, stood in shock and grief.

I went to see Augustus at Kensington Palace as soon as he was able to accept visitors. He was bereft, so much so that he was almost unrecognisable. He'd aged ten years in a single week, and he was distraught over his brother's handling of the whole tragedy.

"Augustus, you don't look well. When was the last time you slept?" I said, looking at him, his hair unbrushed and his clothes disheveled. I also noticed several empty bottles of gin littered about the library, implying that perhaps he'd even banned the servants from coming in to clean up.

He ignored my question entirely. "You know, Margaret, there are times when I don't much like my brother, and then there are times when I truly despise him like no other. I've just discovered that Caroline learnt about the deaths of her daughter and grandson from a passing messenger in Milan who was on his way to inform the pope. Apparently, when asked by his couriers as to how he'd like them to notify Caroline, my dear brother told them that 'she could read about it in the newspapers.'"

"My word, that's dreadful, Augustus! I would hate to think what might happen if that got out in the streets of London. But what about Caroline—what's she to do? Should I go to her, do you think? Do we even know where she is?"

He paused for a long time, and then said, "No, I don't think you should go to her. She was in a bad place before this, but now I don't know how bad things are, or where she is. Let it sit for a while. She'll write again when she wants you to find her."

I knew Augustus was trying to protect me, and he was probably right. I had my own children and my school to think about. I agreed that it would be best to stay put in London, so that's what I did.

40

BESIDES THE JUBILATION THAT THE wars with France were finally over, the postwar years were difficult for most people in Britain. London, in particular, was a desperate place to try to live. Unemployment was rampant with all the men returning from the war and more and more country people flocking to the metropolis, hoping to find a better life in the city. This foul mood was further compounded by a horrible fever epidemic that seized the city and reached a crescendo in 1818, bringing the entire London hospital system to its knees. Jane Marcet's husband was involved in trying to hold it all together, but many thousands died. There were simply very few resources available to the 'common' man, with little hope for any material change in sight.

As we turned the calendar to a new year in 1819, life for most people was nothing short of miserable. With the years of war, trade restrictions, and tariffs, the standard of living for the average British family had been declining for decades. Whilst we had become used to seeing beggars on the street when we first moved back to London, their numbers must have increased tenfold since the war ended. There were entire families, including children, with their hands out on the streets. It was hard to walk past even one of them without feeling the guilt of their hunger pangs in our hearts.

This downwards economic pressure on the labour market was further compounded by the fact that machines were starting to replace people, such as in the textile industry. A friend of Augustus's had invested in the new loom technology that had eventually replaced textile workers in a factory in the north country. The replaced workers had become so angry that they burned the entire factory to the ground, killing two of their own.

The House of Lords was also fuelling the flames of revolution by passing legislation that protected and preserved only the privileged existence of its own members. The masses were mobilising for major parliamentary reform, or war. My nervous nature didn't like reading all the details about the tensions, but Elizabeth couldn't get enough of it. She would cut articles out of the newspaper and track progress in various parts of the country. I think she also attended secret meetings, but she never let on—presumably to stop me from worrying about her, which, of course, I did. She certainly attended all the large and regular public demonstrations, demanding change at best or revolution as a last resort.

One such demonstration occurred on the 16th of August, 1819, at St. Peter's Field in Manchester. The crowd was sixty thousand deep and raucous. The demonstration was supposed to have been controlled by the local yeoman cavalry, but things quickly got out of control when a small child was knocked down and killed. Upon hearing about the now dangerous and growing mob, the Crown immediately dispatched the Fifteenth to the site, attempting to try to control the now rapidly expanding crowd. Thomas left immediately, with no idea what he was riding into. It was a massacre, the likes of which the country had never seen, and at the end of it, or soon thereafter, eleven innocent people were dead. Hundreds were also wounded.

Elizabeth and I had gone to Chelsea to console Sarah as soon as we heard the news. About four hours later, Thomas walked through the door, almost unrecognisable. You could see the blood stains on his uniform, and he was as angry as I have ever seen him.

"That bastard king set us up—the whole bloody mess! He would have had us murder every woman and child in that square if he thought he could get away with it."

I looked at Elizabeth, who was also fuming, digging her fingernails into the palms of her hand and starting to pace. I could feel myself having trouble breathing, so I just reached for Sarah's hand and let the two of them be in the sitting room. We went outside and sat in the garden, and I watched Sarah cry.

Because of the Fifteenth's affiliation with the Crown, they were entirely blamed for the human carnage. The papers likened the battle to that of the Battle of Waterloo, except that this one was called the Battle of Peterloo, and the Fifteenth had now become butchers of the ordinary British workingman. The truth was, it was the local yeomanry, many of whom were allegedly drunk, who had incited the crowd into violence. By the time the Fifteenth arrived at the scene, there was already melee everywhere.

It befuddled me why the Crown had sent in the Fifteenth to begin with. These men were trained assassins, whose only military training was to maim and kill foreign enemies in the name of protecting our way of life. How, then, could they have been the right resource to disband rioting British social reformers peacefully? It reminded me of Thomas's rage the day we'd thought we were going to lose Sarah during childbirth. These men weren't totally human anymore, and the Crown knew that. I'd seen that myself in Thomas that afternoon in their garden in Chelsea as I watched him weep on his knees. At the risk of stating the obvious, any scholar of war might reasonably agree, therefore, that the peaceful dispersion of the protesting crowd was the Crown's last intention that fateful day in Manchester.

That hypothesis could be further supported by the Crown and parliament's retaliatory action to the Battle of Peterloo: the introduction of legislation called the Six Acts. These acts completely outlawed future public gatherings that proposed social reform, peaceful or not. Punishment included fines, incarceration, and even death. What was the point of the heavy price we'd just paid for victory in Europe if there were no civil liberties for the common man in Britain itself? This arrogance further infuriated the reformists, and sent its leaders underground to reorganise, expand recruitment, and purchase more weapons. The country was now in a slow boil, bracing itself for the future, whatever that might be, with the total certainty that the status quo was totally out of the question.

Elizabeth sometimes got so animated reading the paper that I had to ask her to go into the library privately so as not to upset Jessy Anne. I am quite certain I heard a couple of fists against the wall or the desk at times when she was in there by herself.

Then, to add such devastating insult to injury, less than six weeks after the Battle of Peterloo, our dear Sarah Bryan (née McLoughlin), Thomas's wife and Elizabeth's sister, died. The dreadful incident in Manchester, almost with certainty, contributed to her death. There was no clear cause of her death, except maybe just a will not to be of this earthly world anymore. She was fifty years old.

Thomas was devastated and retired from the Fifteenth immediately. He looked like he had aged a generation: wrinkled brow and now totally white hair. I also noticed he was, more often than not, drinking whiskey whenever we went to visit. Whilst he still lived on Church Street in Chelsea with his two youngest children, he spent most of his time after Sarah's death at the Royal Pensioners' Hospital with other veterans from the Fifteenth. What they did there, all day long, I don't know, but it seemed to make him happy.

This was all very hard on Little Sarah and Little Thomas, though, who were left on their own for long periods of time. George had moved out several years before to become a printer's apprentice. Lucy Elizabeth, now seventeen, spent most of her time teaching music lessons to young ladies at our apartments in Portman Square. Sarah took reasonable care of her little brother, but she wasn't even fourteen yet.

Jessy Anne, now fifteen, helped Little Sarah a couple of times a week to maintain the house on Church Street. Jessy and Sarah were both quiet souls, and more like sisters than cousins. They were also less than a year apart. I thought that very nice of Jessy, and it made me feel like we were helping in some regard.

Elizabeth and I had suggested more than once to Thomas that it might be easier if his two youngest children came to stay with us, even if for just a little while. Thomas would have no part of any of that, though. His family belonged with him—full stop.

Those days were dark for all of us, as if a cloud had descended over us that didn't have any place else to go.

41

I F 1819 HAD BEEN A YEAR of strife and personal loss, 1820 would certainly rival it, with regards to the future direction of Britain itself. The Year of Our Lord 1820 began with the sad finality of King George III's death. The national grief was palpable, and further exacerbated by the fact that his son, George IV, formerly Prince Regent, was now officially the King of England, without any kind of supervision at all. This would surely mean more abuse of power, and, quite likely, another increase in public taxation.

The only good news arising out of his accession to the throne was that Caroline, as his legitimate wife, was now the Queen of England. This really made me laugh out loud. I can't begin to imagine how much this must have infuriated Georgie Porgie pudding and pie. He'd been trying to get rid of her for nearly twenty-five years. The depths that he would go to try and destroy her this time, though, went beyond even my own imagination of how vile this man could be.

Many of the newspapers were speculating that parliament would try to pay off Caroline quietly to encourage her to stay on the Continent. I could have told them, "Don't waste your time and money." Whilst, admittedly, Caroline had taken an unsupervised and, frankly, dangerous hiatus from Britain, Caroline Amelia Elizabeth Brunswick would always have shown up on the ultimate battlefield, and she didn't disappoint. By early spring, it was reported in the newspapers that she'd left the Continent to take her rightful place as the legitimate Queen of England. The title alone significantly increased Caroline's power and influence, and George IV, her husband and now king, was furious beyond measure.

Augustus tried to be proactive in intervening on Caroline's behalf, so he arranged a meeting with his brother at Buckingham House to see what the king intended to do about his wife's now seemingly imminent return to England to claim her right to the British throne. I vividly remember him describing the bizarre meeting afterwards.

"When I arrived, I was told he'd see me immediately, which doesn't happen often. Most of the time he won't see me at all. It was almost as if he wanted to see me, wanted me to warn Caroline to stay away. It was clear, when I arrived at his quarters, that he was in the company of a woman. I heard muffled voices behind the door—it could have been Gee's sister, Harriet, but I can't be sure. By the time someone opened the door, though, the woman was gone. George was lying naked in the bath, belching frequently and obviously very drunk. It was frightening. I know I could lose some weight, but he looked awful. I poured myself a drink and tried to look the other way. When I asked if he knew about Caroline's return, which of course he did, I said, 'Well, what are you going to do about it?' What he said was that he wasn't worried about Caroline at all because he'd been investigating her since she'd left England, nearly six years ago, and he was certain he had enough evidence—apparently there are bags of it—and, more importantly, parliament's support in finally obtaining a divorce from her."

I gasped, thinking back on the *Delicate Investigation* of 1806. "Augustus, we've been down this road before. How could two investigations of this magnitude ever plague one human being in their lifetime? Does Caroline know about any of this 'investigation' and that it's apparently been going on for years? She did seem paranoid in her last letter. Do we know when she's due to come back? I think you should start looking for a barrister for her."

Augustus looked somber. "I fear my brother has learnt from his mistakes, and I'm certain that the evidence he now has will not be circumstantial. He is the King of England now, so no one can stop him. I think the only person who can save Caroline now is, perhaps, Caroline herself—that, and her popularity with the British people. I will, though, try to find out when she is due back in London."

When I arrived back in Portman Square later that afternoon to tell Elizabeth what was happening, she was already in the know—at least about Caroline's imminent arrival and her husband's nefarious intentions. She even said that some of the evidence may already have been leaked to the press.

"This is awful news, Margaret. I wish we knew where Caroline was so we could warn her. I fear the papers are being spoon-fed by the Palace. According to *The Times* this morning, Caroline has allegedly had many lovers in Europe, but there's one Italian man called Pergami who's going to be a real problem for her. Several of her servants have seen them bathing together. Another claimed to have seen them together in the same bed and to have seen her playing with his genitals."

"What?" I said, interrupting her. "Has she learnt nothing from the *Delicate Investigation* that nearly cost us all our welfare?"

"Apparently not," she said. "The papers are speculating that the king will take legal action against her as soon as she arrives back in London. There's talk of a bill being introduced in parliament."

"A bill in parliament? What does that mean?"

"The fear amongst particularly the House of Lords is that Caroline has been a nuisance for nearly a quarter of a century, and now she has more power simply because of her new title. Nobody wants her revving up the masses and throwing her weight around regarding material parliamentary reform, so they intend to introduce a bill in the Houses of Parliament that will likely result in a trial."

I was dumbfounded. "A trial? Is he mad? We're close to civil war in this country, and he wants a trial just to be able to get a divorce from his wife? Does he not remember the word *guillotine*?"

"We can only hope someone else does," she replied, without showing any emotion at all.

I ignored her implication. "What happens to Caroline if the king wins, in the absence of an independent juror?" I continued. "She'll have nothing, or even worse, perhaps be put in jail or executed!" I felt my chest getting tighter, and I leaned on the nearby chair for support. "This is her worst nightmare, all over again, and I'm not sure there's anything we can do to help her."

Elizabeth just nodded. "I'm quite certain there is nothing we can do to help her. It is rumoured that King George is also planning to embarrass her before she even gets here by demanding that the Archbishop of Canterbury remove her name from the liturgy at Sunday services."

Finally able to catch my breath, I said, "That'll probably work to Caroline's advantage, but George is probably too stupid to realise. We'll just have to wait until she gets here to know what to do. Let's talk to Augustus in the morning."

QUEEN CAROLINE, INDEED, RETURNED TO Britain's shores several months later. On June 5, 1820, as she approached London, riots broke out all over the country in support of her return to claim her rightful place on the British throne. Elizabeth and I were both amongst the well-wishers on the streets of London, anxious to find out where she would be staying so we could offer our support.

Within a day of her arrival, as promised, King George delivered his complaint to both Houses of Parliament, accompanied by the 'green bags of evidence' collected during the 'Milan Investigation.' This, apparently, was the official title of the disgusting six-year intrusion into Caroline's private life whilst she was attempting to seek refuge and peace on the Continent. Elizabeth was methodically doing research on a daily basis and now had a system to clip all the newspapers into some sort of organised manner, which she intended to share with Caroline to help her be better informed as to what she was up against.

As expected, the king's legal action from the 'green bags of evidence' eventually resulted in the need for a Bill of Pains and Penalties to be heard in both Houses of Parliament, against Queen Caroline.

Whilst, on the surface, all this vengeful nonsense seems but a privileged king just trying to divorce his wife, as an educator, it is important for me to explain the role Queen Caroline's legal troubles of 1820 played in advancing the cause for structural political and social reform for all the citizens of nineteenth-century Britain.

The newspapers were full of examinations of Queen Caroline's rights under the Magna Carta, a thirteenth-century British charter of civil rights signed by King John himself nearly six hundred years ago. Whilst the charter was only ever intended to protect the rights of wealthy white men, this was an invitation to try to expand those protections for potentially everyone. Queen Caroline became the entire nation's best hope for real change.

In preparation for the proceedings, Caroline stood steadfast and stoic. I didn't know how to help her, but then an idea bloomed. Immediately upon hearing of the 'bags of evidence' being delivered to both Houses of Parliament, I walked to Kensington Palace to find Augustus. Fortunately, he was in residence and otherwise unoccupied. I was immediately shown into the drawing room, where he was deep in a pile of German papers and drinking gin.

"Margaret, my love, what a lovely surprise. To what do I owe this privilege?"

"I am sorry to come unannounced, Augustus, but I am completely distraught over Caroline's situation. This is all happening so fast, as I am sure King George is intent on being rid of her before the coronation ceremonies. I know you will be obliged to attend the proceedings in the House of Lords, but is there any way that I could accompany you when they read this Bill of Pains and Penalties, even if I wait outside the chamber? I want to show my support, and I am a diligent scribe."

"Margaret, I am sorry, even I can't do that. No women have ever been allowed inside the House of Lords proceedings. They used to let women into the 'strangers gallery' in the House of Commons, but there was a row during the loss of the American Colonies when one woman refused to vacate her seat. That was the end of women being allowed in any House of Parliament, and that was nearly fifty years ago."

I felt dejected.

"I could, however, get you a seat in the 'ventilator shaft' above the House of Commons," he continued. "I have heard it is a dreadful, claustrophobic space, but you will hear the proceedings on the Bill of Pains and Penalties directly from there, if that is what you wish."

I felt my lungs start to tighten. "The 'ventilator shaft'? I have never heard of such a place."

"I am sure you have not. It is a well-kept secret, but it is the only place women interested in politics can understand directly what is being said in the House of Commons. It gives them ammunition to fight their causes and, perhaps more importantly, to understand who is with them and who is against them."

"Well, then, I would certainly like a seat in the 'ventilator shaft.' Thank you very much."

This made Augustus laugh out loud. "You are a bold woman, Margaret, only to be matched by that partner in crime that only you get to call 'Lizzie.' You know you shouldn't be in that 'ventilator shaft' with those weak lungs of yours, but far be it for me to be the one who tries to stop you."

So, on July 5, 1820, I entered this rather sacred space, where women were silently permitted to witness what happened in the hallowed halls of parliamentary, male power. I heard the Bill of Pains and Penalties of 1820 read against Queen Caroline in the 'ventilator shaft,' high above the House of Commons. The air was hot and stuffy. I poked my head out like a parrot, trying to escape the intense steam emanating from the scorching pipes. There were, however, seven other delightful women doing the same, and we all took copious notes.

I can still remember some of the words spoken. "This bill is intended to deprive Her Majesty Queen Caroline Amelia Elizabeth of the Title, Prerogatives, Rights, Privileges, and Exemptions of Queen Consort of this Realm and to dissolve this marriage between His Majesty and the said Caroline Amelia Brunswick. The charge is committed adultery with a foreigner of low station."

I remember thinking, *Would it have mattered if the man in question were a foreigner of high station?*

The introduction of the bill essentially then created the need for a public trial in the House of Lords. Whilst Augustus attended the trial, he recused himself from the vote to try and sway others to do the same. George Canning also tried to resign from the House of Lords in protest to the unfair treatment of Caroline. This I thought particularly admirable, as he'd been named as one of her possible lovers in the *Delicate Investigation*. He stood alone, however, in not being a hypocrite, despite the potential of losing his lucrative political career. It did give me a singular glimmer of hope that there was some sort of ethical backbone left in the now rapidly decomposing institution called the House of Lords.

Caroline was allowed to attend the trial but wasn't allowed to speak. She sat, silent and composed, with hundreds of men wagging their fingers at her for the crime of adultery. A crime, I might add, that most, if not all, of them committed on a regular basis. Neither this nor any of King George's behaviour mattered, though. Whilst one could petition for a divorce on the grounds of adultery if you were a man, no such reciprocity existed for a woman whose husband had committed the exact same offence. The rest of the Hanoverian band of beasts were also up there in the balcony, as were Granville Leveson-Gower, Charles Grey, and the Earl of Bessborough, just to name a few. All with an *equal* vote, and all with an equally sanctimonious, wagging finger.

Caroline, whilst perhaps quiet at trial, was never more vocal than in the press. She employed, how should I say, *more verbally talented friends* to dictate quotes on her behalf, which were then leaked to the *London Times* as having come from Caroline's tongue directly. I have two particular favourites, the first of which incited calls for the guillotine and

King George's head in the streets of London, and the second of which I penned for her and Elizabeth leaked.

> If the highest subject in the realm can be deprived of her rank and title—can be divorced, dethroned, and debased by an act of arbitrary power, in the form of a Bill of Pains and Penalties—the constitutional liberty of the Kingdom will be shaken to its very base; the rights of the nation will be only a scattered wreck; and this once free people, like the meanest of slaves, must submit to the lash of an insolent domination.
>
> *The Times*, August 1820

> A government cannot stop the march of intellect any more than they can arrest the motion of the tides or the course of the planets.
>
> *The Times*, October 7, 1820

Despite her mask of emotional indifference, I knew the pressure was tearing Caroline up inside—the injustice of it all; such a huge burden to carry on her own two shoulders. The entire country was now betting on her, and if she lost, she might also lose her head. There was absolutely no consideration of what her rights should have been at a trial under the letter of the British law, and at the risk of pointing out the obvious, she was also now the Queen of England. She wasn't even given a list of the prosecution's witnesses who would testify against her at trial.

THE TRIAL LASTED INTO THE AUTUMN and divided the country like a foreign enemy. It did, however, lose considerable momentum during its five-month, circuitous journey. It certainly wore the entire country down to complete exhaustion. Then the news came on the 6th of November that the bill had passed in the House of Lords 123-95 in favour of King George. Elizabeth and I couldn't believe it and feared the worst of what was to come next. We didn't need to read it in the newspaper; we could hear it in the streets. We held our breath as to what would be next for Caroline—and the entire country, for that matter.

We heard nothing more for days, and then we got the results of yet another vote on November 10 in the House of Lords, 109-99 in favour of the king. At least the margin was closing. Next we got the big news: In fear of public outcry and an inability to get the bill through the House of Commons (because of the small margin), the bill was summarily vacated in the House of Lords. Queen Caroline was then acquitted of any and all wrongdoing.

Augustus personally escorted her out of the House of Lords. As they approached the main doors, they could hear a low roar, which grew louder with each step they got closer. When the doors finally opened, the thunder of the assembled crowd became deafening. They were chanting repeatedly, "The Queen and Sussex forever! The Queen and Sussex forever!" Her victory was celebrated in the streets of London for days, although not always peacefully. Sympathisers to King George often found their windows shattered and their businesses ablaze. There were peaceful signs of support, though, as well. Some nearly half-million people came out to support Queen Caroline when she attended a service of Thanksgiving at St. Paul's Cathedral several weeks later.

It was not only a resounding victory for Caroline, but a victory for the ordinary British people as well, both women and men alike. Through her very public and protracted trial, she became an icon for all the oppressed. Her lost rights were her people's lost rights, and her victory was their victory as well. The Rubicon had been crossed, and the rightful Queen of England and her people had spoken. Life would be forever changed in Britain.

I can remember getting the news from Elizabeth, barging through the front door and nearly out of breath. "They got scared, Margaret; they dropped the charges. She's free, she won! Get your coat," she screamed with whatever air was still left in her lungs. "They are celebrating in the streets. This is a victory, for all of England!"

I couldn't actually absorb all that she was saying at first. It just seemed impossible that Caroline had won. We had thought three days before that she was going to be executed.

"Give me a minute, Lizzie. I will meet you down there," I said quietly. I then paused to reflect on what Caroline had accomplished. Like me, but on a much grander scale, she had chosen her own path and, against all odds, won battle after battle. She, like me, had reached beyond the strictures of British society, which said that women were worth less or nothing, had no rights, and were held to a higher standard than men. She was told she couldn't when she knew she could and, my God, did she ever prevail in the end.

As if she knew I'd finished my thought, Elizabeth said again, "Come, Margaret, let us celebrate this victory with the entire nation."

AUGUSTUS TOOK ME TO VISIT CAROLINE a few days after the trial ended. He warned me that the trial had been hard on her, not to mention her daughter's untimely death three years before, and that her health was frail.

"I don't think I'll mention Princess Charlotte unless she does," I said. "What do you think?"

"I think that's wise. I'll tell you now she's not ready to talk about it. She hasn't even been to see her at St. George's Chapel. I don't know if she knows that her grandson is buried at Princess Charlotte's feet there. I wouldn't want that to be a surprise for her. Let's just keep it upbeat, about the trial," he finished, as the door magically seemed to spring open.

Whilst Caroline did look very drawn, her spirits, thanks to the recent victory, were high.

"Margaret, I'm so delighted to see you. What do you think about my day in court?" she said, bellowing with laughter.

"Amazing, Caroline. By all accounts, you were amazing. I'm so proud of you. The entire country is celebrating with you. You've given us all something to hope for, in your steadfast victory. I'm so happy for you." I gave her a gentle hug and kiss. It was so lovely to see her again, and to my mind, the trial had only made her stronger.

This was not, however, to be her last stand. In July of 1821, she made a valiant attempt to take her rightful place at her husband's ridiculously opulent coronation ceremony. She arrived by carriage at six in the morning, very ceremoniously, to respectfully attend the services. She first tried to enter Westminster Abbey via the hall, where a crowd was gathering. She was met with opposing bayonets in her face, so she retreated to the back of the church and tried to enter through an entrance near Poet's Corner with someone else's ticket that had been graciously offered to her. She was eventually dissuaded, though, and returned to her carriage, retreating back to Brandenburg House defeated, but not without her supporters creating as much chaos as humanly possible on her husband's big day. They lined the street to throw offensive objects at the king's carriage during the post-ceremony procession. He was so fearful of the crowds he actually slept in the Speaker of the House of Commons's house the night before so he wouldn't have to see any of the 'commoners' before the ceremony. There was also rioting all over the streets of London, objecting to Caroline not being included, and the Light Cavalry had to be eventually dispersed.

Less than a few weeks later, though, this icon, and my 'forever friend,' became deathly ill with an intestinal infection. It was clear she was in great pain, but she made sure all her affairs were in order before she took her final breath. Queen Caroline of Great Britain died on August 7, 1820, with her beloved Willie Austin by her side. She left most of her estate to him and his heirs. There were rumours that the king had poisoned her, but I think if he'd been capable of that, he'd have done it years before.

Nonetheless, after so much heartache in her life, and then her final victory over King George IV only a few months prior, this felt an unjust end. She, my 'forever friend,' had changed the lives of so many, one of which was, indeed, my own. *Please take care of her, Georgiana, and please behave yourself, Caroline.* Her body was sent back to Germany for burial in her family plot, which was her last dying wish. Her coffin bore a small plaque that simply said 'Caroline—The Injured Queen of England.'

'Big' Harriet also died that year, 1821, in Florence, Italy, after the death of her youngest grandchild. It was said she died of a broken heart. I could comment on that, but my Christian soul tells me to move on. Her body was labouriously brought back from Florence, and she is buried next to her sister, Georgiana, in the Cavendish vault in Derbyshire. I wrote immediately to Little Harriet to offer my condolences, at what must have been a difficult time for the entire Leveson-Gower family. It was the end of an era in many ways.

42

THE YEAR 1824 TURNED OUT to be another difficult year for my brother, Thomas. His son, Little Thomas, was a constant disappointment to his father, and his mother's death, five years earlier, had taken its toll on him. As many talents as my brother has, rearing children isn't one of them.

Little Thomas was in constant defiance of his strict military father, who was as immovable as a statue when it came to compromise. As I mentioned previously, Thomas spent most of his days at the Royal Pensioners' Hospital in Chelsea until he met his new wife, Rebecca Ann Gooden, who he married last year. Just before Thomas married again, his youngest son ran away from home, and we were unable to find him anywhere.

I will be honest: I have no time for Rebecca Ann Gooden. She is twenty-six years younger than Thomas and just four years older than his daughter Elizabeth Jekyll would have been, had she lived. That comment is rather critical, I realise, given the age gap between Augustus and me. Nevertheless, I experience Rebecca Ann Gooden as incredibly opportunistic. Whilst I, better than anyone, understand the financial security a husband brings to a woman's life, discarding a potential suitor's children in the process is an entirely different matter. Rebecca made it very clear from the beginning that she had no desire for children of her own but also that she had no desire to be in the presence of children at all. I've often wondered if the soon-to-be 'Mrs. Bryan' packed Little Thomas's bag herself.

After Little Thomas had been missing for months, at the tender age of twelve he was arrested for larceny. He was incarcerated in Newgate

Prison, only steps away from where his grandpapa had built longcase clocks for royalty—clocks I had helped him build. Eventually, he was beaten and released, but it was all over the papers, and Thomas couldn't bear the shame. George, his elder brother, Elizabeth, and I all tried to intervene, but to no avail. Thomas disowned his youngest son then and there and hasn't seen or spoken to him since. Sadly, neither have we, despite Elizabeth constantly scouring the streets of London looking for him. It's still hard for me to realise that Little Thomas is a convicted criminal. I pray for him every day, wherever he might be.

On a much happier note, Little Harriet moved to The Hague in 1824 when her father, Granville Leveson-Gower, became British ambassador to the Netherlands. It was one of those times when I acknowledged the privileged opportunities Little Harriet had been given by being in the care of her father and Harryo, however raw that wound still is. We were even more jubilant when we learnt she was betrothed to be married to the heir to the Dukedom of Leeds.

Little Harriet and the Honourable George Osborne were married in a private ceremony at the British embassy in The Hague, on the 21st of October, 1824. She was twenty-four years old. The couple welcomed their first child, Harriet Emma Godolphin Osborne, just less than a year later. I am now officially a grandmaman, better known as 'Mamie.'

Elizabeth, Lucy, Jessy, Emma, and I all went to see them shortly after the baby was born. It was a heavenly visit. Little Harriet never looked happier, and she's taken to motherhood like a natural. I also adore her husband, seemingly a perfect gentleman. After our visit to the Osbornes, Elizabeth, Jessy Anne, and I returned to London, whilst Lucy and Emma stayed on in Europe. They're still thick as thieves. Emma is touring Europe with her mother, who has very kindly also offered to chaperone Lucy Elizabeth as well. I acknowledge the irony of that, but I'm very grateful to Lady Augusta for her gracious invitation. I have come to know her quite well over the years, and I've nothing but the kindest of words to say about her. The friendship our daughters share is also nothing short of magical.

Lucy Elizabeth, now twenty-four, continues to pursue her musical career. Her plan is to eventually get to Florence, where she's going to learn to speak and sing in Italian. Her goal is none other than the Italian opera. She's my wanderlust baby, and I'd never try to hold her back. It does, however, make me feel better to know that Augustus is looking out for them on the Continent, should they ever find themselves in need of assistance. It is probably one of the few perquisites of being a 'royal spare'—that the Palace and the government provide significant security measures to extended to members of the royal family whilst overseas. Emma is eligible as a niece to the king, even though she is illegitimate.

When we returned from Europe, Elizabeth and I decided to finally retire from teaching and close the doors of Bryan House forever. The London air has been progressively getting worse for my aging lungs, so we've decided to leave the city and make a fresh start for ourselves yet again. We have purchased a new terraced home in Kentish Town, which is being built for us as I write the pages of this book.

In closing, I realise in writing this memoir that I have had the uncommon and cherished opportunity to see my own life through a different lens, like looking down on Earth from a powerful telescope in the kingdom of heaven. I see clearly now how the individual threads of many different colours and thicknesses have tied the whole tapestry together, like Mamie's patchwork quilt—some patches have been present from the very beginning, and some have been woven in throughout the years. My love of the stars, my love of maths—these curiosities surely came with me into this life, carried through from my European ancestors, but hopefully I have sown my own unique seeds that will continue to flower in the scientific books I have written that will survive me.

My desire has been to live my life based on the principles that *I* find worthy, rather than those the world tells me are so. I could not have lived my life traditionally 'in the gilded cage,' as my very being would not have allowed it. I would not wish it to be any other way. I have loved my family, I have loved my work, and I have loved a man with all my heart. Even though I've made sacrifices to live as I wished, I hope that perhaps I have also paved a way for other women to do the same.

As I reflect particularly on our legacy of the Bryan House schools 'for the education of young ladies,' I recognise that our next monarch, in all probability, will be a woman. She is, indeed, the Crown's only legitimate heir: Princess Victoria. Her unlikely succession to the Throne as a woman is purely the accidental consequence of none of the previous king's nine sons being able to produce a legitimate male heir, despite the existence of dozens of illegitimate children, both male and female, scattered around the country. I say no more, as at least three of these children belong to Augustus himself. Whilst Princess Victoria is still just a little girl, it's my sincerest hope that when she does take the Throne, she will be more supportive than her male predecessors in expanding the educational and occupational choices available to women. Augustus happens to be her favourite uncle, so I have no doubt he'll be a strong influence on her reign.

I dare to dream of a new generation of young ladies under the leadership and guidance of such a clever and measured queen—the most important of these young ladies being Harriet Emma Godolphin Osborne, my granddaughter.

I dream of a day when she is free to pursue acceptance into any university of her choosing, in whatever subjects she desires to be educated in, on her own merits.

A day when she's accepted as an equal member of whatever society she wishes to belong to because of the wisdom she carries with her.

Perhaps, most importantly, a day when she has the support of all those around her *and* the courage to tell any man wagging at her to please put down his sanctimonious finger.

I pray for this with all my heart not just to be a celestial illusion.

IN CLOSING, I WISH TO THANK MY READERS for their indulgence and contemplation in the consumption of this intimate memoir of my private life.

Most respectfully,
Margaret Bryan

Epilogue

Margaret Bryan died on March 30, 1836, at the age of seventy-nine—thirty years later, to the very day, that her dear friend Georgiana Cavendish, the Duchess of Devonshire, died at Devonshire House. Unlike Georgiana's elaborate send-off, though, Margaret Bryan's obituary simply read:

AT FORTRESS-TERRACE, KENTISH-TOWN,
ON THE 30TH ULT., MUCH BELOVED AND LAMENTED,
MRS. MARGARET BRYAN, AGED 79

She was buried in St. Luke's, Chelsea, on April 7, 1836, five days after Charles Dickens was married there. She was survived by her three daughters and nine grandchildren. Unfortunately, Harriet Emma Godolphin Osborne did not survive her childhood.

The Endless and Unnecessary Battle for Gender Equality (1836–?)

PRINCESS VICTORIA, INDEED, ASCENDED to the Throne the following year, 1837, at the tender age of eighteen. She ruled as Queen of the British Empire for nearly sixty-four years. As misguided as the British colonisation of the world was, Queen Victoria was almost singularly credited with its undeniable success. By the end of her reign, the British Empire ultimately controlled or largely influenced nearly two-thirds of the world's population. If you've ever visited Central London, you'd be hard-pressed to find a single street that doesn't pay some homage to Queen Victoria's reign. That homage, though, also serves as a painful reminder of the wealth Britain acquired from the rest of the world during it.

Despite being the creator of the modern world's most formidable economic and political empire, Queen Victoria did nothing to advance any kind of equality for other women. When asked about the subject, she is quoted as saying:

> If ever were women to 'unsex' themselves by claiming equality with men, they would become the most hateful, heathen, and disgusting of beings and would surely perish without male protection.

Perhaps it was only she who had 'unsexed' herself? One might alternatively conclude that the absolute corruption of power sees no line of gender demarcation. Without any support from their queen, parliament certainly wasn't going to act independently to advance any civil or political liberties for women.

This lack of leadership for the support of women's rights in the world's political institutions then enabled its most prestigious universities to also curtail the advancement of their education. These revered institutions of 'intellectual enlightenment' colluded, across continents, to limit the matriculation of women to shadow schools, with narrow and frankly worthless curricula. 'Just send them to a different place, and don't teach them anything that has any commercial or political value' appeared to be the 'co-op' mantra—not of the day, but perhaps the entirety of the following two centuries: seventy-three thousand days, just to put that in the context of the appropriate scale.

Cambridge University didn't award degrees to women until 1948. Harvard University wouldn't sign a merger agreement with Radcliffe College, its sister and very separate school, until 1977. Full integration between Harvard University and Radcliffe College wasn't actually completed until 1999.

I was born in 1967, in a small town at the end of Hadrian's Wall in Newcastle, England, and delivered by a midwife. As a child, I immigrated to the United States with my family. I have a bachelor of science in engineering from North Carolina State University and an MBA from Harvard Business School. In addition to being a graduate of Harvard Business School, I also recently enjoyed a position there as a teaching fellow. I was, however, born five years before the first woman was admitted to Harvard Business School.

While attending North Carolina State University as an engineering student in the mid-1980s, I often found there wasn't a female bathroom readily accessible to me. "Yes, ma'am, cross the street; it is the brick building right in front of you, second set of stairs, and turn left" was one protracted and annoying answer I remember getting after politely asking for the nearest toilet. Funny, as I look back on it, I don't think I even found that strange at the time. I just made a mental note to do a little more advance planning.

Despite the obvious obstacles, with a bit of luck and hopefully some measure of determination and intelligence, I've been fortunate to have had a successful and lucrative career as a 'C-suite' executive for companies large and small. Much more importantly, by the grace of God, I'm married to a loving and supportive man and am called *Mother* by two beautiful children to whom I did not give birth. I have also recently become known as *Grandma*.

I, like Margaret Bryan, have experienced profound gender discrimination and harassment in my own now thirty-plus-year career, nearly two centuries after her death. It is, however, discovering the richness and purpose of Margaret Bryan's life and her selfless and anonymous legacy to the scientific education of women that gives *me* the courage to ask my sisters in arms to tell any man wagging at her to please put down his sanctimonious finger.

Researchers have speculated for decades, if not centuries, as to who Margaret Bryan was and from 'whence she came,' including the Royal Society in an article published as recently as March 2023. She was certainly enigmatic, by her own design. It is interesting, though, how things depend on your perspective. The majority of this largely unlucrative research has been spent trying to find her husband, as opposed to understanding where she could possibly have acquired such an education *as a woman in the eighteenth century.* I believe Margaret Bryan is my fourth great-aunt. Her 'brother,' Thomas Bryan, was my fourth great-grandfather. They both descended from at least six generations of mathematical instrument-makers and clockmakers, originally Huguenot refugees from the Continent.

'Field Trip' Reflections
from the Author

Whilst this memoir is clearly intended to reveal the private life of Margaret Bryan, I'm sure, with her complete agreement, that it would be without conscience not to pause and reflect on the story of Queen Caroline of Brunswick. Her win at the 'Trial of the Century' in 1820 unequivocally unified the press and the masses to forevermore reset Britain's political and civil liberties, for men and women alike.

The 1832 Reform Act was passed in both Houses of Parliament only twelve years after her victorious acquittal at trial. The bill was ironically championed by then prime minister Charles Grey, Georgiana the Duchess of Devonshire's lover and father to her illegitimate daughter, Eliza Courtney. The bill itself only improved voting access for middle-class men. It, indeed, made the suffrage problem worse for women, by defining a voter's eligibility to be only that of the male sex.

Having said that there was no direct benefit for women in the bill itself, though, it certainly got a great deal of British women 'still on the fence' maniacally aligned around a single North Star called their own emancipation. The point was that the needle was moving in a more democratic direction for all. Otherwise, parliament would have had a civil war on their hands. Images of the French Revolution were still very fresh in the minds of the British aristocracy, and more importantly, amongst the masses, as were the calls for 'Guillotine!'

Queen Caroline's significant contributions to early nineteenth-century political reform in Britain are undeniable. This, as you might imagine, was not a popular narrative with the House of Lords. They had been brutally embarrassed by her, so they certainly weren't about to give her a bigger microphone, dead or alive. If she died 'The Injured Queen of England,' she now holds perhaps the most unenviable title of 'The Most Forgotten One.'

When I went to visit Montague House in Greenwich Park in 2021, I discovered that it had been destroyed, with all its contents, by her husband, then Prince Regent, after Caroline left for the Continent in 1814. The only remnants of her entire existence there are the crumbling remains of her sunken bathtub. This now-rotting, makeshift monument was first discovered accidentally in 1909, covered up again in the 1980s, and then re-excavated in 2001. *I mean, really?* It is now so well hidden behind a row of hedges that I walked past it three times before finding it. It's not clear what purpose the hedges serve at all, as the bathtub was originally housed in a very expensive and elaborate glass conservatory. Talk about a voyeur's paradise! I'm glad it was only Willie Austin's mother creeping around in her back garden.

When I paid the required admission to visit the still-standing Ranger's House, formerly Brunswick House, next door to Montague House, I enquired about Queen Caroline. "Oh, Caroline. No, she was never the Queen of England; she was never crowned. She was always just the 'Princess of Wales.' There is really no trace of her here after she left her husband to return to the Continent in 1814, apart from a small bust of her on the mantelpiece in one of the downstairs rooms. Some say it was sculpted by one of her lesbian lovers while she was living at Montague House. I think that is it, though, if you have already seen the bathtub" was the response I got before being asked, "Did you have any questions about the Wernher Art Collection?"

That is all there is left of her here *after she left her husband to return to the Continent in 1814?* A crumbling bathtub and the tiny bust, sculpted by a woman who apparently doesn't even bear a name? I was pinned—I mean, spit-nails pinned. What about the trial? Doesn't anyone remember that she came back from the Continent and won the 'Trial of the Century' with all odds against her, which changed British history forever? I wanted to scream at the top of my lungs at her, but of course I did not. I, myself, was born a Brit, and it's a hardwired thing: Say nothing, with a hint of a smile on your face, and don't show any teeth.

I remember thinking, though, *My God, she was the Princess of Wales, and eventually the Queen of England, crown on her head or not.* This is how we pay our respects to her for her important contributions to the so necessary nineteenth-century social and political reform? A crumbling bathtub and a small bust, by an unknown sculptress who perhaps had ulterior motives? I have no explanation, then, as to why the memory of such an important British monarch has been lost without a trace, other than to state the obvious: The site in Greenwich Park, where Montague House once sat, is still owned and controlled by the Crown Estate, as is Ranger's House next door.

Queen Caroline of Brunswick's excavated bathtub, at the once site of Montague House, Greenwich Park, London (September 2021)

I have no explanation at all, though, as to where the rainbow in the photograph that I took came from, which just happens to be almost perfectly symmetrical to the actual bathtub itself. I say I have no explanation for the rainbow as I am an engineer, and it did not rain that day in Greenwich Park. I should mention, however, that it's rumoured by some locals that Queen Caroline's spirit still haunts Ranger's House, along with apartment 1A at Kensington Palace, where Caroline also maintained a residence after the end of the *Delicate Investigation*. This theory isn't one I can offer any insight into other than to say, were I ever to meet a ghost, Queen Caroline would be at the top of my list, for entertainment's sake alone. BYOB to bed! All humour aside, it is my sincerest hope that someone will recognise the gross injustice that's been done to Queen Caroline's legacy and return her to the history books, giving her the credit that she is surely now long overdue.

I apologise; now I have digressed. I return to Margaret Bryan's story. Like Queen Caroline and her decaying bathtub, I believe Margaret Bryan's legacy would also have been lost forever but for that infamous frontispiece of her first book. There can be no doubt that Margaret Bryan's textbooks became a standard in scientific education, for boys *and* girls alike, in the nineteenth century. They are just textbooks, however, which, by definition, mostly become obsolete and forgotten. It is the 'Belle' frontispiece, though, that likely showed up in many a 'gentleman's' (and I use that term loosely) study in the name of supporting the 'above-average-looking porcelain doll who plays the piano with some mastery but doesn't speak at all.'

When Margaret Bryan's *A Compendious System of Astronomy* finally found its way to the British Museum in September of 1965, more than 160 years after its initial publication, an inscription of unknown origin was included on the inside cover that simply reads 'Fine Portrait by Nutter.' I mean, absolutely nothing about the scientific content of the book at all. Talk about a sustainable marketing strategy, though! The Duchess of Devonshire certainly gave Walt Disney a run for his money on who should keep that blue ribbon in perpetuity. I think she still has him beat by at least a hundred years. No disrespect, of course, to Mickey Mouse, and he has had the benefit of at least a dozen makeovers! That, indeed, is the final irony of that controversial and beautiful frontispiece. It made the 'real' Margaret Bryan disappear. Despite her name and image surviving the test of time, along the way, the world lost the story of who she was and from 'whence she came.'

Having said that, I believe it may have been Margaret Bryan's wish not to be 'found,' or perhaps more importantly, not to be 'found out.' While in the height of her career she had her brand and reputation to protect, by the end of her life, this was likely more in the name of protecting all three of her 'own' and very 'real' daughters from their illegitimate and/ or impoverished beginnings. Despite the groundbreaking choices she'd made early in life, after the arrival of Little Harriet, Margaret Bryan was first and foremost a loving and protective mother.

The fact that the frontispiece of her first book became her legacy also meant that the problem of the 'children' never really went away. Those 'children' in the 1797 frontispiece, 'packaged' or not, are still imaginary. That was clearly something that bothered her and her sense of truth. The original engraving was redone in 1805 by a man named MacKenzie to eliminate the 'children' from the picture altogether. I'm just not sure that Margaret Bryan could have ever disclosed the true origins of her family and education, without risking her own reputation and that of her 'own' children. She'd already disappeared into the night once before to protect her family from the *Delicate Investigation* at Blackheath. These issues of legitimacy and lineage were of great importance in Britain then, particularly for women, and perhaps still are.

You need look no further than Jane Austen's *Emma*, which arguably could have also been a semi-fictionalised version of the true life of Little Harriet Osborne (née Bryan). You need not examine the characters nor the story very closely to see the similarities. Little Harriet acquired the middle name *Emma* later in life and graced her daughter with the same namesake. I have no explanation as to why; she certainly wasn't baptised *Emma*. She was christened solely as her biological mother's namesake, Harriet.

How Margaret Bryan would have penned her own memoir, we will never know. I will comment, though, that as much as she despised the House of Lords, by the time she died, all three of her 'own' daughters had now married into the British landed gentry. Whilst Little Harriet has a separate story after she went to live with her father at Tixall Hall, Lucy Elizabeth and Jessy Anne were clearly 'packaged' for their gentrified husbands and the rest of the world as having been born legitimately into that most revered and elite class of British society. When pressed to provide some evidence of Lucy Elizabeth and Jessy Anne's gentrified father, Thomas Bryan, Esquire, is the name that always shows up in the press clippings. No disrespect to the actual Thomas Bryan, but it probably helped Lucy Elizabeth and Jessy Anne that their adopted uncle/father had died by the time they both married in different British embassies on the Continent.

I'm happy to report, though, that as Thomas Bryan, St. Luke's parish clerk, had intended, all three of Margaret Bryan's daughters remained loyal and loving sisters, even after Little Harriet's departure to Tixall Hall. They were certainly all together in Paris at the British embassy in 1828 to witness Jessy Anne's marriage to an Irish gentleman from Kilkenny. Little Harriet was now twenty-eight years old and living in Paris with her husband at the time. She was also heavily pregnant with the future 9th Duke of Leeds. Little Harriet was notably a witness to the marriage as Harriet Bryan, despite being styled Lady Godolphin after her marriage. Some secrets are worth finding a good hiding place for, particularly for those of us trying to follow the crumbs two hundred years later.

Jessy Anne and her new Irish husband, Pooley Abel Warren, Esquire, were also witness to Lucy Elizabeth's marriage a year later in Florence, Italy. She married an English gentleman from Hounslow by the name of Frederick Goddard, Esquire. Jessy Anne and Lucy Elizabeth both had daughters in Florence, Italy, in 1829 and named them after each other, with Florence being the shared middle name for both little girls. To that end, Margaret Bryan also had her grandchildren's reputations to think about as well, as perhaps she pondered how important her own educational and publishing legacy were to her.

Whether Margaret Bryan deliberately chose to fade into the books of history or if she just left us with a great number of clues, we can only speculate. Because of the 'Belle' frontispiece of her first book, though, and the popularity of her widely read scientific textbooks, despite no one knowing who she was or from 'whence she came,' her legacy remains and is prominently displayed in some remarkably impressive places. She can be found at the British Museum, the Science Museum, and the Royal Observatory Museum, to name just a few. The famous miniature painting has also survived and is on permanent display in the drawing room of the Herschel Museum in Bath, of all places. I wonder what Augustus, the Duke of Sussex, would have said about that? Perhaps, more importantly, I wonder what Caroline Herschel would have had to say? Talk about squatting on a competitor's real estate in perpetuity! Georgiana would have been particularly proud of that, even if it happened purely by accident.

What I assume is one of Georgiana's, the Duchess of Devonshire's, original copies of *A Compendious System of Astronomy* has also survived amongst the other seventeen thousand volumes of books still housed at the massive library at Chatsworth House in Derbyshire, the country seat of now the 12th Duke of Devonshire. Most of the remains of Sir Henry Cavendish's scientific library in Bedford Square are also still there, as well as some of his original astronomy equipment from Clapham Common.

I cannot say but how gracious they were to me on my visit to Chatsworth House in the summer of 2022. It was a quintessentially rainy British day. As the taxi driver approached the magnificent estate, I closed my eyes and tried to imagine what it must have been like for Georgiana to arrive at such a place to marry a man she hardly knew at the tender age of seventeen. When a gentleman in a bowler hat with an umbrella was kind enough to point me in the right direction, the archivist looked up the book and then brought the original copy to show me, on a protective cushion.

Original copy of Margaret Bryan's A Compendious System of Astronomy *(1799), now housed in the libraries of Chatsworth House, Derbyshire*

While at the Chatsworth House archives, I was also fortunate to see some letters written from Little Harriet to her Uncle Hart—then the 6th Duke of Devonshire and Georgiana's only son and Harryo's brother— just before she married George Osborne in The Hague in 1824. It certainly brought it all to life for me.

About the Author

 JAYNE WAS BORN IN ENGLAND and immigrated to the United States with her family as a child. She holds a bachelor of science in engineering from North Carolina State University and an MBA from Harvard Business School.

After earning her MBA, she worked as a strategy consultant for Bain & Company and then held various C-suite leadership positions at Dunkin' Brands, Gulf Oil, Planet Fitness, and Alex and Ani. While at Alex and Ani, she had the privilege of partnering with First Lady Michelle Obama on the 'Let Girls Learn' campaign. It was here she developed her passion for raising awareness for women's lack of access to higher education and education in general. Jayne was a teaching fellow at Harvard Business School before she penned *The Gilded Cage of Woman*.

Jayne and her uncle rediscovered the lost story of Margaret Bryan when they were working on an ancestry project together. An eighteenth-century relation and trailblazer in the education of women in the sciences, who found *her* path when there was no path for *her*.